Old Sorcery

James Callan

The Arcanist: Fantasy Publishing

The Arcanist: Fantasy Publishing, LLC

Bloomington, Indiana, United States.

Websites: thearcanist.net | magazine.thearcanist.net

Contact: business@thearcanist.net

Support: support@thearcanist.net

First paperback and hardcover editions: March 2026

First ebook edition: March 2026

Paperback ISBN: 978-1-971706-01-6
Hardcover ISBN: 978-1-971706-00-9
ebook ISBN: 978-1-971706-02-3

Some cover elements by Kim Holm, used with permission under Creative Commons Attributions 4.0 Unported License.

Interior art by Sonulcaster, used with permission.

Cover design by Cody Sexton.

Map of Garden by James Callan, used with permission.

Editing by James D. Mills

In memory of Jack Vance, Lord of the Dying Earth and the kingdoms of Lyonesse

ALSO BY CALLAN

Novels

Neon Dream (Atmosphere Press)
A Transcendental Habit (Queer Space)
ANTHOPHILE (Alien Buddha)

Anthologies

Those Who Remain Quiet (Anxiety Press)

Special thanks to the Great Cosmos that wove everything into existence. Without the stardust and the vacuous tides of the eternal void, nothing would be possible.

More specifically, my gratitude goes out to all the authors and artists who have supported me or inspired me along the way. Among the many souls who have enriched my own, I would like to acknowledge my deep appreciation and thanks to Coy Hall, the grand master of historical horror, crime fiction, and owl men inhabiting far-off worlds. I would also like to thank Alistair Rennie, the true Highlander, the stoic BleakWarrior of the north.

I thank these fine gentlemen for their warmth and generosity, as well as the gifts they have given in their wonderful works.

Lastly, I would like to shower praise and devotion upon the Lords of Synth, the dungeon minstrels of Cryo Crypt, among others. My ears and mind honor the musical wonders of Mountain Realm, Atlantean Sword, Ulk, AMBIENC3, and let's not forget, Old Sorcery, whose name and dark wizardry sparked my own inner enchantment.

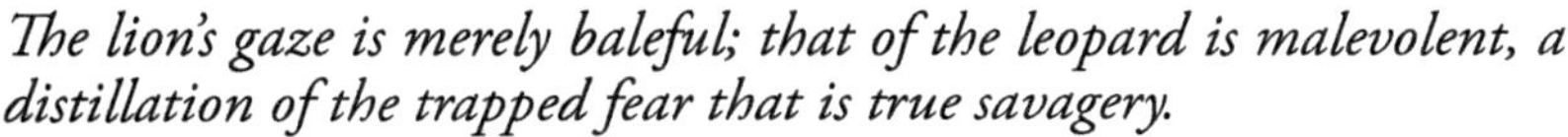

The lion's gaze is merely baleful; that of the leopard is malevolent, a distillation of the trapped fear that is true savagery.

— Peter Matthiessen, The Tree Where Man Was Born

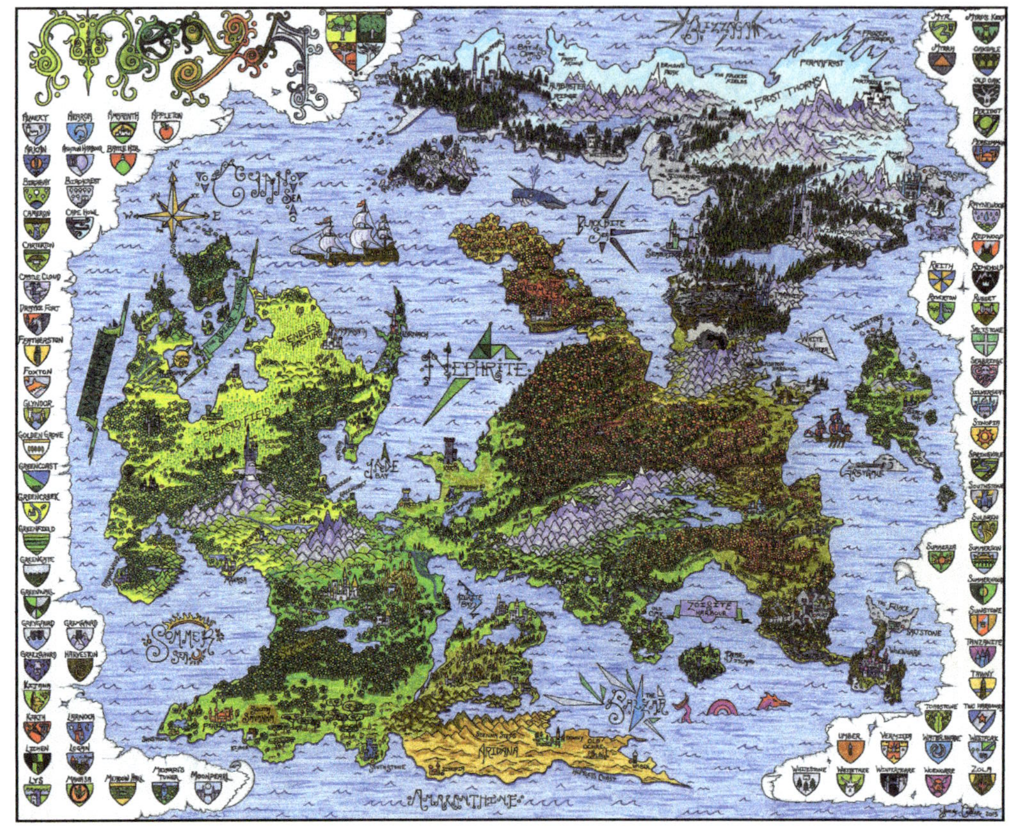

Nephrite
Emerald Field
Endless Pasture
Jade Bay
Sommer Sea
Aridana
Zoizite Harbour
Black Bite Sea
Frost Thorns
Permafrost
White Water
Amaranthine
N
E
W

Contents

I

SEED

In the days of yore, when the old, strong sorcery was more than myth, spells required blood, their potency strengthened by the lives put into them, their power amplified by an offering of souls. Magic made heroes of men, and many men, heroic or otherwise, met their deaths at the wrong end of magic. There were those born with the gift of wizardry, natural enchanters blessed with inherent talents. There were those, too, who passively benefited from trinkets imbued by the sorcery of others. It cannot be overlooked: there is a great divide between the man who launches fire from his fingertips and the man who brandishes flame with the aid of a wand, staff, or scroll.

Some men have aptitude for the sword, the plough, the pen. Others find their aptitude standing on the weathered planks of the prow, or sitting in the oiled saddle of a destrier. Many have little aptitude at all—paltry skills that can scarcely be dredged from the depths of their worthless shells. Fewer still possess the rare aptitude for arcana, the occult and the mysteries of magic. Some men—rarest of all—are born of magic, owing not their reputation to its potency, but their very existence.

Some men stand out among their generation. Some even stand out among the many generations before them—the once-in-a-century mage who rises high, elevated to godlike status. Women, on occasion, rise as high as men—though the ways of the world work against them. It is often said and widely known to be true: behind every great man is a great woman. And while the hammer and the sword may favor the heavier build of man, magic holds no distinction, no discrimination in favor of the configuration of those who wield it. Yes, women have been known to rise as high as men. One in particular, higher still, set the bar so far above the clouds to make any man, past or present, seem as small as an insect underfoot. She was a dreadful sorceress who had no equal, who seized the world of Garden in her relentless grasp. But her tale comes later—much later—and her prodigious wrath is no way to start a story.

This story begins with men. Men powerful in magic, but so bereft of wisdom as to render their talents dubious at best—a double-edged sword held by the blade. Few men are truly powerful, and fewer men besides are wise with the power they do possess. In the days of yore, when the old, strong sorcery was more than myth, there was a man who used only what was required: blood, life, and many souls. He was a man of rare power, and he hatched the rarest man of all: a man who was born of magic.

* * *

Tamarillo of the Bitter Seed, a scion of his master, Persimmon the Great, grew from the rotten fruit of his predecessor's garden. Persimmon had soaked the roots of the tamarillo tree in the blood of vermin he attracted with enchanted cheese. The rats, before they were sacrificed, grew to the size of toddlers. Charmed by the cheese luring them to their fates, the overlarge rodents walked to a nearby village like human children, laughing and playing among the locals. After weeks of visits and much play, cultivating bonds of friendship, the rats coaxed the human children to tag along for a special game of ring-around-the-tamarillo-tree. It was then all parties partook in their deaths, slain by Persimmon to feed the tree with their lifeblood, to germinate the Bitter Seed that would become his corrupted copy.

Tamarillo was born, not as an infant boy, but a full-bodied man. A natural adept, he learned magic from his master and excelled as if a long-toothed scholar of arcana. But he was Persimmon's double, not his child, and he refused to obey the magician who created him. He took his own stances, pleasures, and passions. His study diverted from the paths Persimmon had laid out before him. Tamarillo was rebellious—naughty by nature. Inherently magical, his curiosity grew and soon he dabbled in dark arts and demoncraft. As was the wizardly custom of his time, he indulged in old sorcery, which was not old then, but remained undoubtedly cruel.

Within the first year of his conception, dozens of the nearby villagers came to Persimmon's castle complaining of his tarnished offshoot, the perverse Tamarillo, who they called not he, but it. "It stole my cattle!" "It cut off my cat's tail!" "It comes in the night and seduces my wife!" "It took my daughter's sacred virginity!" "It took my son's!" "If we see it again, Persimmon, we are obligated to kill it."

A stern look from Persimmon might have been enough to lay the villagers' complaints to rest. For good measure, he transformed the boldest of speakers, a turnip farmer, into sea foam, which held its human shape for a half-second before it fell to the floor and seeped into the grotty cracks of ancient stone. But even as Persimmon was a malevolent bastard, so too was he fair. He bade the villagers stay to witness the summons of his grafted soul—his son, so to speak—whom the villagers called "it."

"It," Persimmon called Tamarillo, to chide his scion, but also to appease the fear-stricken villagers. "It shall no longer trouble you, or any people, on any lands beyond the grounds of this castle, the acreage contained by its outermost walls. It shall obey, because if it does not, it will suffer most horrifically by my hand." Persimmon flashed a yellow grin through his white beard. "And it knows, just as you do, my good people, that my word is law. And the law… Well, it is unforgiving."

"Now return to your hovels," he dismissed the villagers, who left the castle with one less member to their numbers. "And you," he glared at Tamarillo, who had been sulking while hidden behind the crowd. "Let it be known: life, mercy, kindness—what giveth may taketh away. You shall play nice, or I will unravel your soul just as I wove it into existence."

Tamarillo bowed to his master, masking the venom within his heart with courtesy and smiles. He quieted for a year—well behaved by all appearances—but his silence was a ruse, a nest for breeding the most despicable disobedience he could muster. Tamarillo was so devout to his disobedience to Persimmon that it became his religion. And he prayed, long and hard. He prayed, night and day.

After Tamarillo prayed for a year and a day to the demon known as Darkstain, after trading a quarter of his soul to invite the sinister prince into his heart, he used his newfound powers to taint the Clearwater River with hell-forged poisons and Hadean curses. Tamarillo's actions led to the death of half a kingdom, spreading blight to The Endless Pasture, The Emerald Fields, and the decay of the great mountain fortress, Castle Cloud.

These dire sins committed by Persimmon's scion did not go unnoticed, though Persimmon remained ignorant to the demon living in the quarter-vacancy of Tamarillo's soul, the dark menace making such vile acts of power possible. Had Persimmon known, he would have slain his son outright, sating the villagers' requests for his death the year before. But awareness of demons aside, mercy gathers dust among the unpracticed tendencies of Persimmon the Great. In the end, he decided to banish his crude copy to a realm where time is a virtual standstill, an astral province where seconds stretch to eons, and ultimately, where Tamarillo would endure eternity, removed from mankind—a fate far worse than death.

But Tamarillo had foreseen his master's plan. Driven by paranoia, moved by his mad intuition, he slit the throats of a thousand frogs and transferred their consciousness into the mind of a geriatric fruit bat. The bat, fueled by black magic and ten-hundred amphibian souls, became prophetic before burning out its newfound power and dying within the hour. In its limited time, the fruit bat scratched the words in dirt that divulged Persimmon's intention to encapsulate Tamarillo in a sea glass stasis coffin. The enchanted coffin, with Tamarillo inside, would be dropped into the deepest trench of the deepest sea and sit there, unchanged, until the sun expired and the world withered into space dust.

With this knowledge of his otherwise intolerable fate, Tamarillo fled, traveling beyond the once-fertile fields he had reduced to ash, beyond the shadow of Castle Cloud's ruinous husk, beyond the reach and influence of his former master and creator, Persimmon the Great.

* * *

Tamarillo fled to the gloomy haunts of The Greenwood, a forest spanning 900 miles in a crescent across the continent of Hyacinth. There, in the ancient woodland, he subsisted on mushrooms and moss, becoming deranged and skeletal, but otherwise at peace in his new, arboreal home. For years, among the trees, he led an ascetic life, abstaining from indulgences and avoiding all pleasures. Often, at night, dappled by the ivory moon, he would lay on the damp leaf litter gazing up to the silver-etched canopy and silently weep, deeply regretful for the terrible sins he enacted against the innocents of Clearwater Kingdom.

In the daytime, his sadness dissipated with the dew, and contentment came as commonly as the little brown mushrooms that sprouted after the rain. Peace was plentiful—rife to point of smothering—and serenity ate quietly away at Tamarillo's rotten heart. The quarter demon in him poisoned everything he experienced, so the great wizard's scion left the depths of the forest to seek absolution in suffering, hardship among the cold chaos of the Cloudy Mountain's cave-pocked, goblin-plagued slopes.

Tammy, as he began calling himself, established his home near the treeline in the easternmost crags. There, among a copse of bristlecone pines that were reputed to be several millennia old, he broke his do-gooders streak with the blood sacrifice of a sacred white stag.

No man shall fell the celestial white stag, for it is the holy animal of life. This is the shared decree of all kingdoms of Hyacinth.

No man shall take the life of the celestial white stage, lest he suffer death by the righteous wrath of God, by the King's law and the headsman's axe. He who harms the sacred white fawn, the snow white doe, or God's own alabaster stag, will undergo swift execution or slow torture: death by the means of the local lord's whim. This is the Greenwood Chapter in the Book of Hyacinth's Common Laws.

Tammy summoned a bolt of icy magic from the cold depths of his black heart. It materialized between his fingertips, glowing radiant and cruel. He nocked the volatile bolt to a bow of fine yew and whispered incantations to guide its noxious malice into the breast of the albino hart. Drawing back, he took his aim, and released—Twang! It flew between the tall trees, behind boulders and shrubby obstructions, weaving to find its target, which fell dead upon the magic arrow's impact over a mile from where it was shot.

The only downside to this spectacular technique was Tamarillo's need to travel a mile to harvest his kill, and, even worse, a mile back the way he came with a mighty stag in tow. He sullied the sacred deer's body by dragging its corpse by its hind legs, its antlers, even its ears, tarnishing its pristine pelt over the jagged rocks and twisted roots. Even after its molestation, the white hart was astonishing to behold: a regal beast of mighty pulchritude.

Tamarillo drained the creature of its blood, drawing out

its soul with dire hymns sung only in Hell. He beseeched himself, "Tammy, please," begging the darkest portion of his character, Darkstain within him, to awaken the trees with the rare life he had offered, the purest of souls he partitioned at their petrified stumps. The bristlecones trembled, uprooted themselves, and moved closer to the depraved man who had awakened them from a peaceful trance only a tree could ever know. They spoke slowly, not in audible words, but in groans and vibrations directly transmitted to the mind.

* * *

Tamarillo, with his band of bristlecones, terrorized the eastern ranges of The Cloudy Mountains, his menace seeping northward from its great, granite roots. The humans of the mountain villages appreciated Tamarillo's mass murdering of the cave goblins, who routinely raided the villagers. The humans did not, however, appreciate his mass murdering of them, which he did for no apparent reason, unless that reason was to satiate some sadistic hunger.

Northward, Tammy spread his infamy, warring with the wise forest trolls to collect their lives and, more importantly, their horns—objects with potent magical properties needed to augment his devious witchcraft. Likewise, he victimized the human forest dwellers, pulverized by marauding bristlecone sentinels, or by the wild, indiscriminate carnage of Tamarillo himself.

Eventually, Tammy's disreputable acts betrayed him—his whereabouts were revealed by his dastardly acts. A conspiracy of ravens blackened the sky above The Greenwood treeline, casting a shadow over the eastern slopes of The Cloudy Mountains. They witnessed the foul deeds of Tamarillo, The Bitter Seed, and flew westward to Persimmon's castle to inform the great wizard of the atrocities carried out by his pseudo-son.

Caw! Caw!

A wave of Persimmon's gnarled fingers, and the carrion

feeders' discordant music transformed to decipherable speech: "The dark shadow that you birthed into this world has sullied the white stag's soul. Hark! He murders men and trolls alike. And lo, he has awakened the oldest of trees and stripped them of their ancient wisdom, reducing them into mindless thugs, brainless cronies to act on his malevolent commands."

Persimmon felt slighted, deeply insulted. "My own self!" He raged. "My own copy!" More than that, he felt responsible. "I planted the Bitter Seed. I nurtured my scion, bringing this wretched menace into the world. I laid a foundation to its roots, applied what wisdom I had, gave all of my craft of magic. I offered Tamarillo the world, and this is how he uses the gifts I have bestowed upon him?"

In a mindless conflagration of rage, Persimmon engulfed the ravens in flames. Cerulean fire, tinged with enchantment, danced on their black feathers, yet kept them alive, in constant torment.

Caw! Caw!

The dark-winged heralds screamed in agony, too bewildered by their pain to contemplate their confusion, unable to ask in resentment: Why, o merciless gods, do we burn, yet do not die?

Caw! Caw! Caw!

A wave of Persimmon's spidery fingers, and the carrion feeders' harrowing music translated to comprehensible accusations: "Why, great master, have you singed us with this unearthly blue flame? Why this betrayal when we bowed to your every whim?" It was all the birds could manage. Speech, magically enhanced or otherwise, became lost to them. Their bodies were on fire, and their minds were ablaze.

It was simply a case of killing the messenger—or, more specifically, not killing the messenger, but setting them afire with a magical flame that inflicted unbearable pain, but not death. Persimmon overreacted, unfairly and impulsively, but what was done was done, and he would make use of his blunder in what way he could.

"Go, ravens of fire! Set the sky aflame! Fly east, and burn the bristlecone pines to ash. Do this, and I will allow death to take you to a restful end. Take care of Tamarillo's minions, and I will take care of The Bitter Seed himself."

Desperate to expire, hoping to end their torment, the ravens cawed in furious delirium, flying east.

* * *

Tamarillo abandoned his diet of frugality, forgoing the consumption of mushrooms and moss. Giving up asceticism, he gorged on troll brains and human stew. He filled his belly on the slow-cooked bones of man and beast, and dulled his senses with hibiscus wine. He lay with the bristlecones, fornicating with them in strange ways, engaging in biologically futile pleasures. He killed needlessly, any animal or man that crossed his path. Darkstain, lodging in the darkest quarter of Tamarillo's soul, was comfortable in his current host. Through countless misdeeds and depravities committed by The Bitter Seed, the demon within him became satiated, and grew far stronger.

And so the day's events repeated themselves: full on troll flesh and human soup, the marrow of man and beast, Tammy slaked his thirst on hibiscus wine and made incomprehensible love to enchanted bristlecone sentinels. The bark was rough on his flesh, but he enchanted himself to endure the pain along with his pleasures. Heavy with food, dulled by wine, and busy in the engagements of his perversions, Tamarillo did not notice the eastern sky aglow with cerulean fire.

Too late, he heard the frantic cawing and torturous shrieking of the ravens dive-bombing his camp. The bristlecone sentinels swatted the sky, darkening their boughs with raven blood, but the blue flame of the birds set fire to the trees, reducing them to lifeless charred husks. Caught off guard, naked and exposed, Tamarillo was attacked at great disadvantage. The ravens' offensive, however, was targeted at the ancient trees, and the young wizard managed to avoid any injury.

His bristlecones were lost, his army burned to cinders, his dendriform lovers slain. Tamarillo was devastated, and his counterstrike was fierce. Through furious tears of frustration and grief, The Bitter Seed intoned to the demon within him, and Darkstain, obliging, ended the flaming ravens with a black belch of sulphurous plumes. The birds fell to the ground, cawing no longer, trailing black smoke and black feathers.

* * *

Not far behind his vanguard of flaming ravens, Persimmon flew east over the Greenwood canopy, carried by Nephele, a cloud nymph, magically bound to answer his summons. With fists full of her flowing, silver hair, and legs clamped tight around her slender waist, the old wizard rode the nymph at lightning speed while the trees blurred below with their furious aerial advance. Unbeknownst to their approach, the great threat looming nearer, Tamarillo brooded over the death of his bristlecone army, weeping on the side of the mountain. Unprepared and unaware, he sat defenseless, totally exposed.

Enchantment, however, has a way of coming back, igniting post-mortem even after its supposed expiration. Sorcery and luck are closely woven, the soothsayers preach, and luck, it would seem, favored the Bitter Seed in his most desperate hour. Resurrected by the faint residue of magic in its withered corpse, Tamarillo's old prophetic fruit bat animated to unlife, activated by his master's need. The fruit bat abandoned its sheath of papery skin, leaving its chiropteran husk and brittle bones behind, flapping into the night on ghost wings that carried it just ahead of Persimmon and his cloud nymph, Nephele.

It arrived luminous like the stars above. Little more than

silver mist and white vapor, it whispered warnings on gentle gusts of cold, night air. Tammy, naked and pitiful among the scorched remains of the ancient bristlecones, heeded the words of the fruit bat spirit, its notification that Persimmon would arrive at any moment.

"Save your tears for another day, my lord, for you must prepare yourself—prepare yourself, quickly—for the sinister intention of your sire." The fruit bat slowly vanished, dissipating on the chilled, mountain breeze. Fading from view, its fragile voice becoming fainter by the syllable, the bat's final message warned his master of Persimmon's old promise, the great wizard's resolve to encase his tainted copy in a stasis coffin, to deposit Tamarillo into the deepest chasm of the widest ocean, or the core of the greatest mountain, or up and away to orbit the planet in the cold and vacuous nothingness of space.

The bat's afterimage lingered, its message echoing in the bitter, silent night. Tamarillo looked west over The Greenwood, deciphered a silvery cloud approaching faster than any weather could carry it.

"Persimmon!" he spat his creator's name as if uttering the foulest of curses. "You gave me life, yet you would not tolerate my individuality, my soul. You gave me life, yet all you ever wanted was a puppet, a golem to mimic your every aspect, to obey your every command." Tamarillo ran to his hovel on the side of the mountain, donned his mage robes and his spell caster's fingerless gloves.

"Persimmon, you fiend!" Tamarillo shouted to no one but himself. "The prowess of your magic is second to none. I have no doubts: I will die by your dire incantations before the moon crests the mountain. But hear this, you lank misfortune of a harpy's miscarriage: though you may take me to hell with your magic, I will not fall to the fire without fighting tooth and nail, without spell and sword and righteous malice."

He wrapped his wrists in pale silks and cloth of gold, enchanted fabrics plundered from the ancient tombs of goblin royalty. Their magical properties tingled against his skin, augmenting his power. He painted runes on his palms and across the center of his forehead, opening the channels of magic that surged within him. He donned a bronze circlet, a headpiece taken from a faerie prince, and as it rested on his brow, he felt its potency amplify his own inherent gifts. Lastly, he took the troll horns he had collected from his warring with the wise and magical folk of The Greenwood clans. He arranged them in a circle and stood in its center, praying to Darkstain, the demon who tainted his soul and had granted him great power. Crackling with magical energies, charged and ready to erupt, Tamarillo left his hovel and stood poised on the steep side of the mountain.

He could see it now, the close approach of a living cloud carrying Persimmon on its back. It descended, a nymph in cirrus skirts and a cumulus cloak, from high above the canopy of The Greenwood. The elemental spirit settled above the treeline, next to where the bristlecone husks lay charred and smoking. There, the great wizard who saddled Nephele dismounted to face his seething scion.

"Tamarillo," the old man addressed his younger copy.

"Persimmon," his mirrored, youthful version responded.

"You must know that my coming here before you is synonymous with your death."

Tammy nodded. "I am aware you would try your best to make it so, yes."

Persimmon laughed heartily, bitterly. "Trying and accomplishing are one in the same for a wizard of my power. There is not one without the other."

"So it would seem, as well, with arrogance and ability, or old age and foul smell."

"Or, in your case, my despicable, blighted duplicate: perversion and chaos, sadism and ruin."

Tamarillo waved his hands in dismissal, prompted by his sheer annoyance and lack of patience. "Shall we commence with killing one another?"

"Let me answer your question with a question: are you

prepared to die?"

Tamarillo spat back at his maker, his genetic facsimile. "Allow me to answer your question with a murderous incantation," he replied, and without a single second to separate his last spoken syllable with the volatile magic he unleashed upon his opponent, the space between them filled with an arc of molten rock, spewed from the bowels beneath the mountain.

"Child's play," Persimmon mocked his would-be assassin, his child-turned-adversary. Before the lava could scorch his skin or singe his robes, the great wizard erected a luminous shield, flickering and sparking upon contact with the magma, stopping it short where it oozed to cool upon the ground.

"You guard yourself well," Tammy admitted with a grin. "But what of your pet?"

"My pet?"

Too late did Persimmon reason that the cloud nymph, Nephele, was the "pet" in question. Too late to save her from Tamarillo's secondary volley of lethal pyrotechnics. Before the old wizard could respond with a spell of his own, a defensive counter, Nephele was gauze on the wind, evaporated beyond any hope to coalesce ever again. Her scream was a high pitched gust of wind, loud at first, then ever so faint. Her piteous call may have trailed off for a while, but it was drowned out by Tamarillo's laughter, which drew the irate attention of the most powerful wizard ever to walk the world of Garden.

"And now, you die." So matter of fact were the words of Persimmon that one may have mistaken it for arrogance, an ego-driven bravado akin to the puffing out of one's chest. But the ease with which he weaved his fingers to trace a golden rune of light, a radiant symbol that widened a portal to some distant, unearthly dimension, commanding a horned dragon, black as shimmering ink, to crawl forth from whatever hellish realm existed on the other side, bespoke of mastery beyond the need for chest-puffing machismo.

This was no show of arrogance, but ascendancy. All at once, face to face with his death, Tamarillo understood the wide gap between his proficiency in magic and his creator's near-divine supremacy.

"And now, I die," Tammy echoed the words of his former master. The last image he saw in life was the wide maw of a monster from a bizarre, astral realm. Seconds later, many well-chewed, separate pieces of him travelled down the gullet of a dragon born across the cosmos. And that was that... Or so it seemed for the briefest of interludes.

* * *

Tamarillo had died, obliterated by his master, and yet part of him lived on. The dragon who had devoured him coiled into a tight knot of midnight, plated scales, twisting its serpentine body in on itself, groaning in agonizing discomfort—its meal, it seemed, was not to the monster's liking. It belched acrid, black smoke and hacked up the blood and bones of Tamarillo's devastated body. Among the ruined jigsaw of the scion wizard's corpse, an apparition rose amid the disheveled gore and mutilated limbs. A small figure the size of a child, horned of head and hoofed of limb, laughed maniacally at the astral dragon's plight, its obvious anguish as it writhed across the face of the mountain.

"What fresh corruption is this?" Persimmon faced the small, demonic figure. "What rancid devil rises from the belly of the dead?"

The child-size horror grinned to reveal sharp fangs and a forked tongue. "I am your own copy," it declared. "Tamarillo of the Bitter Seed."

"Nonsense!" Persimmon waved a hand in dismissal and disgust. "Do you take me for a fool? I can see quite plainly you are not my scion son, but a dismal creature from the netherworld."

"I am Darkstain, son of Blemish, Lord of Rot, and child of Goreah, Queen of Anguish."

"A demon of royalty," Persimmon remarked with utter contempt as Darkstain bowed with exaggerated flourish. "You may have been born among the upper echelons of Hell, but even as a highborn prince, a demon is bound to their doomed and desolate realm. Tell me, foul creature, how have you come to this world, far too pure to harbor your blighted soul?"

"I am Darkstain, Prince of Misfortune, Lord of Decay, but I am also Tamarillo, who is your copy, and so I am also you, Persimmon the Exalted."

"You speak in riddles," Persimmon huffed. "Bad riddles, which make little sense. I will not stand here and tolerate games of guessing. Tell me plainly what you mean, and quickly, or hold your tongue and promptly prepare for your death."

If Darkstain feared the great wizard's power—his melange of spells that might undue the demon, fiber by fiber, flesh and soul—he betrayed no evidence of his anxiety. Instead, he laughed, explaining with devious mirth how he had gained entry into the human realm, divulging his union with Tamarillo, the details of their contract that granted him haven under the pure, blue sky of Garden.

"He offered you his soul?" Persimmon's disgust reached the depths of his core.

"One-quarter of his soul," Darkstain declared. "Which is how, in a subtle way, Tamarillo still lives on. Inside of this stunted version of my netherworld whole, resides the fragmented ghost of your son."

"Tamarillo is not, never was, my son."

Darkstain spread his dwarfed limbs, his taloned fingers. "Semantics, old man. Though it cannot be denied, you two are very close—as close as can be. After all, Tamarillo is you, and you, him. Say what you will about your relationship, but you ought to know: you speak as a bitter father who has been estranged from his child."

Persimmon scoffed. "My child, as you would have me call him, has abandoned his father, abandoned all reason, and finally, abandoned humanity. He has committed acts so heinous and cruel that he is more akin to a monster, like you, than a man, like me. And now what of my son? He is three-quarters dead, and the part of him that lives on dwells in the diminutive iteration of a vile wretch, a demon who has crawled out from its loathsome abyss." He shook his head and waggled a bony finger. "Tamarillo has been dead to me since the day he murdered half a kingdom. I may have brought him into this world, but he is not my kin. He is no son of mine. He is all yours, Darkstain—and you are welcome to him." Persimmon spat on the ground before him. "It is just as you say: Tamarillo is now a part of you."

Darkstain chuckled, strangely deep for so small a figure. "It is what makes you, mighty Persimmon, a small part of me as well. I am Darkstain, Demon Prince of the netherrealm, but I am also Tamarillo, the quarter of his soul that gives me viability in this world, and by virtue of this, I am also you, a quarter-copy of the vintage mage who made me."

Persimmon was troubled greatly by what he heard. He recalled the devastation and plague Tamarillo had inflicted on Clearwater Kingdom, the dark magic that now, in retrospect, resonated with demoncraft. So it was Darkstain, and not Tamarillo, who plunged into the chasm of doom, who took the great leap from misdemeanor to mass murder. Persimmon sighed, truly saddened. But one more look at Darkstain, who mocked him with gleeful, unrestrained giggling, and the wizard's sorrow melted away, replaced by rage that simmered to boil over into hardened resolve—he would eradicate Darkstain from existence.

"You do not belong in this plane of reality. Yours is another realm." Magical energies—luminous hues of blue, white, and gold—coalesced to swirl around Persimmon; the residue of raw power agitated his loose robes and long, white beard. "You have no place in this world," he condemned the apparition before him, "and I will not tolerate your presence here for another minute." He glared at the quarter-sized demon, the quarter-soul of his scion, thoroughly corrupted by evil-incarcerate. “But neither will you return from whence you came. Never again will you walk the green lands of Garden, or return to your throne of corpses in the gloomy caverns of the shadow realm.”

“But enough talk.” And without a further word, quick and blinding as lightning, Persimmon traced a series of intricate runes in searing, white light. The symbols hovered in the air before him, growing in luminosity and size.

Darkstain’s impertinent laughter and insolent smirk vanished amidst the foreboding, bright light. He cowered in its glare and, shielding his serpent-slitted eyes, quickly inscribed his own dark sigil, to erect an adequate shield against his impending demise.

Blood, lives, and souls—the requirements for the strongest of magic. With enough blood on his hands to last an eternity, Darkstain summoned a shield of defense forged on the countless lives he had taken, the innumerable souls he had spoiled. Persimmon, who was stronger than the enemy he wished to thwart, had, nonetheless, failed to account for the presence of a demon prince. He had prepared for Tamarillo, an encounter requiring the blood, life, and soul he had applied for the occasion. At this point, Persimmon was tapping from a dry spring.

Still, this was Persimmon, a wizard famed for being the strongest to ever walk among the world of Garden. If he was unprepared, what of it? He would make do, and expeditiously slay the demon before him. And so he raised his gnarled, old hands and unleashed the magical force he willed into reality. A beam of pure, astral energies borrowed from celestial bodies occupying distant solar systems erupted from Persimmon’s withered palms. It hit Darkstain, colliding with the Hellfire shield planted before him in defense, and sent the demon hurtling across the slopes of the cloudy mountains.

And still, Darkstain endured. He rose up from his knees, holding the ragged ruins of his shield, and approached Persimmon for another round of violence. His grin returned to spread across the demon's face, for he determined that the old wizard was spent and unprepared. Darkstain was weak and injured, but no longer saw himself as outmatched. Beneath the layers of his own, demonic spirit, he felt the soul of Tamarillo—what was left of it—imprisoned within him, crying out from the realms between. Sadistic to the end, his old host's plight lent the demon newfound strength.

"Shall we make an end to this?" Darkstain asked Persimmon when he crossed the rocky slopes to face his adversary yet again.

"It is I who shall make an end of you," Persimmon answered, and although his words carried ferocity, his retort came with a sputtering of blood. He hobbled, cradling his torso as if an arrow had pierced his guts. "Though it would seem," he laughed in a blend of amusement and bitterness, "that this might, indeed, be my end as well."

As before, he sighed in sadness, but smiled, too, as he traced more runes, sent forth more blinding light on beams of magical energy. It was the final thread to the tapestry of his vast power, the last drop among his reservoir of potency. Without the blood, the lives, the souls to fuel his summons, he took of himself—Persimmon, a depleted husk, teetered on the brink of death. Had he killed Darkstain? He was not entirely sure.

Knowing his seconds scarce, he targeted his heart while it still beat in his chest, drawing out the last life that remained to it, crafting a spell of utter destruction. Persimmon scanned the mountainside for Darkstain, the blight he would obliterate from the purity of Garden. But the demon was nowhere in sight, and without a target for the use of his spell, nor a single minute of breath remaining to him, Persimmon stored his dire magic in the stasis coffin he had intended to use to imprison Tamarillo.

Tamarillo… it was of his scion that Persimmon's final thoughts lingered on. My dear boy… Oh, how I failed you. With the cataclysmic spell inside, Persimmon sealed the stasis coffin, fell to the rocks at his feet, and expired on the slope of the mountain.

* * *

In the chaos amidst the penultimate moments of Persimmon's battle with Darkstain, the weakened demon escaped the wizard's final spell, which surely would have marked his end. Drawing from the powers of Tamarillo, who shared his existence, and augmented by the untold barrels of blood, the countless souls his cruelty had amassed, Darkstain cast a spell to transfer his soul, abandoning his body which swayed on the edge of expiration. He did not have time to be choosy, his luxury of choice limited to the first living thing that he saw. And so, Darkstain shifted his spirit into the nearest creature, a woodlouse, with aims to recover his vigor.

The transfer of souls was a temporary measure, one that would last no longer than needed. This was, in any case, the intended plan. But intention and plans are fickle things in any world, more so still in a land of magic and demons. Fate, as it were, served its own intention. And fate, as it often is, was a cruel, sadistic bastard.

The woodlouse, who was a demon prince, and the host to a distant part of Tamarillo, too, settled on the bark of a tree of no special significance, a run-of-the-mill conifer. But luck and fate and magic are kin to chaos, and luck and fate would have it that magic once scathed that particular, not-so-particular tree. A deep gash in one of its lower, larger boughs glistened with liquid amber, and the woodlouse, beneath its flow, was encased in the dark resin bleeding freely from the wounded tree. The insect version of Darkstain, and the residual soul of Tammy inside, struggled against the sticky substance as it coated its legs, abdomen, thorax, and eventually, its head. But here was a battle that was truly futile, and the insect-demon-wizard-soul was entombed, buried alive.

Outside of the small, contained space of the stasis coffin

nearby, the rest of the world carried on. All across the lands of Garden, from The Greenwood to The Cloudy Mountains, from the once-blighted Emerald Field to the recovered Endless Pasture of Hyacinth, and beyond, to the continents that spread east—Dahlia, Zinnia, and Dianthus—time behaved as it always did, passing in a series of nights and days that aged people, all living beings, and all objects, items, and places, a constant continuum of movement, change, and decay. The sun rose, crested the sky, lowered beyond the horizon; the moon mimicked her partner's steps. Day, then night. Day, then night. Repeat. Ten thousand days and ten thousand nights—this, only the beginning. Seasons came and went. Epochs and eons fell away like autumn leaves. One million years. Two, three. Tree resin hardened to amber, and a woodlouse was preserved inside, a demon's quarter-soul nestled in its arthropodal husk.

One day, when the sun rose to bathe the world in light, just as it always does, a passing traveler chanced upon a ring of petrified bristlecone trees. It was a curious sight, and diverted the man from his purposes. A trapper who wished to test the eastern slopes of The Cloudy Mountains, its treeline where certain mustelids of snow-white coats were reputed to dwell in healthy numbers; the man was drawn to this spot, but set down his trapping gear when he came upon a strange box glowing at the edges of its sealed lid. The rising sun poked its brilliant crown above the towering mountains and, as if a sign from the gods above, or the guiding hand of fate, its magnificent pillar of light shone to spotlight the smooth, sea-glass casket that radiated aquamarine. As the trapper approached the strange, spectacular coffin, the great shafts of sunlight shifted over and behind his shoulder, whereupon they set aglow an impressive chunk of raw amber, settled among the rocks.

A pure white pelt of a wolverine, a martin, a weasel or a stoat—these are fine things. But one does not idly walk past abandoned treasures sitting unattended in the heart of the wild. One cannot ignore an ornate chest aglow from within—not even a trapper who has mustelids on his mind. And so, the man approached the sealed coffin, oblivious to the power and history locked within its moss-strewn glass.

Using the sturdy branch, which served as his walking stick, the traveler wedged a hardwood staff between the lid and casket, working hard to pry open its seal. After some struggle, the lid came loose, but not gently. The power contained within, suddenly set free, exploded upward as if the volatile eruption of a volcanic blast. The heavy glass lid flew high above the canopy of the Greenwood. It sailed through the air in wild circles, scraping the clouds, and crashed a mile or more down the slope of the mountain. The trapper was blinded by the power of the spell. But he did not dwell on this sudden impairment—quite frankly, he hadn't the time. Seconds after he lost his sight, the trapper was reduced to boiling blood and flaming innards, incinerated to ash and dust.

The spell, which seemed to be sentient with a clear purpose, shifted east, then west, up and down the slope of the mountain. It resembled an angel in flight, but shapeless—a blob, a jellylike creature, made of raw power and light. It weaved through the ring of petrified bristlecone stumps, then suddenly paused, grew brighter, larger, and approached a sizable chunk of amber laying exposed beneath its terrible glow.

The spell, which was sentient, was the last trace of Persimmon's soul, extracted from his living heart a million or more years prior to that moment. Since its conception, the magic stewed in the passing millennia, the indeterminate eons, experiencing no time at all, but waiting, nonetheless, for this fateful moment. It condensed in on itself, concentrated energy packed into the size of a mustelid's beady eye. It shot forth, a dreadful bullet, into the heart of the amber stone that housed an ancient woodlouse within.

Crack!

The amber split into four jagged pieces, shards of stone the color of marmalade. They smoked upon the rock where they had been scattered, trembling with energy, each with its own quarter of woodlouse corpse within. The last phase of the spell took effect, lifting the hot, smoking shards high into the air and dispersing them, each one, into various directions across the vast lands of Garden.

Four shards, one for each continent, distributed across the wide-ranging world. Each fragment was placed, not randomly, but with forethought and purpose, planted in unattainable locations—deep caverns, high mountain spires, the ruins of a haunted, wasted kingdom, and the bottom of a deep, black swamp. To the west, in Hyacinth, and the south, in Dahlia; to the east in Zinnia, and the cold, arctic north of Dianthus; the amber shards settled in their new and implausible places. There, they would rest, perhaps for another million years, for untold millennia, undisturbed through quiet eons.

Or perhaps they would be found. But by who? Legends of the future. Myths in the making. More names, more history, more steps in the never-ending dance of time.

And thus ends the story of Persimmon, the exalted mage, and his scion, Tamarillo of the Bitter Seed, marking the termination of their feud, their misdeeds, their various triumphs, crimes, and perversions. Here is the juncture in time that concludes the story of Darkstain, the demon prince, and the creation of the amber shards, the adventures and calamities that their power would later influence.

But stories, like time (barring stasis coffins), never truly end. They flow and continue, endless, ever shifting, developing, growing. For some, this is the end of the story. But at the end of every story is the beginning of another…

II

HYACINTH

Prince Chervil, second son to the King of Almery, visibly withered beneath his artificial smile. What was there to say? The man was not used to being denied. Nonetheless, he bowed with courtesy, speaking warmly as he bid the allied king and the king's youngest sister farewell. It was only after Chervil had vacated the castle hall, departing without the company of the princess whom he had travelled countless leagues to woo—yet before he mounted his great white stallion and rode out beyond the north gate to begin his venture home—that he allowed an exasperated "fuck!" to escape his unkissed lips.

"Everything alright, Your Highness?" one of the royal escort knights of Almery kindly inquired of his prince.

Prince Chervil moaned. "Oh, shut up, you worthless dog cunt!"

* * *

Wrenna Raynewald, fifth in line to the throne of Raynewood, refused yet another suitor —the umpteenth one. At the age of 30 and not yet betrothed, she harbored little desire to ever marry, unburdened by the slightest ambition to rise among the court of her family name. Husbands, she reasoned, are a fine way to barter freedom in exchange for daily sentences of coital obligations, nine-month stints of pregnancy, and a lifetime of motherhood, which she may want someday—but not now, and certainly not with Prince Chervil of Almery.

"But he is so handsome..." said Twigg, Wrenna's handmaiden, swooning by her Lady's side.

Wrenna stared longingly from the high window of her bedchamber, studying a jade sea of forest stretching northward to a horizon of low mountain swells. "I didn't notice," Lady Raynewald offhandedly mentioned.

"Didn't notice?!" Twigg puffed her round, rosy cheeks. "Forgive me for my uncouth longings, Lady Wrenna, but I confess I had lewd thoughts about that robust, young man. If it were me, my Lady, I'd have been thinking of ways to plot our first rendezvous before the marriage, if you take my meaning."

Wrenna sighed, turned away from the vast expanse of the Raynewood, now bathed in the fiery hues that accompanied the onset of dusk. "Sex, my little Twigg, is something I can have whenever I wish."

Twigg giggled.

"And sex, my dear Twigg, bores me near to death." She turned back to her window, lost in a landscape that brought her both angst and yearning. "Besides," she added, "one hardly requires a prince—much less marriage—if one desires a little sex."

Twigg squealed with delight, blushed, and frantically began dusting the wardrobe that had already been dusted. "And what *does* one require, my Lady?"

Again, Wrenna Raynewald sighed. "Adventure," she said, and did not turn her gaze from the wide world without. "Adventure," she repeated. "And a little magic, too."

* * *

The King of Raynewood endured his youngest sister's request to be granted leave of the castle—her hope to travel north to seek Melorin, a well-reputed wizard whom Wrenna hoped to persuade to accept her as his apprentice in the art of magic.

His Majesty, King Waldorf Raynewald, leaned forward in his throne, squinting at his sister through a gaze of utter stupefaction. "Magic, as in… spells?"

"Among other things, Your Majesty."

King Waldorf held out his hands. "Please, Wrenna, cast aside your formalities. I am your King, yes, but I am first and foremost your brother. Call me Waldo, like you did when we were children. I may be ten years your senior, and your sovereign besides, but that doesn't change the fact that you have always been my favorite; the very best of playmates among our brethren, those rivals and sycophants alike."

"As you command, King Waldo."

"*Just* Waldo, please. And I do not command, but ask of you as a favor."

Wrenna allowed a light volley of laughter to escape her growing smile. "Okay, Waldo."

The King, too, joined his sister in laughter. "Now," he began anew, "as to this magic business—which, I will have you know, I think is folly, dear Wrenna—beyond spells, what *other things* do you refer to?"

Wrenna paused for thought, playing with the hem of her dress as she pondered her brother's question. She bit her lip and looked off to the side, searching within herself for answers she did not rightly know. King Waldorf shifted in his seat, growing impatient in the prolonged silence.

Without really knowing what she was saying, Lady Raynewald spewed out the following list regarding her *business of magic*: "Spells, brother Waldo," she began, "and incantations, too. Enchantments, curses, herblore, potions, and summons. And let us not forget charms and conjurations. Oh, and sorcery—old and new. The fruits of dark arts: necromancy and illusion. The illusion of necromancy. Necromancy to raise an illusionist from the dead." Lady wrenna paused for breath before forging onward. "Healing, of course. Voodoo and general wizardry.

Hexes, Waldo. And to put it rather plainly—occultism, and with it, demonology and witchcraft."

King Waldorf sat at the edge of his throne and scowled. "Witchcraft?!" He pointed at Wrenna accusingly. "Sister or no, I'll be forced to burn you at the stake." Waldo managed to hold his glowering stare for a few seconds before he burst into amused laughter—his acting left much to be desired. "It sounds exciting, little sister. Truly, it does. But why, I wonder, is this business of magic preferable to the business of marriage?"

Lady Raynewald scoffed at her brother's question. "You said it yourself, Lord King."

"Waldo," he corrected.

"You said it yourself, brother Waldo: *It sounds exciting.* Magic is more than exciting. It's, well," she searched for words and failed, "it's… *magic.*"

"Magic *is* magic," Waldorf agreed. "I cannot argue with *that.*" The two siblings shared a hearty chuckle. "But tell me," he leaned once again to the edge of his throne, "in all seriousness… what is marriage to you?"

Wrenna began to speak, but the King interrupted her. "Before you answer, let me tell you what marriage—*your* marriage—is to *me.*" He stood up and walked to his sister's side, laying a hand on her shoulder. Waldorf looked into Wrenna's eyes, spoke sternly, but gently: "Your marriage, to me, would be the strengthened bond between an allied kingdom. Or, no less valuable, the salve applied to an old wound, a mended bitterness shared with a hostile realm. It would offer stability, safety, and assurances—for you, and for the throne. It would give you a life to claim for your own, independence from The Raynewood court, and a secure platform to become a mother to many children, to raise princes who might become kings, and princesses who might—"

"Be bartered to a queue of suitors?" Wrenna interjected. "Each one as impersonal as the last. The elderly, the strange, the ugly, the cruel."

"The kind, the generous, the loving," the king countered.

"Bah!" Lady Raynewald scoffed. "You would have me—have all the women after me, an endless line of daughters and sisters—become puppets to the never ending dance of politics?"

"Of tradition!"

"It is tradition that I wish to break from, Waldo."

"Why? So you may run off to some wizard and become a witch?"

"To find my calling, brother. To become powerful, like you, but in my own right. I am destined to be skilled, dear Waldo, skilled beyond my ability to sew and give birth. I am destined for greatness, and not by extension of the man I will be offered to in marriage, whose sons I will bring into this world and resent for the rest of my life—my own children! I do not want that. But I *am* destined for greatness, Waldorf. I tell you now, and ask you to help me make it so—I am destined for *magic*."

King Waldorf raised a finger, held it in the air. So too, he held a severe countenance that rested below his crown on a face of disapproval. The silence settled in the air, filling the throne room with nothing to drown out the crisp, metallic crackle of wood slowly disintegrating over the flames of the wide, roaring hearth. Above its warm, flickering glow, The Raynewood Coat of Arms twinkled with light, striped with dancing, erratic shadows.

Wrenna followed her brother's sad glance as it rested over the broken shield, its painted emerald tree fragmented in many jagged pieces. She remembered the story, now legend, of how her great grandsire, King Waldon, had fallen to the usurper from the east; how his body, like his shield, lay broken in many scattered pieces by the strike of the marauder King's warhammer, *Doom*.

For half a generation, Dezmond of Kirth held dominion over Raynewood Castle and the lands surrounding. What is now regarded as Raynewood's bleakest period in history, Dezmond's isolated reign became known as The Great Shame.

It was only after Waldon's son, Waldwick the Unforgiving, had turned to magic that he was able to reclaim the throne of Raynewood, leading an army behind his furious, fiery wrath. His command of flame and manipulation of weather turned the tide of battle in Waldwick's favor. Dezmond of Kirth was slain, his warhammer, *Doom*, melted down in magic fire, reforged into the crown that rests on Waldwick's great statue in Raynewood's town square. As for King Waldon's broken shield, the family crest in its ruined jigsaw; the splintered tree hung above the mantelpiece in the royal throne room, a reminder to future kings of the folly of letting your guard down, and, perhaps more than anything else, the vengeful power of magic.

After what seemed to be many minutes, but, more likely, a moment spanning half a dozen seconds spent in a state of anticipation, the king lowered his accusing finger, dropping his stern mantle to reveal not an imposing king, but an open-minded, kind-hearted older brother.

"I have no doubts, dear sister, that you are destined for greatness. Indeed, I noted your greatness from the moment you were born, how you effortlessly outclassed all those brothers and sisters wedged between my own birth and yours." Waldo exhaled a long, surrendering sigh. "You are destined for greatness, we both agree." He sat back down upon his throne and smiled. "It is time I let you take up the reins to your own life, little sister. If it is your will, then show me. Show me, Wrenna, how you are destined for magic."

* * *

"On one condition..."

Lady Raynewald sat upon her fine, chestnut mare, watching the road pass beneath the beast of burden's methodical trot. Wrenna recalled her older brother's stipulation that accompanied his agreement; the king's condition for allowing her to ride north to seek an audience with Melorin, the wizard of reputed power who dwelled in his tower on the far fringes of the Raynewood. The King's command echoed in her head:

Oh, dearest, crazy sister, how I love your spirit, which is as fierce and bright as Waldwick's unrelenting flame. You are free to pursue this mad fancy that has befallen your whim, this fixation on magic, which, despite its dangers, has aided our family in the past—delivered our bloodline from its ruinous fall.

By decree of the King, I grant your request. I offer you leave from the trappings of old tradition, from the walls of Raynewood Castle that hem in your ambitions to a fixed place. I allow you, Wrenna, to make your way north to Melorin's tower, to seek out the wizened recluse who is famed for his eccentricities, yes, but also his prowess of magic. I grant you leave, dear sister, to follow your passions and seek out your fated destiny. But my generosity comes side-by-side with proviso. To heights of greatness or dark depths of oblivion, you are free to follow your untamed spirit to wherever it may guide you, on one condition…

You will return to me, arriving here at Raynewood Castle before this very throne. In one year from tomorrow—one year exactly, beginning at dawn—you will stand here, as you do now, and report to your King. You will inform me of your teachings, your acquired magical abilities, and present ample evidence of your progress in whatever display makes it apparent. If you show me a modicum of magical learning, an advancement of your newfound craft, I will allow you to continue as your whim dictates—your life will be yours to command until the end of your days.

If, however, your year of study bears meager fruit, yielding little magical advancement of any substantial worth… well… then I will make the decisions regarding the remainder of your future. If you fail to uphold your end of the bargain, sweet sister, then you will give up magic once and for all. Under my guidance, you will walk the path of tradition. If you cannot prove you are a witch to reckon with, Princess, then I tell you now… you will serve The Raynewood realm. I promise you, Wrenna, as sure as the sun will rise tomorrow, you will finally marry.

Now, wouldn't that *be magic?*

With dawn a memory of hours past, the sun crawling to heights approaching midday, the year-long clock began to tick for Lady Raynewald. Fourteen months. Four-hundred-and-twenty days, nights to match. Not a single sunrise beyond the full Garden year. One annual cycle, at the very utmost, and she would be riding through the same gates she had this morning left at her back.

Along with her handmaiden, Twigg, riding on a pony by Wrenna's side, and a trio of Raynewood knights on their majestic destriers, Lady Raynewald and her escorts left the towering turrets of Raynewood Castle behind them. Wrenna looked over her shoulder to the open window of her bedchamber high up and far behind her. It was a mere, shadowed speck on a great, stone spire. She knew the view from that window like the dream that invaded her sleep every night since she was a child. She could see it now as she closed her eyes: a jade sea of forest canopy, stretching northward to a horizon of low mountain swells.

Lady Wrenna opened her eyes, but the image of her bedchamber window had vanished. Raynewood Castle was no longer in view. Its imposing walls and lofty towers were engulfed by the forest canopy that swallowed her and her escorts whole.

* * *

The Malachite Sea hugged the western coast of Hyacinth, and Raynewood Castle, situated at the tip of the continent's southwestern peninsula, overlooked its seemingly endless horizon. To the south, the forests tamed into grasslands, terminating in precipitous, sandstone cliffs that dropped into the warmer waters of the Sommer Sea. The Malachite was known for its storms, its seasonal moods that fluctuated between rough and tempestuous. Even within the darkest cell of the deepest dungeon of Raynewood Castle, the sound of Malachite's buffeting waves echoed through every corridor. Though too far away to hear, and with calmer waters besides, the Sommer Sea was still close enough to witness from the high turrets of Raynewood Castle, and the frequent southerlies that blew in from over its gentle expanse provided a warm and welcome reminder of its proximity. Surrounded by trees in three directions, it was the ocean that dominated the sights and smells of Raynewood Castle. Salt, storms, and seagulls—it was the maritime impression that seized the senses.

And so it was, when Lady Raynewald entered The Raynewood forest, that she was startled and more than a little surprised, when all evidence of the western and southern seas left no trace of their presence. The sounds of Malachite's tides and tantrums were swallowed by the emerald swath sprawling thick overhead. The smell of salt was overpowered by the rich and musty aroma of earth, the occasional waft of perfume from flowering trees. The gulls fell silent, their incessant cries absorbed by the enveloping leaves, the sheer and staggering biomass that blanketed the gloomy forest, and all those who walked beneath its canopy.

It was odd to be away from the sea. But for Wrenna, her thrill outweighed her fear. The forest was strange and unknown, and seemed, she thought, to pervade with mystery. And while the raised hairs on the back of her neck suggested she was stirred in some way; the subtle threat of danger that provoked this sensation entirely invigorated her. Wrenna inhaled deeply with her nostrils, savoring the heady blooms and dank, earthy smell.

The forest, she determined, was pure magic.

"Begging your pardon, Lady Raynewald, but the forest is pure shit."

Wrenna laughed at Twigg, who was a constant source of amusement. "Pure delight, I should think."

"Well, far be it for a handmaiden to disagree with her Princess, but here I am, disagreeing anyways, my Lady." She abandoned the grip on her pony's reins to pinch her nostrils.

With a comically nasal voice she explained how the smells brought back memories of Wrenna's "nappy days."

"And what do you think, Sir Trillium?" Wrenna asked the escort knight riding nearest. "Does the forest seem fair or foul to you?"

Trillium looked up at the network of twisted boughs and dark canopy they supported, from side to side at the bark pillars that faded into gloom. Ahead, something rustled in the undergrowth. The young knight flinched, touched the pommel of his longsword at his hip.

"Forgive me, Your Grace. I'm inclined to agree with Miss Twigg."

Wrenna smiled, nodding in acceptance. "Sir Columbine?"

The knight behind her was larger than Sir Trillium; older, more seasoned. "The forest is a fine place to hunt, Princess." Though his voice was gruff, his sentiment was gentle. "But the sea is the sign of home, and the open sky gladdens my heart. The long shadow cast by Raynewood Castle is the only darkness that soothes my soul."

"I did not take you for a homebody, Sir."

Columbine spread his hands. "Adventures are for the young, Your Grace. Believe me, I've had my share of them."

Wrenna bowed to the older knight, then turned in her saddle to address the third escort in her company. "And you, Sir?" She did not recognize this knight, who had remained silent all day. "What are your thoughts on the forest?"

The unknown knight sat atop his midnight destrier, shifting to face Wrenna. He met her gaze with an unrestrained, mischievous stare. In the moments before he spoke, the depth and beauty of his crystalline eyes utterly bewitched her. So blue, so pale, they shone like stars amid the dimness in the wood.

"Dearest Lady," he said, forgoing the accustomed formalities. "I delight in this quiet, tranquil place." He broke his gaze to regard his surroundings, then returned his attention to Wrenna, who was newly besieged by the enchantment of his sapphire gaze. "The forest is a realm of untold wonders, astonishing beauty that does much to open my heart—indeed, my very soul. There is little that compares to the seduction of its charms, except, if I may, the overwhelming pulchritude of Your Grace."

Lady Raynewald blinked in the silence that followed, felt a blush rush over her face. Twigg giggled, swooning on her pony, while Sir Trillium coughed and cleared his throat. Behind them all, the elderly knight, Sir Columbine, chided the third escort for his lack of decorum.

"You will speak to the Princess in a manner according to her station, and yours. Better yet, you will not speak at all. Do not forget yourself, Sir Hawthorn, lest I am moved to remind you by means sterner than words." He patted his sword, hanging by his side.

"Of course," Sir Hawthorn bowed his head to Columbine, though beneath his courtesy remained a poorly concealed grin. The handsome knight turned to Wrenna, bowing deeper. "Apologies, Your Grace." Beneath the curtain of his cascading, dark locks, he met her eyes once more, his own twinkling with mischief and seduction.

For the second time, Lady Wrenna felt a warm blush surging to her face. "Not at all, Sir Hawthorn." She flattened the ruffles of her blouse, suddenly aflutter. "I appreciate your candid nature, and admire your poetic expression and love for the forest."

"Your Grace," Hawthorn bowed once more. And though Lady Raynewald was not entirely sure of it, she thought the dashing knight may have winked before turning away to face the forest path.

Sir Trillium continued to clear his throat. Sir Columbine grunted his disapproval. Miss Twigg twittered in delight. And Lady Wrenna smiled, filled with sensation that made her feel more alive than she ever had before.

* * *

Lady Wrenna had never felt at home growing up as a young princess, belabored by the luxury of Raynewood Castle. She had always found the constraining rules, the high expectations placed upon her, and her royal brother's rigid plans for her to far outweigh the perks and privileges that came with being a child of the King and Queen. And while it cannot be denied, she was a stranger to some of the token discomforts of peasant life—pangs of hunger, anxieties of labor, the need for money, cold nights without a roof to ward the wind or rain, exposure to any and all the elements, to violence and general hardship; the list goes on and on—still... Princess Raynewald felt a kinship with the smallfolk, whom she secretly referred to as the *true* folk.

Her days were filled with daydreams of working in the stables, of serving ale at the local tavern, or even of weary farmers toiling to feed the kingdom. She'd study her hands, soft and pale and clean as prized, imported silk. She wished for calluses, for small embedded thorns, for red tallies where the tall grass had protested against her passing. Her nails were long and smooth, unbroken, pretty. She knew her desires were odd, but she longed for the black crescent of dirt to rest beneath each broken and serrated edge of brittle keratin. She pined for suntanned hands with fingers free of cumbersome jewels. Though most peasants would gladly trade places with Princess Wrenna, it was Wrenna, as much as any stablehand or tavern wench, who was eager to make the swap.

As a child, lost in her unorthodox fantasies—her inclination to abandon her crown, to take up the pitch fork, to join the *true folk*—Wrenna was regarded as aloof, always "wandering off to another realm." As an adult, beleaguered by suitors who sought her hand, to use her as a pawn for political gain, as a stitch to sew old wounds exchanged between begrudging kingdoms, as a body to slake temptations, or a biological machine to produce coveted male heirs; Lady Wrenna became regarded as a cold, hard bargain with a pair of tits.

It was true, Wrenna would concede if pressed, that she *had* met suitors who were kind enough, or young enough, or handsome enough to appease her own tastes for the opposite sex. But the stipulation of being owned was too steep a price for marriage to be worthwhile. At the end of the day—any and all of them—Wrenna was pleased to be free of the bond that her King and brother and tradition continually urged her to accept.

Her dreams of wielding the pitchfork and mugs of ale had faded with time, but her fondness for the *true folk* was resolute.

As her twenties fermented nearer to thirty, Wrenna became more and more fascinated by magic. It was then that strange dreams came to her with regularity; nightly visions of a crown set with an amber stone. Wrenna would awaken, filled with longing and need, all the while realizing that the dream was nothing new. Rather, it had been recurring since the infancy of her memory.

And so it was, that very night while under the stars, their thousands of tiny lights veiled by the thick canopy of The Raynewood, that Lady Raynewald drifted off to sleep in her bedroll on the fringes of a fire, its warm glow illuminating her three escort knights, and little Twigg nuzzled by her side.

More comfortable on the bare earth amid the forest than on her feather bed in Raynewood Castle, Wrenna dreamed of a dashing knight with pale, luminous eyes. She dreamed of a brooding menace made of stone. More dire, yet more distant, she dreamed, too, of a sorceress with the power and rage of a goddess scorned. In the end, she dreamed of what she always dreamt: a pewter crown, and an amber stone that radiated with pure and potent magic.

* * *

The second day of Lady Wrenna's travels went as smoothly as one could hope—until it didn't. The day began with breakfast, as any day should. The rashers of bacon and fried eggs brought from the Raynewood Castle kitchens went down well with the fresh forest berries Sir Hawthorn had foraged the day before. With their appetite sated and blue skies above them, the company travelled in good cheer among good weather.

Afternoon was no less pleasant, no less uneventful. The mild soreness of travelling on horseback was not yet so irksome to render pain, but merely pleasant, especially when dismounting to stretch one's legs and lay out upon the moss-strewn forest floor. Frequent breaks were allowed for the sake of the princess, but it was always Wrenna who stood up first, saddling her horse and urging the company to move on.

It was just before nightfall when the mundane pleasantries and uneventful day escalated into horror. The company had dismounted for another break, debating whether they should stop for the day and set up camp and build a fire; or if they should press on for another hour or so to close the shrinking gap between themselves and their destination.

Sir Trillium dismounted from his brindled destrier, stretching and yawning before he spoke. "For what it's worth, I say we call it a good day's travel and rest for the evening. If Melorin's tower has stood all these years, and the old wizard himself doesn't expire in the next day or two, it should make no difference that we retire a little early and add an hour to the journey tomorrow." The young knight let his travel satchel fall upon the grass and, massaging his shoulders, said through another yawn, "My advice is rest and an early dinner, Your Grace." In his weariness, Sir Trillium allowed a weak smile to escape the constraints of a knight's expected propriety toward the princess he served. "And perhaps a cup of wine. Now, wouldn't that be nice?"

Before Sir Columbine had the chance to reproach Sir Trillium for his youthful fumbling of decorum, Sir Trillium's head, smile and all, fragmented into innumerable shards of skull, untold globules of brain. The grass where he stood was covered in blood, the forest flowers trampled by his lifeless body as it collapsed in a heap across the ground. The devastation of Sir Trillium was followed by the briefest moment of silence before the night air was filled with songs of pandemonium. All at once, a chorus of chaos: the braying of panicked horses, their hooves like thunder on the forest floor as they scattered in all gloomy directions; the metallic rasp of longswords pulled free of their scabbards; Twigg's wild cries, and, louder than all the rest combined, the god awful shrieking of the gargoyles besieging Wrenna and her company.

Columbine was quick, shattering the stone arm of a demon imp with the powerful impact of his sword. Hawthorn was even quicker, beheading the lion head of a chimera, while snapping its serpent tail with a swift kick of his heavy boot. He lifted his shield in time to deflect the murderous rush of some heinous, winged beast, bashing it soundly into crumbs before readying for his next attacker.

Lady Wrenna froze for a time that seemed to her an eternity, but, in reality, was a few seconds. She had the sense to draw her sword, which she carried purely as a matter of course, having never trained with weapons of any kind, nor had she any intention of using one. It was with instinct, then, more than anything, that led the princess to raise up the blade to intercept the approach of a stone harpy, wedging the sword between herself and the monster, felling the foul creature, which crumbled into a pile of pebbles at the hooves of Wrenna's frenzied mare.

Sadly, no such instinct aided Twigg, who was thrown from her pony in the panic of the beast's distress. Wrenna watched on in horror, but turned away in time to avoid witnessing her handmaiden's head rupture on a pile of rocks. Unfortunately, Wrenna could not deafen herself to the sound of Twigg's cranium popping open, a hollow splitting sound like a ripe watermelon dropped onto cobbles.

Wrenna didn't have time to mourn the sudden death of her friend, the loss of her confidant who guarded her secrets, the nurse who tended her needs from infancy into adulthood. Wrenna didn't have time for *anything*—except to flee as fast as she could—as more and more villains, gargoyles by the dozen, materialized from every shadow of the forest.

The last thing Wrenna saw as she galloped away—in a direction she hoped was north—was Sir Columbine besieged by half a dozen stone demons, a melange of swords and axes, claws and fangs denting his armor and tearing at his flesh. She witnessed Sir Hawthorn, too, but only for a moment. He felled a gargoyle, then another, then was lost to sight altogether, buried by the forest separating the brave knight from the princess who fled from certain death.

Wrenna rode for an hour or more, long after the sun had set and the darkness of night had consumed the woods. It began to rain, and all the warmth of the day had leached from her body. Exhausted, bereft, grieving, and terribly frightened, she dismounted and collapsed under what cover she could find beneath the wide, needled hem of an ancient conifer.

Wrenna Raynewald, Princess of Raynewood, cried herself to sleep amid the cold and rain. Without warning, her romantic sense of adventure plummeted to vexation and dread. All of sudden, that feather bed in a warm, cosy castle didn't seem so bad.

* * *

What were gargoyles doing in the middle of the forest? As creatures of stone, how had they materialized from the wood and earth? Is there a graveyard nearby? A decrepit castle? Headstones or ruins that might provide gargoyles with a home, the material to manifest? And why, I wonder, did they attack us?

These were among Wrenna's many thoughts as she awakened the following morning. She wasted little time mounting her horse and riding northward in search of Melorin and his tower of magic. She could think of few reasonable answers to her questions, but none seemed of any importance—trivial, next to the deaths of her escort knights and her dear friend, Twigg. The thought of their sudden, horrible ends brought tears to her eyes. With no time to sit and be sad, Lady Raynewald mourned on the go.

The forest, though just as beautiful as the day before, now seemed to Wrenna a strange and spoiled landscape, a haunted place where ghouls and nightmares might manifest behind every tree.

Still, she had nowhere to go but forward. Wrenna was resolved in her quest to find Melorin, determined to become his apprentice in magic. Though every fiber of her being demanded that she dismount and curl up onto the ground to weep for her dead friend, cowling among the overwhelming fear that filled her soul, Lady Raynewald resisted giving in to these limiting urges.

Her brother, the king, had once told her what he often had to tell himself—a slogan he relied on since he first took up the crown of the kingdom bearing their family name. King Waldorf had told his sister: "Bravery is not the absence of fear, but the action one takes in the face of it." Lady Wrenna whispered those words as she rode on amid the eerie morning mists of the forest. She might have been filled with fear, but her actions reflected bravery.

Bravery and determination are fine things, especially during a quest for magic. Even so, such qualities cannot nourish the body, and Wrenna was entirely without food. The supplies had been divvied among her escort knights, who were either certainly dead as was the case for Sir Trillium; or very likely dead, as was the case for Sir Columbine and Sir Hawthorn. Wherever they were, dead or alive, the food that they carried could not serve her now.

Wrenna would willingly delve into the dreaded netherworld before she turned back to look for the scattered loaves of bread and broken eggs among the severed limbs and ruptured heads of her friends. Her tummy growled, which made her flinch. *It's not a monster*, she told herself. *Not a monster...*

As the day wore on and the sun rose higher in the sky, its light and warmth did much to dissipate the mist and gloom of the forest. The mood fell miles shy of cheery, but at least it was a little less grim, and Wrenna was no longer wracked with chills. She ignored her hunger, the increasingly frequent pleas of her digestion.

Trotting northward, ever resolute, she scanned the endless trees for signs of Melorin's tower.

She found a stream in the early afternoon, dismounting from her mare to drink its clear, cold water. Kneeling on the bank, she drank her fill, and a narrow beam of sunshine fell from a gap in the trees to bathe her in its golden aura. The moment, while peaceful, wasn't meaningful in any unusual way, yet something had captured Wrenna's attention.

Beside her, a butterfly fluttered in the light. The insect was like none she had ever seen before. It was black as black could ever be, as black as a moonless, starless night. As black as the deepest tunnel in the darkest cave. As black as the heart of a mountain.

Yet somehow, even as it presented the epitome of darkness, the winged creature radiated light, seeming to absorb the sun that it fluttered in and out of, trailing light as it took flight further down the stream. Something compelled Wrenna to follow the butterfly, to observe it further—at least, anyhow, while it fluttered north, which by good fortune it did at that moment.

Wrenna took the reins of her mare and guided the beast along on foot. In this manner, she meandered through the forest for an hour or more, all the while trailing the strange and beautiful butterfly that seemed to her, somehow, to be made from equal parts darkness and light. After a time, the butterfly slowed, began to circle. It fluttered up among the trees, then down… landing on the nose of a lion carved from stone, and finally settling on the head of a gargoyle chimera resting in the sun.

Wrenna's eyes shot wide open and her sword was drawn in an instant. She was prepared to defend herself, to attack, to run… to respond in whatever way the next few dire moments determined was the best course of action. But the chimera did not move. It did not budge a single inch.

Maybe it's only a statue? Wrenna couldn't be sure. She waited and watched as the stone chimera remained perfectly still. It didn't even bother to shoo away the butterfly that now rested over its vacant eyes. Frozen with indecision, Wrenna stood with her sword in the center of an open glade.

"You have arrived at last," a voice filled the quiet from very close by, from out of nowhere. *Who is speaking?* Wrenna wondered, looking from side to side, behind her, in front of her. *The ground? The stone chimera?*

"Neither." Wherever the voice was coming from, whoever was speaking, they seemed to have read her mind.

Wrenna squinted at the insect that was paradoxically both dark and light. "The… butterfly?"

"Bingo!" A great purple cloud billowed from the insect, turning blue, then green, then back to purple, back to blue, as if grappling with indecision. In the end, the cloud turned black as ink, as black as that strange butterfly's wings, before erupting in a flash of light. Wrenna blinked away the luminous assault that was brighter and harsher than staring into the midway sun.

Seconds later, when she opened her eyes to hazard a look at whatever might come next, the butterfly was gone, the chimera had vanished. In their place stood a wizened yet distinguished old man. He was dressed in robes dyed the very darkest of black, though his shaggy hair and long beard were white to the point of luminosity. He wore a tall and wide-brimmed purple hat, and held a staff with a great, crystal orb divided into two perfect halves, one dark and one light.

"Melorin?" It seemed stupid to doubt it, Wrenna considered, looking behind the robed, old man to a stone tower that had suddenly risen out of the open glade to soar above the trees at its fringes.

"None other." The wizard smiled playfully, bowing almost comically in extravagance. "Welcome, Lady Raynewald, to my humble abode."

There was nothing humble about the man before her,

neither in his showboating entrance or his spectacular abode. Melorin's tower was made from stones the size of warhorses, soaring so high as to scrape the clouds—that is, if it hadn't been a clear day. Its construction was aided by magic, that much was obvious. From its wide base to its high witch's cap turret, windows and balconies pocked and jutted from the stone. All over, in profusion, the tower was festooned in gargoyles.

Gargoyles?! Lady Wrenna considered the chimera, the butterfly—Melorin—who led her here to the stone monster. Though she had seen Sir Hawthorn slice free its head, kick off its tail, the beast was exactly the same, undamaged and whole. Scanning the heights of Melorin's tower, she saw more of them, recognizing others, too—the imp, the harpy, and many more. Fixed to the stone, they turned their heads to meet her gaze. Wrenna gasped, and was glad that she yet held a naked blade.

She brandished her sword and stepped back from the open glade, away from Melorin, who made no move to defend himself, and was still smiling. "I assure you, Princess, there is no need for alarm."

Wrenna did not believe the old man for a second. "Do you take me for a fool? Or do you think I am blind, wizard?"

"Neither, as it happens. Both your intellect and sight are quite proficient."

"You attempt to assuage me with your honey-coated lies," Wrenna spat, raising up her sword in a show of defiance. "I see your tower, old man, its many gargoyles. I see the stone monsters that serve you, the same beasts that attacked me last night, the same devils that killed my knights and dearest friend." Bravely, foolishly, Wrenna approached Melorin, poised to strike him with her sword.

The wizard sighed in mild irritation, almost as if he thought the whole altercation incredibly boring. He hardly moved—only lifting a finger—sending Wrenna's sword flying from her grip. When the blade hit the grass it took the shape of a serpent, slithering away across the open glade to the shadows of the forest.

Wrenna screamed, more in rage than in fear, shaking a fist at Melorin. "What now? Will you kill me, too? Just like you did Twigg? Well go ahead, you old, withered bastard!"

Melorin cocked his head and studied Lady Wrenna with a long, scrutinizing gaze. "Maybe I was wrong," he finally said. "Well, half wrong, anyways."

Wrenna had heard that wizards speak in riddles, but she wasn't in the mood to guess at Melorin's meaning. "What do you mean, *half* wrong?"

"You're certainly not blind," Melorin said. "I was right about *that*. But I may have been wrong about your intellect. You actually believe that I killed your friend, Twigg." He shook his head and clicked his tongue. "Your misguided supposition casts a shadow of doubt over your deductive reasoning. Still, I think you are salvageable, Lady Wrenna. I will not deny you today."

"What are you talking about, crazy old fool?"

"Fool?" Melorin shook his head again, his long beard trailing his chin left to right like a snow white pendulum. "Not I, dear girl. And not you, either, I think—even if you are horrifically wrong about what I did with Twigg."

"*What you did with Twigg?*" Lady Wrenna considered the possibility of her friend's survival—even so, her doubts were stronger than her hopes. "It is plain to me that you killed her!"

"Are you determined to believe that your friend is dead? Do you truly believe that I murdered an innocent woman?"

"These are your gargoyles!" She gestured to the tower, the stone creatures crowding around her, gradually descending to the tower's base. "The same ones that attacked us last night. I saw Sir Trillium torn asunder. I saw Sir Columbine besieged. I witnessed Sir Hawthorn surrounded by innumerable foes. And I saw sweet Twigg thrown from her pony." Tears welled up in Wrenna's eyes while she carried on shouting. "I heard her impact upon the rocks. I left her there. And if she somehow survived her fall, then she has lain injured and alone since last night, unprotected from your wretched army of monsters!"

No longer could Wrenna hold back her grief, her many tears of sorrow and wailings of rage. "You speak of my proficiency in sight, well, I *saw* these things, wizard! I saw what you did, how you attacked us in the night. I *saw* my friends die!"

Melorin leaned on his staff, gazing at Wrenna. His face was somber as he listened to her pour out her heart and vexations. He looked troubled, almost as much as Wrenna. Then his sad expression melted away, replaced by a mischievous grin. "You forget, Lady Wrenna, that I am a wizard."

"I forget nothing!" Wrenna spat at the old man.

"Ahh, but I think you do," Melorin countered. "For instance, have you forgotten, I wonder, that any decent wizard—and I assure you, I am the very best—is capable of illusion? As a master of illusion myself, it would present no trouble—no trouble at all—to conjure the semblance of your friends. To have their images murdered before your very *proficient* eyes."

Wrenna wiped the tears that fell freely down her cheeks, the rivers of snot that dribbled over her lips. "You mean… you didn't?"

"Kill them?" Melorin smiled. "No. Well… yes *and* no."

More wizard riddles? "Just tell me plainly, conjurer: are my friends alive and well?"

"Come, we shall talk among the comforts of my tower. Come, my dear apprentice. I shall explain all and everything."

Apprentice?

"Oh yes." Melorin read Wrenna's thoughts. "You have passed the test I laid out for you. Your performance was admirable. Now come along, Lady Wrenna. There is much to talk about, and even more to learn."

"Is Twigg alive?"

Melorin chuckled. "Come along, my apprentice..." He started toward the entrance of his majestic tower. "I shall tell you everything, and make you a nice, big dinner while I am at it. Come, let's silence that tummy of yours. It's loud enough to wake the dead!"

* * *

The interior of Melorin's tower proved even more impressive than the outside—and that was an understatement, if ever there was one. The front room widened upon entry, augmented by magic to expand five or six times the circumference of the stones that encased it. In days to come, Wrenna would learn that similar enchantments had been placed to expand the tower upward, as well as down beneath the ground. All told, Melorin's tower was many times wider than the exterior suggested, and boasted three times as many levels.

Size was one thing, but there were also countless wonders filling the tower's magically expanded dimensions. Full bookshelves lined the walls, great tomes with hundreds of pages filled with spells and histories, lore and myth. Here, a codex of cryptids, there, an index of kingdoms, the names and coat of arms of each royal family that encompassed the vast world of Garden. Glass bottles and jars, vaporous vials filled with bubbling potions, caught the light coming through stained glass windows—tall panels of kaleidoscopic brilliance, invisible from the outside. None of it made sense, but magic never does. Magic has its own laws, and its laws, in general, are lawless. Paradoxical? Oh, yes. But paradox and magic are like strawberries and cream, they go together to a tee.

Wrenna looked around in wonder, her eyes darting from one strange and fantastic object to the next. All those many curios and trinkets, the array of wands and crystals, rolled and ribboned scrolls filed away in a sky-high vertical shaft of shelving. The endless catalogue of herbs, preserves, dried berries and seeds. The skeletal remains of countless beasts, some known to Wrenna, others uncanny and undefined.

Among all of that *stuff*, all of that miraculous, magical paraphernalia, nothing held Lady Raynewald's interest quite so ardently as the table laden with fresh food, the feast that Melorin had laid out before her.

If her guts had been growling before, now, in the face of such succulent foods, it was bellowing like a volcanic eruption. Wrenna salivated as she took it all in: fresh, warm bread and great slabs of rich, yellow butter; meat pies, fruit pies, vegetable pies; roasted pumpkin, potatoes, and parsnip; soups and salads and dressings and sauces; olives, dates, and walnuts; food, food, food. And drink, let's not forget! Warm ale, cold ale. Wine, red and white. Mead and spirits, cordials and cold, crisp water. There was milk, too, sweetened and plain. And when, at last, Wrenna broke her fast, no matter what she ate or drank, each ravenous bite and thirsty gulp was replaced by Melorin's mighty magic.

"Eat as much as you like, dear girl," Melorin watched with amusement as Wrenna attacked the food with gusto. "I assure you, this feast will outlast your appetite." He picked up a perfect, red apple and took a loud, crunchy bite. "As a matter of fact," he said while chewing, "this spread would sate a dragon."

Wrenna carried on filling her belly, but stopped prematurely, setting down her half-eaten cob of corn. Now that her hunger had been answered, a litany of questions filled her mind. She wiped clean her chin of a trail of melted butter and asked Melorin, "What has become of Twigg?"

Melorin had eaten his apple down to its core. He counted its visible seeds, "Seven, my lucky number," before throwing the remains through an aperture in the tower wall that opened and closed in timing to its passing. "Your friend is alive," he turned to Wrenna and announced.

"She's… alive?!" She stood up so fast that her chair fell out from behind her. "Then we must go back and help her. Her head… she's hurt… she may be concussed, or worse!"

Melorin waved his hand and Wrenna's chair lifted up and returned to its place just behind where she stood. "Sit," he commanded. "Twigg is unharmed, and needs no saving or aid from you or I in any way."

"But… I saw her… her head…"

"Yes, yes," Melorin shooed her worries away with a brisk motion of his arm. "Illusion, remember? As in *not real*."

"So she did not fall from her pony? She did not strike her head?"

"She did not strike her head," Melorin assured her. "But she *did* fall. She fell straight into a portal I had disguised as a large rock."

Wrenna replayed the scene from the previous night in her mind, shaking her head in disbelief. "But, I *heard* it... oh, that dreadful sound: Twigg's head colliding with the stone."

"Quite similar to the vacuous suck during the moment an object passes through a portal—a distinct *pop*. Your imagination did the rest. You thought you saw your friend hit the rocks, so that is what you heard."

"Then, Twigg is not harmed? Not even a little?"

"She is back at Raynewood Castle, where she has been instructed to inform the king, your brother, that you have arrived here in one piece, and that you have been accepted as my apprentice in the pursuit and practice of the glorious art of magic."

"Twigg has been *instructed*? How?"

"Telepathic messages. You, too, will learn this method in time."

"So Twigg is okay?"

"Perfectly. She is safe and sound, warm and alive."

Wrenna visibly relaxed, but quickly tensed back up. "And my escorts? The knights that travelled with me? Their deaths were also an illusion? They're also okay? Safe and sound? Warm and alive?"

Melorin drew a slow and cautious breath. "Sadly, they failed in protecting you, even if it was preordained that harm would not befall you."

Wrenna pushed away her plate of food. "Then they are

dead? You killed them?"

Melorin made no apologies, offered no condolences. He met the reproachful eye of his apprentice and did not balk when he imparted these words: "Sacrifice goes hand in hand with magic, my dear lady. In the days of yore, when the old, strong sorcery was more than myth, spells required blood, their potency strengthened by the lives put into them, their power amplified by the offering of souls. Magic made heroes of men, and many men, heroic or otherwise, met their deaths at the wrong end of magic."

"You… *sacrificed* them?"

"Blood and souls, my apprentice. Without these, there is no life remaining. Without these, there is no magic."

Wrenna slammed her fist on the table, sending mugs of beer to spill across its surface, a dish of peas to explode with soft, green fireworks. "You are a villian!" She cursed Melorin, reaching for her sword. "You speak as though killing my men was necessary!"

"Yes," Melorin told her plainly. "Yes it was necessary. It will always be necessary. And you must learn to detach yourself from your emotions, Wrenna Raynewald, should you wish to learn and practice magic." A long, empty silence filled the room before Melorin elected to break it. Leaning forward, serious as the grave, he asked: "So, will you?"

Wrenna looked up at Melorin, fresh tears budding in the corners of her eyes. "Will I *what*?"

"Practice magic." The wizard leaned in closer. "Tell me, Wrenna Raynewald, will you do what you must to become a great mage? Will you take the blood, life, and souls that are required? Will you do what is needed to become my apprentice? I will have your answer here and now… are you, or are you not, willing to kill?"

Once again, the room was filled with silence. Wrenna did not speak. She did not need to. Melorin had read her mind.

"Come, my apprentice," Melorin offered Wrenna his hand. "There is much to learn."

* * *

The first lesson of Wrenna's training was on how to open her mind. The process required nothing of her, except that she was naturally receptive to the spell that Melorin cast upon her—which she was. The spell was simple, a single enchantment in the form of a raw magical thread, or a worm, as Melorin liked to think of it. Once conjured, the string-like serpent of magic entered the body under the eyelid, through the back of the eyes, eventually riding on the optic nerves to connect with the greater network of its host's neural pathways. The process was quick, taking a matter of minutes. It was also entirely painless.

"And that's that," Melorin told Wrenna, concluding her first lesson an hour after breakfast.

"You mean, it's done?" She had felt nothing at all during the few minutes Melorin had intoned with focus. Nothing, except maybe the slightest of tingling where his hand lay upon her forehead. "That's it? The spell is complete?"

Melorin withdrew his hand from Wrenna and nodded. "The gift of magic has always been in you. It has been lying in wait, growing all this time. This spell, what I have done here today… has merely awakened it. You will soon feel its power. And when you do, you will recognize a feeling you have known since birth. It will be like looking in the mirror, seeing that familiar face, and yet seeing yourself for the very first time. You will see. And when you do, you will learn. You will learn very, very fast."

And she did. She took to magic with ease, progressing with smooth and accelerated advancement. And just as Melorin had told her she would, she saw herself clearly, *felt* what it meant to live in her body, as she had everyday of her life. She was the same old Wrenna. Nothing had changed. And yet her new reflection was somehow more real than her original self, as if the magical iteration of Wrenna was the genuine version, and the non-magical was naught but a faded copy.

Though an imperfect metaphor, Wrenna likened the distinction to being asleep and being awake. Before magic, she had been sleeping. Now, she was wide awake.

In her new, enlightened state of mind, Wrenna dedicated all her time to the study of enchantment, funneling her efforts into becoming a strong and able magician. She was most proficient, wasting little time mastering the basics: simple illusions, minor bolt spells, and the ability to inflict a state of sleep on those ill prepared to defend against its lulling malaise.

In the cozy confines of her private quarters on the 77th floor of Melorin's 99-floor tower (recall that it only appeared to be 30-storeys tall from the outside), Wrenna worked tirelessly to improve her craft, concentrating her magical essence to produce lifelike illusions of squirrels, salamanders, and spiders. These images, at first, remained stationary, but in a matter of weeks Wrenna was able to make them move. What started as a crude catalogue of static, hazy mirages, blurring at the edges, developed into sharp, detailed illusions that moved with the apparent authenticity of an actual, living animal or physical object.

Bolt spells came easy. They were also quite fun. Wrenna would practice in the open glade spreading around Melorin's tower. There, she would shoot beams of fire, or lightning, or concentrated water, or even air at wooden targets set at various distances. While these blasts of energy could not shatter the gates of a stronghold, nor knock a fully grown troll off its feet, they could harm and distract smaller enemies, making a goblin marauder or even an armored knight think twice before pitting themselves against her power.

It was not long before Wrenna forwent the use of wands, becoming proficient in casting spells from the palm of her hand at will. Be it fire, lightning, water, or air… the elements, aided by magic, projected directly from her body.

Wrenna focused her magic and funneled her intent, taking aim at her target—a dummy stuffed with straw. The raw force that she summoned coalesced in her fist, erupting from her palm to smite her makeshift enemy. The dummy's threadbare cloak set aflame, its innards blasted asunder. Wrenna smiled, while bits of her target smoldered in the grass.

"Not bad for a lady of the court!" Wrenna applauded herself.

Melorin shrugged, glancing calmly at his apprentice. "Your power is sufficient," he let that hang in the air, "… to thwart enemies that are made out of straw!" He chuckled at Wrenna's deflated expression. "You show plenty of promise, young woman. Even so, you have a very long way to go."

He tickled Wrenna just below the ribs and under the armpits, laughing like a maniacal gnome who had drunk his fill of acorn wine.

"In time," Melorin promised his power-hungry apprentice, "your bolt spells will do more than tickle a dragon."

Melorin promised he would teach her greater bolt spells when she was ready, those that borrowed power from the stars, celestial beams capable of stopping a centaur in mid-gallop—and more impressive, reducing its body to an indistinguishable, charred mass.

"But in all seriousness," he told Wrenna after he ceased his tickle spree "Keep practicing. Keep up the hard work. As days fall away and the weeks wither into passing months, years, decades, your power and abilities will only grow. Truly, you will be a magician to be feared."

Wrenna had no desire to be feared. She would not, no matter how powerful she became, purposely instill fear to meet her goals. Unless, of course, she was confronted by raiding pirates or ogre bandits— the "bad guys" of the world who, if they had their way, would squash the "good guys" underfoot. Still, she accepted Melorin's compliment, and took his advice. She continued to work hard, putting all her energies into magic. She couldn't deny the truth of her master's prediction: she *was* becoming powerful.

Despite her advancement, becoming stronger, more

proficient with magic every day, Wrenna carried a measure of guilt that continued to grow alongside her increased ability. Eating away at her was the notion that her magic required living sacrifices—the blood, life, and souls that were needed to fuel its potency. True, she had not taken human life—not yet—but the large population of rabbits burrowing in the glade, their prolific breeding that supplied a seemingly endless glut of bunnies, was constantly subjugated by the wringing of necks and well-aimed bolt spells; frequent murders enacted by Wrenna as a necessity for her magical practice. Indeed, the gaggle of geese that frequented the nearby pond had taken a hit, too, thinned in numbers due to Wrenna's constant need of life-force to keep her studies afloat. She hated taking lives, but she could not abandon her pursuit of magic. As a result, she was riddled with guilt, which was enough to keep her awake most nights.

Still, Wrenna got her sleep, and plenty of it. At night, in her bed, when she could think of nothing but the little bunnies kicking out their long legs as they drew their last breath, or the graceful, snow-white geese as they struggled and honked in a frenzy under the strain of her boot, she would cast a simple spell, an enchantment to help her sleep. Wrenna did not miss the irony of it all, how the lives that she took were both the source of her guilt—her inability to sleep—and also the source of her sleeping spells. Directing these spells at herself, she was aided in finding a sound, if fitful, slumber, courtesy of the lives she had taken.

* * *

Melorin's library, like everything else in his tower, was rife with enchantment. Its physical space was remarkably vast, made cathedral in scope by the magic that warped the dimensions of its architecture. Lighting the vertical shafts of populated shelving were heatless flames; not even fire in truth, but a flickering starlight cool to the touch. The collection it highlighted seemed to stretch on without end.

The size of Melorin's library was well beyond any other that Wrenna had ever visited—far larger, for instance, than the well-reputed library of her home in Raynewood. The sheer number of its texts, the array of volumes that lined the walls, the many shelves stretching as tall and wide as a fully-grown dragon expanding its wings, was staggering, intimidating, *invigorating*. How many books there might be was anyone's guess—not even Melorin knew the exact number. Like drops in an ocean, the total figure was inconceivable, yet every tome contained magic! Such strange and wonderful magic. Terrible magic. Dark and foreboding. Miraculous and beautiful. Each page within every tome, each word on every scroll or scrap of vellum, seemed either to describe, account, explore, or evoke the very essence of magic. All of Melorin's tower was filled with magic, but its library was *erupting* with it, bursting at the seams with so very much to learn.

When it came to finding an ideal place to study, Wrenna loved the library most of all, favoring its cavernous magnitude and palpable magic over the cozier, more intimate qualities of her private chambers. Truthfully, there was not a single room or space to be found in Melorin's tower that Wrenna did not enjoy; her new home was very much beloved to her. Even so, the library inspired her more than any other area, and it was there that she devoted most of her time to learning, spending many hours each day pouring over volumes of witchcraft, wizardry, history, and myth. Much like her magical abilities, her knowledge of the occult was expanding precipitously. Not only was Wrenna becoming powerful, but she was also becoming knowledgeable, cultivating wisdom and education to compliment her sorcery.

Among the dozens, hundreds, of books that Wrenna had read through—an infinitesimal fraction of Melorin's library—there was one book that sparked her interest and stuck in her mind. It was not so large, nor ornate a tome as to strike the eye while sitting up on the shelves, but its title,

"Demon in the Shard," intrigued Wrenna enough that she procured it for her study, and found its contents captivating enough to read through the dull historical preface. Its opening pages were dedicated to the greatness of a wizard from long, long ago, a mage of astonishing power by the name of Persimmon. An account of his exploits were detailed over many pages, including his creation of his scion, a perfect clone. The scion, who went by the name of Tamarillo, did not bend to the will of his creator, betraying Persimmon in the end—indeed, betraying an entire kingdom with his foul deeds and ill-conceived magic.

For Wrenna, all of this added up to a mild interest, who was stirred just enough by Persimmon and Tamarillo's story to read on, which led her to progress to the portion of their story that *deeply* interested her. Tamarillo, who at that point in his tale mostly went by Tammy, was in cahoots with a demon by the name of Darkstain, or Darkheart (scholars are at odds on this account). Wrenna paused to consider her preference, and without much conviction behind her choice, she decided that, among the two schools of thought, she would refer to the demon as Darkstain. Now, with that out of the way… Tammy traded a portion of his soul to inherit the power of Darkstain, and with this newfound power he wreaked inglorious mischief on the Kingdom of Clearwater, and its people. Persimmon became enraged, ashamed of his scion—and himself, too, as he bore the responsibility of Tamarillo's creation. In the end, the great wizard and his scion did battle, and while Tammy was killed outright, Darkstain lived long enough to transfer his soul into an insect or spider. The details are hazy, but the account suggests that Persimmon was killed by the overt power and use of his own magic, and that Darkstain, in the form of a bug, was trapped in amber or some kind of crystal—some sources suggest quartz, even amethyst. Regardless of the material, the nature and composition of the reliquary, the text insinuates that it was blasted into several fragments—exactly how many is the subject of much debate. Some say as many as one hundred fragments have scattered across the lands. Fringe scholars speculate thousands. By far the most common consensus was that four shards of perfectly divided quarters lay scattered in various, hidden whereabouts, with each crystal portion located within one of the four Garden continents. Due to this largely accepted theory, the four shards have been assigned by the names of the lands they are believed to reside: Hyacinth, Dahlia, Zinnia, and Dianthus.

These details did much to pique Wrenna's fascination, but what *really* interested Wrenna about "Demon in the Shard" was its claim to the purported location of one of the crystal shards, a location fairly near to her own—insofar, anyhow, as the whole world of Garden is concerned. And what *really, really* interested Wrenna about "Demon in the Shard" was its claim to the purported power that each crystal lent to the ones who wielded them. Supposedly, according to the text, one of the demon shards would, in the very least, double the power of the sorcerer who obtained it.

Somewhat of a setback to Wrenna's enthusiasm regarding the demon shard, and the notion of seeking it out, was the final pages of information that imparted a rumor: the nearest shard was believed to be set in the crown of a goblin lord by the name of Blightheart, a villainous king and accomplished sorcerer who dwells under the cavernous ruins of Castle Cloud in The Cloudy Mountains. For most adventurers, be they warrior, wanderer, or mage, it was a compelling enough argument to divert the prospect of questing for the crystal shard.

For Wrenna, it only made obtaining the shard more appealing.

* * *

Aware that she was already half a year into her apprenticeship, Wrenna decided she would ask Melorin to charge her with a quest. Her hope was to achieve something great, something truly remarkable, so that she might return to her brother, the king, and make clear to him her advances in magic. Wrenna was already progressing with remarkable efficiency. Even without a quest for further power, she might have already acquired sufficient power to convince her brother that her magical training was worthy of abandoning the tradition of marrying, that her choice to become a mage was well founded. Even so, Wrenna wanted more than to merely appease her brother. She wanted to *astound* him.

A quest would allow Wrenna to prove her worth, to punctuate her power. She would need the endorsement of her master, of course. So she brought the notion to Melorin.

"Master Melorin, if I may interrupt your meditations?"

Melorin levitated in the center of his meditation room, a sparse, small square with undecorated wood paneling and low lighting. It was the most unremarkable room in all of the tower. Months ago, when Wrenna had asked him why this may be, her master did not divulge an answer. Instead, he suggested that she meditate on her question and come back to him when she found an answer. Wrenna did as Melorin instructed, and quickly determined that the room had been left intentionally plain to avoid unwanted distraction. When she told Melorin her answer, he did not reward her with his confirmation, and yet his smile of approval could not be missed.

"No trouble at all." Melorin slowly revolved in midair before descending upon the floor to sit facing his apprentice. "Speak your mind, child."

"Thank you, Master Melorin." Wrenna bowed and sat on the floor across from him. She gathered her thoughts, then cleared her throat. "I've come to ask something of you," she began, "to seek your permission for something I have planned."

Melorin stretched across the wooden floorboards, casual as a cat in the sun. "A quest is a fine idea, my apprentice." He had a habit of reading Wrenna's mind, which saved her the trouble of presenting her case, of choosing the right words and well-crafted sentences to make her arguments.

"The Demon Shard of Hyacinth, is it?" Melorin reached for his large, outlandish purple hat, placing it over his wild, white hair. He nodded, combing fingers through his beard. "The pursuit of this coveted, magical item… I trust you realize… this will be dangerous business."

Wrenna nodded from across the small room. "I am aware of the dangers, Master. I have determined that the risk is worth the reward."

"The risk is guaranteed," Melorin flatly stated. "The reward… well… that is not."

"Your words ring true, Master Melorin. But the risk of no reward just adds to the initial risk we have already made plain. All risks accounted for, I am happy to pursue the proposed quest."

Melorin continued to play with his beard, now making soft humming sounds that reflected his pondering thoughts. The moments stretched on for a time while the wizard seemed to teeter on indecision. Finally, he spoke: "The risk of no reward is an element to the quest that I am willing to accept. As to the dangers you will be exposed to… This is a bitter herb to swallow."

Wrenna waited patiently while Melorin entered another prolonged bout of thoughtful silence. The small meditation room was so quiet that Wrenna could hear her own heartbeat pounding with anticipation for her master's resolution. Just before the moment when Wrenna thought her patience might expire, at long last, Melorin delivered his judgement.

"I grant you permission to go on this quest to seek the Demon Shard of Hyacinth."

Wrenna visibly stirred, allowing a sliver of excitement to escape her composure. Melorin noticed this, and held out his hands to subdue her titillation. "However," he added, letting the surprise stipulation hang in the air for several agonizing seconds, "I absolutely insist that you do not go alone."

Wrenna was fraught. "But, Master, *please*." She stood up in protest. "The accomplishment will not be my own if the quest is completed with your aid."

"Sit!" Melorin commanded. "And do not whine like a child, for Garden's sake!"

Wrenna sat and remained silent.

"That's better." Melorin shook his head before he continued. "I will not be joining you, you might be glad to know."

"Master… I did not insinuate that—"

"Silence, little girl. It is golden. It is what I require. And you shall give me this gift, yes?"

Wrenna did not answer with words, but with a nod that she understood.

"Good!" Melorin beamed. "As I was saying… I will not go with you on this venture to obtain the shard of Hyacinth, but neither will you go alone." Melorin stood and stretched. He procured a pipe from the deep pockets of his robes and took his time packing it with a wad of tobacco. He lit it with a small, blue flame that appeared at the tip of his finger and, once inhaling the tobacco, notably relaxed. "Meditation is a fine way to unwind the frazzled tangles of a busy mind, but nothing does the trick half so well as good tobacco." Melorin grinned, blowing impressive smoke rings across the room.

"Now… Where was I? Yes, of course. Your companion in travel." Melorin paced the room as he spoke, pausing now and again to savor the contents of his pipe. "Sorcery is made stronger by the sword," he explained. "Magic and muscle go hand in hand, complementary halves to form a greater whole. Mage and warrior, working together, are greater than the sum of their talents. Trust me, young apprentice, you will do well to travel with The Azurite Knight."

Wrenna was no longer able to maintain her silence. "The Azurite Knight? Who is that?"

Melorin chuckled in private amusement. "You have met him before," he told Wrenna.

"Have I?"

"Yes, though you know him by another name."

Wrenna had no idea who this "Azurite Knight," a man she had supposedly met, might be. "And what name is that?" She heard footsteps behind her, but before she could turn around to see who the newcomer might be, her question had been answered.

"Hawthorn, Your Grace."

Wrenna stared into the familiar face of one her escorts knights, a man she believed to be dead. Sir Hawthorn was just as handsome as she remembered him. And those eyes! Those stunning, sapphire eyes—*azurite* eyes!

"But ignore the old fool." Hawthorn winked playfully across the room at Melorin. "The Azurite Knight is his silly nickname for me. I am no true knight. Merely a humble warrior, Your Grace."

"And *Her Grace,"* Melorin chimed in, "is merely my humble apprentice. She is no longer a princess—not here, not while under my direction. So drop the formalities, Hawthorn, which you are so very good at on most occasions. Cast aside the "Your Grace" and try out Wrenna, instead. After all, it *is* her name, and a pretty one, too. A pretty name for a pretty girl, don't you think?" Melorin laughed as he watched Wrenna blush, Hawthorn shuffling his feet self-consciously.

Wrenna pried her own eyes away from Hawthorn's set of bewitching blue optics. She managed to escape the web of their beauty only to become lost in the chiseled contours of his jaw, the shadow of his coarse stubble, and luster of his luxurious, dark locks. "I had taken you for dead," she finally managed to say. "Yet here you are before me"

"Wizard tricks, Your Grace—*ahem*—I mean Wrenna."

"Illusion," Wrenna whispered.

"And a fine illusion *you* present, my lady. You are as beautiful as I remember, and I am most pleased to see you once again."

Melorin butted in, rescuing Wrenna from her embarrassment, which had been aroused by the delicious agony of flirtation. "Come," he announced behind his two young underlings. “Let us leave this small, drab room to convene somewhere fitting for a happy reunion. To the dining hall, I should think, where we might feast and prepare for your impending journey. After all, I have made up my mind: your quest begins tomorrow.

* * *

Sleep did not come easy that night while Wrenna tossed and turned in her bed. For once, it was not guilt that kept her awake in the dark. What was it? Nerves? Excitement? Fear? A cocktail of all these feelings? Wrenna wasn't sure herself. A poor night's sleep is no way to start a journey, she determined, and so, as she often did during those last seven months, she conjured up a slumber spell, inflicting restful sleep upon herself.

With dawn came a rude awakening, the rooster's crow an irksome reminder that a groggy morning often followed self-inflicted snooze enchantments. Wrenna rose, reluctantly abandoning her warm bed. The cold stones on her bare feet were extra icy, she thought. The magic of Melorin's tower seemed subdued, Wrenna was sure of it.

Getting dressed in travelling garb felt like a perversion to her routine; the vice-like riding boots and close-fitting jerkin was an outfit most constricting, almost claustrophobic, next to her loose wizard robes that she had become accustomed to wearing these last two seasons. She was forced to remind herself: this was *her* idea, this notion of quest and adventure. Despite this fact, she was filled with emotions she had not anticipated, and, when shutting the door to her bed chamber, knowing it would be some time before she would return, it took all of her will to hold back her tears. As Wrenna wandered down from the 77th floor of the magical tower in a paradoxical ten steps that transported her to its ground level, she was struck by the fact that she was already homesick. Too emotional to face her food, she skipped out on breakfast, wondering if there was a spell to simulate apathy. If there was, she would have surely cast it on herself.

Melorin was not one for long goodbyes. He had told

Wrenna and Hawthorn as much the night before, declaring that he would abscond from any sentimentality that might lead to becoming mopey. "Good luck," he had said to his apprentice and the warrior he had assigned to protect her. "And stay safe," he added as he left the dining hall.

As Wrenna followed Hawthorn beyond the open glade, and once the forest obscured any evidence of Melorin's Tower, she felt a pang in her heart that brought to light just how much that strange, magical place now meant to her. It had become her home. As much, and probably more so, than even Raynewood Castle, the walls that had confined her for thirty years.

* * *

Heading northward, they rounded the western neck of The Raynewood Peninsula. For Wrenna, leaving this landmass behind them marked a singular milestone: the first time she had traveled beyond the kingdom that bore her family name. Symbolically, the transition to new lands was dramatic. Physically, *actually*, it was as if the change had never occurred. The sky was still blue overhead. The grass remained green underfoot. The air was still breathable, and the sun still painted the world in its warm, buttery hues. There was a brief interlude of grassland and low, rolling hills occupied by farms, the quaint settlements that tended them. This domestic landscape terminated within a half day's travel, evaporating into memory as the great forest of The Greenwood enveloped them in its ancient growth and immensity.

"I hope you like trees," Hawthorn remarked. "And lots of them."

Wrenna loved trees, and didn't understand why sarcasm and a bitter tone accompanied Hawthorn's statement. "Who doesn't like trees? They are beautiful."

"Well," Hawthorn scoffed, "you've certainly come to the right place." He explained to Wrenna that The Greenwood was among one of Garden's largest forests, a woodland crescent spanning 900 miles east to west across the continent of Hyacinth. "I like trees, too, as it happens. But I prefer them with edges, with exit points and conceivable ends."

Wrenna looked up to the old-growth trees blotting out the sky and swallowing her whole. Lost beneath The Greenwood's dark canopy, she recalled a phrase she had once heard, one that suggested there are, in fact, scenarios that exemplify *too much of a good thing*. If that were true, Wrenna had yet to witness such scenarios herself. She shrugged, ignoring Hawthorn's unbecoming pessimism. Deciding not to comment, she quietly admired the innumerable trees.

Darkness fell early in the wood, and dusk, while fleeting, was remarkably beautiful. Billowing motes of spores, lazy clouds of pollen, and a profusion of busy, tiny insects scintillated in what few shafts of low sunlight threaded the endless trunks. Here and there, luminous sparks of bronze and gold drifted in the green gloom, horizontal pillars of light that formed and faded in a matter of minutes. As the last semblance of daylight ebbed into night, and with it, total darkness, Hawthorn built and fed the flames of a campfire that held the shadows at bay.

"Wine, Your Grace?" Hawthorne uncorked the bottle with his teeth and held it across the fire in offering.

"It's Wrenna," she reminded him. "Just Wrenna. And you, as I recall, are Hawthorn—*just* Hawthorn. Though do forgive me if I let slip the *Sir*. After all, I have to unlearn the false habits that have been founded on deception."

"The deceptions of *your* master, Your Gra—Wrenna."

"And yours, I wonder?"

Hawthorn laughed, a failed attempt to mask his resentment, and, becoming careless in his agitated state, spilled some wine into the fire. "Do you want a drink or not, Wrenna?"

Wrenna took the bottle and swigged a hearty gulp. She coughed, wiped her chin, then took a second glug. The wine was strong, and felt good when it hit her belly. It was like liquid flame, doing much to unravel the nerves and tension of her first day on the road.

She handed the bottle back to Hawthorn. "Well," she prodded, "is he?"

"Is 'who' what?" Hawthorn took a large quaff. Wrenna thought he might be hiding his emotions—perhaps even secrets—behind the bottle.

"Why have you joined me on this quest?" Wrenna asked. "Is your motivation money? Gold? Fame? Friendship with Melorin? A means to settle some debt to him? Is your will your own, I wonder? Or, as I suspect, like me, is Melorin your master?"

Hawthorn set down the bottle and stared across the fire at Wrenna. His eyes were so unusual, so arresting, so unworldly in their beauty. But they were not warm, just then, even as they reflected the amber firelight in their vivid, icy blue. They held in them boundless depths, brimming with mystery, tinged with bitterness, and filled with pain.

He took another sip. Swallowed. Sighed. "Melorin is my master, aye. But not like you, Wrenna. Not by a longshot." Again, he drank deep before passing the bottle back to Wrenna, who surprised herself by accepting and indulging in another long glug that worked wonders to dispel her homesickness. As the effects of the drink warmed her, unwinding the tight coils of her withdrawn nature, the handsome warrior sitting across from her became even more alluring, more captivating and provocative.

"I would like to know your story, Hawthorn." She hiccuped. "Would you share it with me?" All at once, the wine caught up with her, and the bright fire began to blur into the dark forest around it.

"Get some rest, Lady Wrenna," Hawthorn urged. "We have another long day of travel on the morrow." He looked up into the high canopy obscured by darkness. "And more trees…"

Wrenna did as Hawthorn said, having little other choice but to lie down and allow sleep to fall over her. Drifting off, she noticed Hawthorn watching over her, his hand ready on his sword while gazing out into the impenetrable gloom beyond the fire. The last thing she saw before sleep took hold of her senses was Hawthorn gazing down to smile upon her, and, when he turned away to continue his vigil, how the firelight caught his remarkable eyes, almost as if they radiated light from within.

For once, there was no need of incantations to aid her to her dreams. Wrenna closed her eyes and slept. She did not wake until the morning.

* * *

Wrenna woke to the soft sound of rain, though the dull throb in her temple told her a hangover would accompany her morning—perhaps most of the day. She blinked in the low, misty light and groaned.

"Here." Hawthorn held out a small bottle filled with pale liquid. Wrenna squinted up at his offering, noting that he was already dressed, packed, and busy combing the horses.

"What is this?" She held the vial at arm's length. "Please, no more wine."

Hawthorn laughed. "Not booze, Wrenna. An elixir. For hangovers. Distillation of ginger and peppermint, with a touch of honey. Trust me, it works wonders."

"If you say so."

"I do. So drink up. And after that, have some breakfast. Fried mushrooms with butter await you. Sliced apples, too."

"Thank you," Wrenna wrestled herself out of her bedroll. "You are too kind."

"Maybe so," Hawthorn grunted. "But the road won't be. So hurry up. And after your breakfast, get dressed. We ride as soon as you're finished."

Wrenna willed herself to her feet, yawned, and drank the distillation of ginger and peppermint. Her eyes watered at the elixir's strength, and she keeled over, coughing.

For some moments, Wrenna continued to struggle,

clutching at her throat. And all the while, Hawthorn chuckled in amusement. “Not the whole bottle!” He filled the forest with his laughter. “You’re only meant to take a small sip.”

Wrenna finally caught her breath and, hunching over, glared at Hawthorn through a wild mane of disheveled hair.

“You know something, Wrenna?”

“What, Hawthorn?” Somehow, she knew she’d regret playing along.

“You’re really cute when you let yourself go. Something between a haystack and a pretty princess.”

All over again, Hawthorn erupted with jolly laughter. And though Wrenna was the butt of his joke, she couldn’t help laughing herself. When the two of them finally settled down, Wrenna looked around among the silvered mist of the vast and beautiful Greenwood. Though she couldn’t believe it, the elixir had worked. Her hangover faded with the fog as the sun rose and the rain settled to make way for a clear and sunny day.

* * *

Good weather and good cheer do much to aid in the ease of travel, but regardless of sunshine or favorable mood, the arrival of an ogre sours even the most tranquil moments in one’s journey. More than that, the arrival of an ogre presents danger—significant, *sizable* danger. Luckily, Hawthorn had spotted the ogre before the ogre had spotted him and Wrenna. But this didn’t spare them from an unwanted encounter. Not yet. The ogre, likely by design, had positioned its camp at the end of a narrow gorge where the buttressing foothills of the The Cloudy Mountains funneled all northbound travelers to a single point. To turn around and go another route would add days to their journey, perhaps as much as a week. Not only this, but it would present them with other obstacles, additional dangers, ushering them deeper into the heart of The Greenwood, which was known to be haunted and was teeming with spiders as large as cattle. Wrenna and Hawthorne resolved to go forward, staying their course. They resolved, as well, to sneak past the ogre, rather than test its strength (and their own) in battle.

Observing the large brute through patches of shrubbery that clung to the walls of the gorge, Wrenna noted with disgust that the ogre picked its nose, which was the size of her leg, digging out boogers as large as her head. It was cooking a meal over a large fire. Something alive. Something struggling against the vines that had been used to keep it bound.

A goblin? No. A human? Sadly, yes.

"Well," Hawthorn whispered, "so much for avoiding conflict. Unless, of course, you still want to try and sneak past the beast."

"No," Wrenna shook her head. "No, we can't." As much as she wanted to tiptoe quietly away, she knew that she could not ignore the plight of a human who would, without her aid, become an ogre's lunch.

"Okay, Wrenna," Hawthorn lay a hand over her shoulder. "Are you ready?"

She took a deep breath, tapping into the core of her magical prowess. Her arms and the back of her neck tingled with energy. She could feel the bolts of flame and lightning begging to be released from her body, aching for a target to sear and split asunder.

Wrenna nodded. "Ready."

Hawthorn drew his longsword, slow and steady, and Wrenna could hear his grip tightening on the leather straps around its hilt. He leaned in close and whispered, "You're really cute when you're on the edge of battle. Something between a demon and an ogre's next meal."

"I guess my love spell is working then." She whispered back to him.

"Maybe," Hawthorn grinned. "Maybe it is."

"Hey, Hawthorn?"

"Yeah?"

"Try to keep up." And with that, Wrenna burst from the bushes in a headlong rush toward the ogre. It was only then, after closing the distance between herself and the monster, that she realized that the human figure the ogre was about to cook was a decoy, an empty suit of armor with a melon for a head, loose strands of stuffed straw poking out from its quilted trousers.

"It's a trap!" Hawthorn shouted, rushing up from behind her.

Wrenna stopped and looked up at the twelve-foot tall, hideous bastard before her. She gazed at the boogers that amassed at its feet, each one the size of her head.

"It's a trap!" Hawthorn echoed.

The ogre let its human decoy fall squelching to the ground in a pile of its disgusting collection. It stood its full, towering height and, looking down at Wrenna, hefted its cudgel.

"It's a trap!" Hawthorn cried out a third time.

"Yes," Wrenna whispered. "So it is."

And so too, she thought, *it is time to test the might of my magic.*

* * *

The cudgel came down with a resounding thud. Trees shook, leaves and branches trembling. A pillar of dust rose up from the ground where Wrenna had only just stood, but when it cleared away, she was no longer there. And neither, Hawthorn was relieved to discover, had her body been crushed to fill the wide divot that now dented the earth.

A crackle of raw, magical energy manifested in the cradle of Wrenna's palm. Formless, delicate as smoke, like gauze on the wind before settling, it condensed to form a sphere. Her sorcerous energy glowed, even among the light of the day, illuminating Wrenna, who had safely maneuvered behind the unsuspecting ogre.

Now, let it be known: Wrenna was a fantastic student of

the occult, a natural that showed the promise of an adept in the making. But as good as she may have been, as fast as she advanced in the art and proficiency of magical craft, her experience was limited to a seven-month stint. True, she had what may be the most powerful living wizard in Garden as an instructor, which only accentuated her fast-track to excellence, but facts remain facts, and facts reveal one glaring truth in regards to this encounter between an ex-princess, apprentice mage and a fully grown, battle-tested ogre...

Wrenna was sorely outmatched.

That said, it should come as no surprise when the lightning ball, though expertly manifested from the core of her current abilities, failed Wrenna's expectations to warrant significant impact on the outcome of the battle she had been unexpectedly thrust into. Kudos to Wrenna for avoiding the cudgel, for sidestepping the mighty ogre's assault and sneaking behind it to expose the brute's unguarded backside. This action was performed with masterful guile. But the magical bolt, while well-formed and quickly conjured, lacked sufficient *oomph*. One launched to collide with the ogre's ass, the orb split its foul sheepskin trousers, but drew only a modicum of blood. It was, shall we say, immensely inadequate, akin to what may add up to a bee sting, or a playful slap on the butt.

Despite its looks, the ogre was no fool (at least, concerning its battle-instinct, which has nothing to do with overall intelligence). And so, electing to ignore the "bee sting"on its rump, it did not turn around, but focused instead on the seasoned warrior with a drawn sword charging from the front.

Unlike Wrenna, Hawthorn was not a newcomer to his abilities, having first trained with a sword at five years old. And so, even with the full might of an ogre before him, he was not out of his depth. When he arrived at the scene he swung at the ogre's cudgel, rather than the ogre itself. He did this to throw the monster off balance, and to maneuver himself where he might better protect Wrenna.

"Back up!" he shouted to his companion. "Throw your bolts from afar, but do not get close." When Wrenna did not move, but stood as if frozen in place, Hawthorn shoved her away. "Go, you fool! This isn't one of your lessons, you know? This is battle! Life and death!" Behind him, the ogre poised for another attack. "Princess or no, in this, you follow *my* command." Again, he shoved Wrenna. "Now go! Get the fuck out of here!"

Hawthorn rolled to the side with centimeters to spare, narrowly avoiding the downward swing of the ogre's tree-trunk cudgel. He found his feet just in time to jump backward, feeling the wind on his face from the near-passing of a blunt weapon the size of an elephant's thigh. Hawthorn cursed, spat in the ogre's direction, and readied himself for further onslaught.

Combat was a dance, Wrenna realized—methodical, brutal, beautiful. And if combat was a dance, then Hawthorn had tangoed and waltzed at countless balls. He ducked, he dodged, he parried, he thrust. He dove and rolled when need be. He ran when it was required. He sprinted away, then toward his enemy, darting between the ogre's tall legs while dragging his longsword along the inside of its knee. The ogre grunted, screamed, and rose up its epic, oaken club. It, too, was a dancer. It, too, knew its own ogreish arrangements. And it showed its expertise by leveraging both its bulk and the terrain to its advantage. Hawthorne cut off one of the ogre's toes as it kicked at him, but the great brute had backed its human opponent against the granite shoulder of the gorge.

Now, the monster had total advantage.

Wrenna watched on, her heart in her throat—then snapped out of her stupor. She thought outside the conventions of battle, how she could apply her magic in unorthodox ways. She considered the spell that she knew best, had the most experience using. She brought forth the energies required for its making, and summoned a sleeping spell with enough potency, she hoped, to make even a cyclops feel drowsy. Wrenna boldly thrust herself into the dance she both admired and feared. She confronted the ogre, aimed, and fired.

The result wasn't dramatic, but *adequate*—only just. While the ogre, bombarded by Wrenna's most intoxicating sleep spell, wasn't swayed into a state of slumber, the magic's effect was enough to cause the beast to slow, to pause for a second, and yawn.

It was its yawn that slayed the beast, for a simple yawn in the throes of battle can certainly put someone to sleep—the eternal sleep of death, that is. Her meager spell gave Hawthorn enough time to summon the finishing blow, an act of combative violence that was as perplexing as it was fierce. Wrenna watched in confusion, in amazement, in fright. She held her breath as she witnessed Hawthorn raise up his blade, drawing strength from some strange, unknown source of devastating power: a blue, vaporous light that emitted from his eyes. By what means, Wrenna did not know, but she watched as Hawthorn channeled the luminous, blue mist to fuse with his gleaming longsword. Augmented by this mysterious force, a simple sword became a tool of cataclysmic power.

What had seemed a dire situation, which may have ended in Hawthorn's demise, had instantly become his overwhelming advantage in battle. Despite its looks, the ogre was no fool. When it comes to instincts in battle, even brutes can become scholars. So it was, with total acceptance of the inevitable, that the ogre dropped its massive cudgel to the dirt, receiving its deathblow with grace.

Hawthorn obliged and, ending their dance, split the monster in two.

* * *

That night, by the fireside at their camp, Wrenna broke the sullen silence that she and Hawthorn had shared since their unfortunate encounter with the ogre that morning.

"Sir Hawthorn," she spoke timidly from across the flames.

"Just Hawthorn," he reminded her. "No *sir.*" He did not look at Wrenna, but busied himself by poking the fire with a stick.

"Hawthorn, then."

"Yeah? What is it, lady?" Though she would have corrected him either way, Wrenna could tell by the way Hawthorn said "lady" that he did not mean it formally.

"Wrenna," she said. "Have the goodness to call me by my name, if not my titles."

Hawthorn drank from his bottle, spat wine into the flames. "Well, Wrenna, what's on your mind?" His voice strayed from decency, Wrenna thought, and lacked kindness. "No, wait. Let me guess... You want to know what happened back there with the ogre. You want to know about my *eyes.*" He did not state it as a question, and as he spoke the word, *eyes*, he flashed his in Wrenna's direction. There was no question regarding their unique and unnatural beauty. As the campfire reflected in Hawthorn's bold stare, she realized that his eyes were not merely sapphire-like, but actual sapphires, or something similar—polished stone, or cut gems.

"Yes," Wrenna nodded. "Yes, I would like to know about your eyes. I think it's come to a point where it would be perverse—and impossible, besides—to ignore them any longer. Surely, that was magic pouring out of them today, magic with the power to smite a mighty ogre—very *potent* magic."

Hawthorn's defiance melted away. His blatant, challenging stare withered into a relaxed state—not friendly, per se, but no longer guarded. "Well, if the cat's out of the bag..." He drank more wine, then offered some to Wrenna.

"Not tonight," she told him. "Tonight, I keep my wits. And tomorrow, I avoid the hangover."

"It's just as well," Hawthorn managed to crack a smile. "You drank all of our distillation of ginger and peppermint."

"It shall not be missed!" Both Wrenna and Hawthorn laughed, which worked as well as magic to ease the tension between them.

"Okay," Hawthorn began. "My eyes…" He took a prolonged glug from his bottle until it was empty of the wine within. "Let me tell you about these eyes of mine…" And he did. Long hours they talked—Wrenna mostly listening—as Hawthorn's tale unveiled the mystery behind his weird and gorgeous eyes, but more than that, too. He lay bare his soul, allowing droplets of his secret history to collect into a trickle, and from there, building into a torrent.

He revealed the nature of his bond to Melorin, the origin of how he and the great wizard forged their acquaintance, the brutal justice that Wrenna's master had inflicted upon the warrior who travelled by her side. Hawthorn shed angry tears from eyes made of stone, revealing not only his violent past, but dimension to his character. All the while, as the tortured warrior told his story, Wrenna gazed into those enigmatic eyes of his, bewitched by their strangeness, but also by the man himself, his warmth that lay just beneath the cold, hard layer of his affected armor. As Wrenna listened to Hawthorn's history, she became aware of something that she felt for him, a deep connection and interest that none of the countless suitors who had sought her hand in marriage had ever inspired in her. What was this feeling, Wrenna wondered? Infatuation? Lust? *Love?* Her heart pounded with some inner stirring foreign to her. It pounded, as well, with the thrilling details of Hawthorn's story.

Wrenna had learned that Hawthorn's bond to Melorin was not one of mutual making, nor one of gentle origin. Long ago, when Wrenna was still a child, Hawthorn had been a thief, a soldier who had abandoned his liege lord's army to follow his own path, pursuing the life of a wandering rogue. As a deserter, only the noose awaited him should he return to his homeland in the kingdom of Peridot. And so, his travels brought him down from the north of Hyacinth, where he was from, to the warmer climes of southern Greengate, and the northern borders of The Raynewood Forest. It was there, in his arboreal wanderings, that he discovered a magical tower among the wood, an architectural marvel festooned with gargoyles. Intrigued, but wary, Hawthorne made a semi-permanent camp nearby, and, keeping tabs on the activities surrounding the magical tower, decided to attempt a heist when its resident wizard, Melorin, left for some unknown errand.

"Well, this is where the story takes a dark turn." Hawthorn reached for more wine, but, recalling that the bottle was depleted, sighed in disappointment before continuing with his tale.

"As it stands, I am little more than a slave," he said with sorrow and deep bitterness. "Without sugarcoating my role, I am merely a pawn, a magician's thrall. But let me start from the beginning, that fateful day that I thought to rob the most powerful wizard in Garden."

Hawthorn divulged that his attempt of thievery started and stopped at the front door of Melorin's tower, that the gargoyles decorating its structure came alive and descended upon him. "Had there been three or four of them, had there been a *dozen*, I would have escaped the ambush that awaited me," he said, now on his feet, pacing around the fire. "Alas, there were many dozens—nay, hundreds of the stone bastards. I am good, Wrenna," he assured her. "But not *that* good. I fell in battle. And Melorin returned to deal with the thief who had dared encroach upon his property."

Hawthorn detailed the account, the words and deeds exchanged between himself and Melorin.

So you would rob me blind, would you? The wizard had said. *Well, you know the old saying? An eye for an eye. You would rob me blind, but now it is I who will rob you of sight, leaving you blind.* And without a moment offered to retort or beg for his life, Hawthorn's eyes were taken from him, melted by magic fire, dealing pain beyond the register of his senses.

"You are... blind?" Wrenna could hardly believe it,

so competent was Hawthorn in battle, in riding horse, in guiding her through the forest, and enchanting her with his targeted gazes.

"Not blind, dear lady. Not anymore." He gazed into the fire with eyes that were not the ones he was born with. Firelight danced on their smooth, uncanny surface. "Melorin gave me new eyes," he looked up from the fire at Wrenna. "He gave me *these*."

"They look like sapphires," Wrenna said.

"Azurite," Hawthorn told her. "Polished stone. They are imbued with magic—powerful magic—so that I might see."

"The Azurite Warrior," Wrenna whispered.

"Yes," Hawthorn smirked in resentment. "Melorin's little joke."

"It's terrible what he has done to you."

Hawthorn shrugged. "I suppose it is," he agreed. "But it's terrible what I planned for his tower, Melorin would argue—stealing his valuable, magical items. Pawning them to rogues like me, or worse. And besides, nothing but the noose awaits me back in Peridot. Life as a nomadic thief is no picnic. Perhaps, as a servant to Melorin, I am better off."

"Is that what you are? A servant?" Wrenna was agitated, troubled by the golden image of her master which had now been sullied by this grim and violent story that painted him in an entirely different, darker shade. "Aren't you angry, Hawthorn? Aren't you *furious*."

Hawthorne sighed. "Sometimes I am. Sometimes I am not. Often, I am too tired to give the thought any regard."

"How long?" Wrenna asked.

"Sorry?"

"How long must you remain bound to Melorin as you are? Surely, your punishment comes with an end? Is there some term that Melorin has made plain? Is there an end to your…"

"Slavery?" Hawthorne filled the gap where Wrenna had struggled to find the right word. "I'm afraid not, Lady Wrenna. My fate hinges on the whim of a mighty wizard. As it stands, there is no end to my charge. I made no oath, but am bound to one, nonetheless. I can feel it."

"A spell?"

Hawthorne shrugged. "Melorin *is* a wizard, after all. It seems a spell is likely."

"I will talk to him," Wrenna proclaimed. "I will persuade him to let you go."

Hawthorn scoffed. "Good luck with that."

"He will listen!" Now Wrenna, too, stood up to pace the edge of the fire. "In the very least, I will urge him to place an end to your sentence—a reasonable term. Melorin is a good man," Wrenna said with conviction, but then wondered if her statement was true. "Melorin is a good man," she repeated. "You will once again be free."

Hawthorn looked up to the dark canopy, sighed deeply, and sat back down by the fire. Somberly, dejectedly, as if recalling some battle where he had been soundly defeated, he shook his head, and calmly said to Wrenna as a matter of fact: "Melorin has branded my soul, charged me with a lifelong task that has no end. I am bound by magic, Wrenna, bound to fight on behalf of the protection of The Raynewood. As it is, I am also bound to its borders, unless Melorin allows me to wander, which is how I join you here on your quest. As a servant to Melorin, his *sword slave*, I am the blade to accompany his magic, and the guardian, whether I will it or not, to his woodland realm. This is my task, Wrenna, my task until the day I die."

Even though it was Hawthorn's sad story, and Hawthorn's tragic plight, it was Wrenna who was crying at the edge of their campfire when the warrior concluded telling the tale of his past. Wrenna watched Hawthorn as he drew his longsword and set the weapon across his lap, grinding a whetstone across its blade, sharpening it in a repetitive motion that may have been employed to distract him from his own, sad story.

Wrenna stared into those bizarre, boundless, azurite eyes. "So beautiful," she could not help but say aloud.

Hawthorn looked up from honing the edge of his blade. He met Wrenna's wet eyes with his own, and tapped them with a finger on their exposed surface. "Beautiful, they may be. But they are deadly, too." And it was true, Wrenna had seen the magic they had unleashed upon the ogre. "And while they allow me sight, there is something you should know."

"And what is that?" Wrenna wondered.

"Through these eyes, I am gifted vision," Hawthorn calmly stated. "But know, too, that Melorin watches. He follows me wherever I go." He tapped at the hard surface of the pair of azurite orbs embedded in his head. "Whatever I see, Melorin sees. Remember that, Wrenna, should you wish to hide something from your master."

Without warning, Hawthorn turned over to get some sleep. "Wake me in an hour," he instructed. "You have the first watch."

* * *

The next four days went without incident. No goblins, no trolls, nor marauders in the night (or day). Thankfully, there were no more ogres, either. The sorceress-in-training and the seasoned warrior with magic gemstones for his eyes traveled in relative comfort, and with good speed. Accentuating the calm and quiet was an overt lack of discussion. Hawthorn led and Wrenna followed. Little words were shared between them.

It was understandable, Wrenna thought, that after Hawthorn had shared his dark past, his deepest secrets, he should become distant and withdrawn. With this in mind, she held back from unleashing her plethora of questions, her teeming curiosities and comments about Hawthorn. So too did she refrain from pondering aloud the unfamiliar world of Greenwood, the strange flora and fauna that engulfed them in its natural wonder. There were toadstools taller than she was, taller even than the ogre that Hawthorn had ushered to the netherworld. There were mushrooms that glowed in the night, luminous hues of orange and green, and moths that visited them in unfathomable numbers; furry creatures as wide as dinner plates, others that were small, but translucent, like glass. On one occasion, while skirting the treeline of the northeastern slopes of The Cloudy Mountains, they passed what appeared to be a lone tombstone, or a strange, glass coffin that was molded over and festooned with moss. A snow-white mustelid—a marten or a mink—sat atop the lip of the open container. Wrenna wanted to know what the coffin was, why it was there, and what sort of mustelid perched on its open edge. Despite her interests, her growing queue of unanswered questions, Wrenna remained quiet, allowing Hawthorn's brooding silence to run its course.

That night, they made camp in a man-made hollow on the side of the mountain. It had clearly been lived in before, but so very long in the past as to show few signs as to who or what occupied the lodgings. There was an old trunk locked with a great, metal clasp, but it was so long neglected, so very ancient and unused, that when Wrenna touched it, it crumbled into dust. Among the pile of detritus that remained was a broken, curved object of unknown origin.

"A troll horn," Hawthorne spoke for the first time that day. He stood behind Wrenna and reached past her to take up the item she had found. When his fingers clutched the horn, it dissolved into dust, and an eerie, whispering sound filled the cavern before fading into nothing.

"So old…" Wrenna reached out to touch the remnants of the horn, running her fingers through the particles lingering on her palm.

"Very ancient," Hawthorn agreed. "Whatever magic it held has now been released into the ether."

Again, a soft, whispering sound.

"A ghost?" Wrenna tensed.

"I think not," Hawthorn's magical eyes lit up as he scanned the cavern. "A trace element… A lingering memory."

"The troll?"

Hawthorn shrugged. “Or the man who wielded its horn. Perhaps a sorcerer. Perhaps a demon. Or none of these things. Time has worn away any notion of ever finding out.” And indeed, they would never find out. They would never discover that this was, in fact, the same cavern that Persimmon’s scion, Tamarillo, had once stayed in.

Wrenna shivered and leaned into Hawthorn, who stood close behind her. “It is good to hear your voice again.”

Hawthorn did not balk from the intimacy that Wrenna offered him. He reveled in her proximity and affectionately squeezed her shoulder. “It is good to speak,” he agreed. “And not just in my head, to myself, in an endless loop of berating, shameful accusations.”

Wrenna did not ask for particulars. She knew, now, that Hawthorn’s past haunted him. She knew that whispers in a cavern were of little consequence next to the real ghosts that dwelled within troubled minds. Searching for her own source of comfort, as well as alleviating her companion, she soothed Hawthorn with soft strokes of his hair, and traced his jawline with her palm. She leaned in closer, embracing him in earnest. Then she stood back from her hug, smiled as brightly as she could manage, and suggested that they set up camp.

“If you build the fire,” she offered, “I will make the stew.”

Hawthorn’s stony expression—the same one Wrenna had seen him wear over the last four days—melted away into a warm and easy smile. He set down his travelling pack and sword. “I’ll tie up the horses. You gather dry wood.”

“Then *you* build a fire,” Wrenna playfully poked at him.

“And *you* make a stew worthy of an emperor’s banquet,” he tussled her hair.

One last time, the icy whisper filled the cavern with its spectral sound. Wrenna and Hawthorn shared a look, shrugged, and got on merrily with their business of setting up camp.

* * *

The morning found Wrenna and Hawthorn lying side by side. They hadn't shared the same bedroll, but they had lain close enough that their arms and legs touched, one body brushing up against the other. It was a good way to keep warm after the fire had died down and the embers began to fade. It was a good way, as well, to spark certain intimacies that had been growing between them. It was a fine way, Wrenna discovered, to pluck at her heartstrings, which made sweet music in her soul. She recalled her many suitors, men like Chervil, the prince of Almery, and compared the man, and others like him, to Hawthorn, The Azurite Knight. The gap between their allure was a wide canyon in her estimation. Presently, she watched Hawthorn asleep beside her. Then, as he began to stir from his slumber, she turned away and blushed, privately visiting the notion of marriage, remarking in her mind that maybe, after all, it isn't such an unfortunate fate.

After breakfast, they left the cave behind them. Outside, the morning was cold and gray; a hard, steady rainfall made travel less than pleasant. They did not have to endure the weather long, however, for an hour or two further northeast along the treeline brought them to the wide maw of a bleak and black cavern opening into the side of the tall Cloudy Mountain cliffs.

"Darkness awaits." Hawthorn gestured to the black hole in the mountain. "Behold: the goblin city of Under Castle."

"Under Castle?" Wrenna had not heard that name before.

"Dark Root, Bitter Gate, Blackmorre… The goblin kingdom bears many names," Hawthorn told her. "Though Under Castle is its local name."

Wrenna knew that high up above, nestled on the peaks of The Cloudy Mountains, the ruins of Castle Cloud lay scattered, like so many tombstones. She also knew that the goblin city lay under its roots, and the wide network of the city's tunnels and linked caverns worked their way upward, not down as one might expect, worming higher into the heart of the mountain, and beyond, above, opening to the outside world, where the skeletal remains of Castle Cloud precariously stood.

"Under Castle," she said and nodded. "It makes sense."

Hawthorn shrugged. "Under Castle, Bitter Gate, Turd Bucket… It makes no difference. It's a rotten shithole of a world in there. And whatever you choose to call it… it's all the same… it's still Blightheart's lair."

Blightheart. Now *that* name was familiar to Wrenna. *Blightheart.* The goblin lord who ruled the kingdom under the mountain. *Blightheart.* The dark sorcerer who wore a crown adorned with the Hyacinth Demon Shard. *Blightheart.* The reason Wrenna was there. *Blightheart.* The bastard she must kill.

"Fancy a day trip to Turd Bucket?" Hawthorn said.

Wrenna stared into the black abyss that opened into the face of the cold, towering mountain. "Lead on," she commanded. "Take us beyond the Bitter Gate. Guide us deep into the vile arteries of Blackmorre. Lead on, good man, and take us into the forsaken city of the goblins, to wretched Under Castle, the sprawling, sordid kingdom of Blightheart's lair."

* * *

The subterranean "city" was little more than a network of naturally occurring caves, unrefined chambers linked by tunnels forged by goblin industry. Beyond these raw, hollow chambers, the narrow arteries connecting them, there wasn't much else save for an odd sconce here and there, offering meager flame to dimly light the way. There was virtually no evidence of habitation. All in all, there was a total lack of intricacy to the goblin kingdom of Under Castle, no indication whatsoever of its fabled urban complexity.

Until they reached its central chamber…

The sight before them stole Wrenna's breath. And Hawthorn's, too. Beside her, he placed a hand over his heart, allowing his tightly clamped jaw to fall open in unrestrained awe. *This* was intricacy. *This* was urban complexity.

This was what Wrenna and Hawthorn saw:

A cavern so wide and tall as to swallow ten Cathedrals, one beside the next, or perhaps stacked upon the other. An entire castle, along with its village and surrounding farms, would easily fit into the mountain's vast belly. Here and there, great towers soared to unknown heights, lost in the blackness of a vertical shaft that ended who-knows-where. Modest buildings, too. *Hundreds* of them. *Thousands?* Very possibly. They spread out for miles, some lining cavern streams, others neatly organized along well-built roads. Above them, birds flew in great flocks, swiftlets and swallows that were unhindered by the enclosed space for all its vastness. And bats, so many bats, their guano in heaps as high as hillocks, yet confined to corners as if the goblin residents took pride in managing their fecal deposits. More arresting than everything else, the *lights!* Globes of blown glass dotted the cavernous landscape, each one encasing a tiny flame that danced upon an oil-soaked wick within. The result was an array of colors, each hue of every glass sphere bearing its own subtle distinction. And the flames within, as if alive, emitted animated light, a paroxysm of illuminated brilliance, all colors of the rainbow. This light-show did not omit a single shade among the full spectrum of color as it bathed the stone-carved Gothic architecture favored by the goblins, their legendary stonework and masonry.

It was hard to swallow, but the fact could not be denied that Under Castle was as beautiful as any human city among the open air of the outside world. Wrenna stood, weak at the knees with wonder, and with thought of her own city, Raynewood. There was just no comparing the two... Under Castle was somehow leagues ahead.

Wrenna found her voice. "I had prepared an illumination spell to light the way."

Hawthorn found his composure, finally closing his jaw. "If ever there was an unnecessary use of magic…" He chuckled.

"You're telling me," Wrenna agreed, squinting in the kaleidoscopic array of colored lights.

"Darkness, as it happens, would have aided us," Hawthorn said, looking out over the fabulous, illuminated city stretching out below them. "We need to get there," he pointed across the urban expanse to the far cavern wall. "That road leading up and away from the city. That's where we need to be."

Wrenna followed his gesture to their desired path. It was miles away, a faint, distant line crawling up a steep slope across a cavern so large that it offered a sense of horizon. "Why there? Won't Blightheart be here among the city?" Wrenna pointed to the largest, most formidable and beautiful tower among the cityscape. "Surely, Blightheart will occupy one of these great fortresses here."

Hawthorn shook his head. "The Lord of Blackmorre is known to spend his time among the ruins of Castle Cloud. We will find him high up on the peaks of the mountain where the sky is not made of rock, but of cold, open air."

"Why?" Wrenna asked. "And how do you know this?"

"How do I know this?" He echoed her question, tapping his azurite eyes. "I see in the places I deign to look, but I see much more. I see the sights that Melorin wills to share with me. Sometimes these images come to me in dreams, other times they come when I am wide awake. It is a gift, some might say. A powerful tool, no doubt. But these visions come to me unbidden, and most of the time, unwelcome. A powerful tool, yes, but one I am never free to put away."

"As to *why* Blightheart spends most of his time among the cold and blustery mountaintop ruins of Castle Cloud? Well… to that I say this: he is a sorcerer, and it is common knowledge that all sorcerers are either mad or deeply eccentric. Why does Blightheart—or any sorcerer—do what they do? You tell me, Wrenna. You are training to become one. You are more qualified to answer such a question." He nudged her and grinned. "You skirt much closer to madness."

Wrenna shrugged, accepting the playful insult in good humor—she had to admit: Hawthorne had a point.

"Come on," Hawthorn tugged at her sleeve. "Let's go." As they began the alternating rise and descent of a long trail that would lead them in a wide berth around the goblin metropolis, they stared out over the magnificent sight of the city once more.

Taking it in, Hawthorn shook his head in wonder. "Never again shall I refer to this place as Turd Bucket."

* * *

In the sunless interior of the cavern, it was impossible to tell time, but Wrenna wagered it took half a day to safely skirt the city of Under Castle. They had made the long loop around its brilliantly lit homes and tall towers mostly without incident. True, there was an encounter with goblin sentries, two spear-clad warriors guarding a trail that Wrenna and Hawthorn had every intention of taking. But it was trivial for Wrenna to conjure a beam of condensed air and send it rocketing away to knock them off their feet, ushering the pair of goblins off a ledge plummeting from untold heights to splatter on the rocks below. There was another encounter, an incident with a goblin brute who wielded a stone hammer and proclaimed that "all humans must die!" But the goblin's statement turned out to be the most dramatic thing about the encounter, as Hawthorn, almost bored, stepped forward and, drawing his sword rather calmly, chopped off his adversary's arms, hammer and all. The screams that followed might have alerted unwanted attention, but they were quickly muffled by Hawthorn's repetitive striking fists, which buffeted the goblin's skull until it looked like something resembling raspberry-swirled oatmeal. In any case, Hawthorn and Wrenna made their way across the city safely.

They ascended higher and higher up the mountain, putting miles and many tunnels, caverns, and hollow chambers between themselves and Under Castle, which was now hours behind. Much like in the beginning of their subterranean sojourn, they found themselves, once again, in a totally unadorned, raw hollow within the mountain. The place they made camp was, without embellishment, a nondescript cave, where they would dine in silent darkness before rising to face Blightheart on the top of the mountain.

Not wanting to risk the unwanted attention a fire could bring, they cuddled for warmth, relying on each other's bodies to abate the dank and dingy chill. Wrenna felt the strength in Hawthorn's arms as they wrapped around her, holding her close. Embracing one another, they recounted the incredible marvels they had witnessed since leaving Melorin's tower. Wrenna had lost count, but it could not have been more than ten days spent in the forest, and an undetermined few more within the darkness under the mountain. And yet it seemed as if she had been on the road forever, travelling with Hawthorn for a lifetime. She leaned into him, angling up her head to meet his strange, spectacular eyes.

"Kiss me," she said, surprising herself with words that she had not consciously chosen to say, but words, rather, which seemed to escape her lips anyhow.

Hawthorn had no words to speak at all. He simply did as Wrenna had bidden him to do. He kissed her. What followed was a matter of course. But before all their clothes were removed, before the deepest of intimacy was shared between the cursed warrior and princess sorceress, Hawthorn took a ribbon from her long, dark hair and tied it around his eyes.

"What are you doing?" Wrenna whispered between kisses.

"I do not want him to watch," he said. "It is no privilege of his to look upon you without your clothes. It is no privilege of his to live vicariously by our private passions."

Wrenna almost asked who Hawthorn was talking about.

But she knew who he was referring to. Melorin could see through Hawthorn's eyes, and Wrenna agreed with what Hawthorn said.

"It is no privilege of his," she said. "But it's a privilege I would not take away from you." She untied the ribbon around his eyes and removed the remainder of her clothes. Hawthorn greedily drank in the sight of her bared body and exposed, intimate regions. He allowed himself to savor the beauty and intoxication of a woman whom he desired even more so than his longing for freedom from his accursed bonds. Then, he closed his eyes—and kept them shut—all throughout the long and impassioned throes of love lasting the night.

* * *

Wrenna and Hawthorn gathered their clothes in the morning, and, stealing glimpses of each other as they dressed, their eyes inevitably met, speaking volumes without the exchange of words. Without discussion, their clothes dropped to the floor once again. Wrenna may or may not have moaned "I love you" as she ascended to high summits of physical pleasure. Hawthorn may or may not have responded "I love you more than life itself" as he collapsed in his own climax of bodily ecstasy. The details of lofty proclamations were lost in the tussle of sweaty limbs and loose strands of disheveled hair. Regardless of the clumsy few words they exchanged, they shared many other non-verbal sentiments, as well as... more intimate things—deep gazes, exploratory prodding, bodily fluids, et cetera.

They managed better in their second attempt to get on with the day. They got dressed, kept their clothes on, then prepared and ate breakfast. After that, they packed their belongings, and with a new, greater sense of depth to their relationship, continued up the dark tunnels of the mountain, making their way closer to the final peak of their journey.

They felt the cold of the outdoors long before they saw

any of its light. Though they were warmed by their arduous, uphill trek, each time they stopped for a rest, the freezing air quickly settled into their bones. It was more trouble than it was worth to stop and catch their breath, and so they kept moving, pressing on toward dangers far worse than the cold.

"Look," Hawthorn was the first to notice daylight, something they had not seen in many days. "Do you see what I see? I can see cave walls ahead."

Wrenna had been staring at her feet, bent over with exertion, but as she looked up she noticed what Hawthorn had pointed out. Apart from passing through the goblin city, its brilliant colors illuminated by innumerable glass bulbs, she had not been exposed to any light beyond the anemic flicker of torches set intermittently, infrequently, along the dark tunnel paths. The daylight pouring in from the exit of the cavern was received as a blessing—even if a curse awaited them beyond.

When they emerged from the cavern, Wrenna and Hawthorn found themselves standing on top of the world. Far below them, the lands of Hyacinth spread out like a map: the forest in a broad swathe miles beneath them, the sea a distant blue smear on the western horizon. To the north, a great expanse of yellow-green spread without end; The Emerald Field and, beyond it, the Endless Pasture. From their vantage, heavenward among the clouds, the world below looked like a great mosaic, an art project of the gods.

Loathe to do so, Wrenna pried her eyes from the spectacular sight, compelled to turn away from the bitter wind that gnashed at her with its icy fangs. Now, with her back to the world of Garden spreading out behind her, she became aware of the towering ruins that vaulted drunkenly above. Castle Cloud, or what was left of it, stood devastated and charred before her. It seemed as if it may blow over in the next gust of wind. Looking up at the great corpse of a castle that had once stood dominant among the heavens, Wrenna shivered, and felt very small.

The sound of Hawthorn drawing his longsword stole her

attention from the blackened, castle husk. Wrenna followed Hawthorn's deadly glare to a figure that materialized from the snowdrifts—an enemy she knew she was destined to face. Even so, as the moment finally arrived, she doubted her destiny, and wrestled the urge to run away. In the end, that option was unavailable to her. With enemies all around her, and Blightheart at their lead, there was nowhere to go. There was nowhere to run.

"Why look! A pretty, little girl." Her fated adversary said with mockery in his tone, and a disgusting, shark-tooth grin across his hideous face. There he was… Blightheart, Bastard of the Blackmorre, vile mage of The Goblin Horde. He stood among his train of several dozen goblin warriors, each one wielding a bared sword, spear, or axe. He was a head taller than the rest —uglier, too—and he wore a pewter crown set with a sizable amber stone.

The Demon Shard of Hyacinth. Wrenna knew the stone for what it was, and she felt the power it contained.

"Blightheart, I take it?" Hawthorn took a step forward to stand between the goblins and Wrenna.

"Oh my!" Blightheart tittered perversely. "And a pretty, little boy, too!" He shared a salacious glance with his cronies. "We will certainly eat well tonight, lads!" The mountaintop erupted with goblin cackling.

"If your sorcery is twice as good as your comedy, it still won't be enough to save you, Blightheart." Hawthorn was grinning, Wrenna noticed. Though she could tell by the way he clamped his jaw that he was agitated, furious, and probably afraid. She had seen him clench his jaw in the same way on the night he shared his tormented past with her, and when he battled the ogre, too. She had come to know it as a sign of distress.

If Blightheart was offended by Hawthorn's insult, he did not show it. If anything, he seemed to be enjoying himself. His grotesque smile widened, and his easy composure suggested confidence, complete control. "Is that what they're calling me now? Blightheart?" He laughed into the cold mountain air, his amusement riding on wafts of white mist. "Oh, you humans sure are a dramatic bunch of fools. *Blightheart.* Ha! Actually, I kind of like it."

"Well, what *is* your name?" Wrenna asked, stepping out from behind Hawthorn. "Or should we just call you Ass Face? Now that I've seen you, it seems an appropriate name to match the image." Her own bravery astonished her, and it must have astonished Hawthorn as well, because he gave Wrenna a look that seemed to both berate her for her reckless action, and applaud her for her ruthless insult.

Blightheart finally dropped his smile, and introduced himself with a new, darker energy to match his scowl. "My birth-name you need never know, for the ancient tongue of Goblinese is indecipherable to petty, human ears. But in your own, limited language, it crudely translates to... Death." He raised his hands, causing his many obsidian bracelets to fall tumbling down the length of his pale arms. Between his palms, held high above his head, a crimson cloud of magic began to take form. "Yes," Blightheart concluded, "that name fits. You may call me Death."

* * *

It suddenly occurred to Wrenna while standing there among a goblin sorcerer renowned for his cruelty and power... Her life was very much at risk. She couldn't speak for Hawthorn, but Wrenna was keenly aware that she was very much out of her depth, that the opposition assembled before her was beyond her ability to defeat. Her situation, at best, looked precarious. Realistically, it appeared quite dire. She scanned the array of enemies before her, their collective presence amounting to her certain doom.

Things looked quite bad. And then they got worse.

The scarlet cloud billowing like noxious vapor molded to the whim of Blightheart's magic. Moving his hands erratically, he shaped the mist into the form of a serpent. He called out loudly in a strange, foreign tongue—Goblinese, perhaps?—

and in response, the snake-shaped vapor wiggled away in the air, burrowing into a crevasse beneath the mountaintop. Hawthorn made a move to attack, but stumbled before he could raise his sword. Wrenna swayed, falling over beside Hawthorn. The mountain seemed to move, and then it split asunder.

The crevasse from which the crimson cloud had slithered widened with great, cataclysmic force. From the abyss of its unknown depths, a new beast emerged, and this one was in no way vaporous, but solid. It looked like a dragon, red and scaled and winged. Yet it bore no limbs, and as such, resembled a serpent.

"A cave wyrm." Hawthorn struggled to his feet. "This just got a whole lot more fun." Wrenna watched his eyes ignite, felt the residual power radiating magic from his azurite orbs. "Stay back," he commanded. "This is far worse than any ogre." The blue mist pouring out from his eyes seeped into his blade. Raising it before him, it shone bright enough among the daylight to cast long shadows. "Stay back," he repeated to Wrenna. "And be prepared to run."

How else can it be put? All hell broke loose.

The wyrm was devastating. Its raw, physical strength was beyond redoubtable. As it thrashed its armored body, and lashed its blunted tail, its attacks rent the rock where it narrowly missed Hawthorn, who was deeply engaged in dodging for his life. Well-trained or bound by magic, the beast was beholden to Blightheart. It reserved its attacks for the sorcerer's intended target, carefully avoiding the accidental destruction of his goblin troop, or Blightheart himself.

Now, as for Blightheart, he was living up to his Goblinese name, which roughly translated to *Death.* Because death, it would seem, was sure to visit both Hawthorn and Wrenna within a matter or minutes. Still, where magic is involved, unpredictability reigns, and magic was *en force* in the company of wizards, warriors, and wyrms. Regardless of how things were likely to turn out, this is what happened next:

The cave wyrm hurled itself toward Hawthorn, who dove out of the way in time for the would-be-dragon to run past him, crashing headlong into the ruins of Castle Cloud. A massive stone pillar wobbled precariously. Had it fallen, rather than stabilized, Wrenna and Hawthorn would surely have been crushed. What little debris had fallen was enough to injure them, but the fist-sized stones and rainfall of pulverized mortar fell around them, not on them. It was a close call, but no one was dead—yet. And besides, the incident gave Wrenna an idea.

She knew the limitations of her magic, and did not squander her attacks on Blightheart, who would deflect her spells with ease, or the wyrm, who would simply absorb them as if they were mosquito bites. Instead, she made herself useful by firing bolts at the goblin warriors. In their numbers, they were a nuisance to Hawthorn, and it was easy enough for Wrenna to take them down, one by one. But what she really wanted to do was shift Blightheart's position. She knew she couldn't challenge him directly—not with her magic—but she devised a way that would do more than harm him.

Now, if only she could get him to stand in the right place.

Behind her, the wyrm recovered from its collision. It roared and belched black smoke that hinted at fire. Hawthorn feigned charging the beast, then made a dash for Blightheart, who lazily swatted the warrior away like a puppet on strings. Using telekinetic threads, the sorcerer picked Hawthorn up by his ankles and threw him across the rocks to the edge of the mountain.

Hawthorn scrambled to avoid falling over the edge. Finding his feet, he swore mightily: "Fuck!"

Despite what the storybooks tell you, there's no time for elegance when it comes to words in the heat of battle.

With the cave wyrm preparing for another charge, and Blightheart's amber jewel lighting up with signs of renewed conjuration of magic, Wrenna decided to force the issue, and implement her plan. She would either succeed or she would die. This notion made the choice to act much easier than it may have otherwise been.

The plan was simple: get Blightheart to stand where the castle ruins would topple upon him. But first, baiting the sorcerer to stand in the correct place, a position where he would be soundly crushed. And second, to goad the wyrm into another concussive rush, a collision with the massive pillar that balanced on a razor's edge.

As Wrenna ran into action, several factors complicating her plan suddenly became apparent—how to bait Blightheart, how to provoke the wyrm, and how not be blasted by magic or crushed by the monster in the meantime—but none of these concerns were so glaringly problematic as when Blightheart smiled at her and said, "You are pretty, young girl, but you are very, very stupid. Do you honestly think you can trick me into being crushed by a falling castle? Do you really think you can use my wyrm against me? And before you answer my question, let me answer the one that is circling this moment in your pretty, little head: yes, I can read your mind. Isn't magic a lovely thing?"

Well, Wrenna's plan hadn't worked. But in the end, it didn't need to. Remember unpredictability? Recall magic's almost predictable unpredictability?

What followed is a fine example of exactly that:

"Hey Ass Face!" High above her, Wrenna looked up to where Hawthorne balanced on the tip of a crumbling turret. "You didn't read *my* mind, did you?" His eyes were alight like two sapphire flames, and his sword was charged with that familiar blue light that was Melorin's signature magic. He swung his blade, which shed an arc of raw, destructive force. Well aimed, the projectile collided with the base of the tower he occupied, slicing the stone like butter. The tower, and Hawthorn within it, fell crashing upon the unsuspecting wyrm below.

Wrenna could hardly believe her eyes as she watched

what happened next. Hawthorn, it would seem, had aimed the tower precisely, riding its downward arc to land with his legs around the cave wyrm's neck. Driving his enchanted blade deep into a wedge between its armored scales, Hawthorn rode the wyrm almost like a horse, guiding its movements by the hilt of his blade, jutting from the beast's neck. With the element of surprise, and the power of a cave wyrm now at his command, Hawthorn battled toe to toe with Blightheart, who bombarded the mountaintop in a foray of offensive magic.

It's hard to say who may have won the battle had things gone a little bit differently. But as Blightheart dedicated his full attention to the threat of Hawthorn and the furious cave wyrm that he rode, Wrenna took advantage of the sorcerer's preoccupation. Sneaking behind Blightheart, she casually plucked the amber-set crown from his ugly head.

And thus was the moment that the fate of Garden shifted. But all that would come later. At present, it was enough that the battle had shifted very much in favor of Wrenna, who now possessed the power of the Hyacinth Demon Shard.

As the Bastard of Blackmorre cowered on the ground at her feet, Wrenna, head adorned with a pewter crown set with an amber jewel, stood over him and smiled. "Who's a pretty, little girl now?" she asked, but did not await for Blightheart to answer.

* * *

Their return journey to Melorin's tower was many times smoother, and faster, with Wrenna's newfound power at her disposal. They had not run into any more ogres, but if they had, the crown that Wrenna now wore would have lent her sufficient power to obliterate it without breaking a sweat. When they rounded the neck of The Raynewood Peninsula, heading south and leaving The Greenwood behind them, Wrenna felt the joy of coming home. When they reached the open glade of Melorin's tower she greeted the hundreds of gargoyles as if they were her children, and when she saw Melorin she embraced him as if he was her father.

Only then did she remember Hawthorn's troubled past, and Melorin's grip on her lover's soul. "We need to talk," she told her master.

"I cannot let him go," he said. "Not yet." Wrenna should have known… Melorin had read her mind. "He will taste his freedom, I promise that to you, and to him. But not now, my apprentice. Now, we celebrate. Now, we feast. Now, I will hear all about your adventure."

* * *

Wrenna returned to Raynewood Castle with five months remaining in her allotted year of magical study. She was joyfully greeted by Twigg, her old handmaiden, who embraced Wrenna with gusto, and her brother, King Waldorf, who misinterpreted the reason for his sister's early return.

"I see you have returned to us with time to spare, Lady Raynewald." On his throne, King Waldorf smiled in deep satisfaction. "Though your failure to complete your studies must come hard for you, know that your return to court blesses us with your presence, which has been sorely missed. Know too, sweet sister, that a marriage suitable to your station and favorable to a happy future will be arranged. It pains me to know that your high hopes of becoming a great magician have come crashing down. Though having you back with us here at Raynewood fills me with utmost joy. And knowing , as well, that you will lead a fine, traditional life of a princess."

Wrenna could not sustain a small bout of laughter.

"What amuses you, sister? Have I said something funny?"

"No, Your Grace."

"Please, call me Waldo. I am your brother, after all."

"Forgive me, Waldo. I didn't mean to laugh. Your words are most kind and none of them are funny."

"Why the laughter, then, sis?"

"It is just… you have mistaken the motives behind my early return."

"Have I?"

"Yes, Your Grace, brother Waldo. You have."

"I do not understand," the king shifted uncomfortably upon his throne. "Will you tell me what you mean?"

Wrenna smiled. "I will do more than that, dear brother. I will *show* you." She removed a pewter crown from the deep pockets of her traveler's cloak. As she placed it upon her head, its amber stone lit up brighter than flame. The power lent to Wrenna through the magic of her headpiece was something she would never take for granted—the feeling thrilled her every time.

"Now watch," Wrenna instructed, and showed the king the magic that she had mastered. She lifted her brother, throne and all, with a casual lift of her smallest finger. Setting her king safely down, Wrenna whispered with unspoken words directly into his mind, "Do not worry, dear Waldo, my magic will never harm you." After that, Wrenna gestured to the hearth, wove her fingers in a command that manipulated its fire, creating an elemental stag of roaring flames as it trotted in a circle around the throne room. With a gentle flick of her wrist, the fiery apparition dissipated into smoke, rising up to drift away among the high rafters.

"And now something useful," Wrenna said as she gestured to a broken heirloom that hung above the mantelpiece.

"King Waldon's splintered shield," the King whispered as he watched its many fragments float upon the air to hover in the center of the throne room.

Wrenna grinned. "Splintered, no longer." And then, like a thousand puzzle pieces coming together all at once by the aid of invisible hands, the broken shield was put together, and made whole.

"Well?" She asked her brother, the king. "What do you think?"

King Waldorf was speechless for a while, but he soon

found his voice. Leaning forward on his throne, his stoicism ruptured into a wide smile of mirth. “I think, Lady Raynewald, all prospective marriages can be disregarded from this moment forward.”

III

DAHLIA

South of The Summer Steps, whose purple mountains divided Hyacinth from the southern continent of Dahlia, The Summerwood was vibrant, adorned by dusky refractions of sunlight bouncing off the surface of its lake, Everpool. The many mountain rivers threading the sun-scorched valleys only added to its depth.

Beyond this vast, wet woodland, The South Savanna spread west and south to seas, which defined its coastline; The Sommer and Amaranthine, respectively. To the east, a bifurcated landmass stretched far into The Salzar Sea. Its northern branch was populated by modest kingdoms among The Roanwood Forest, and its capital city, Glyndor, whose famed beauty was evident in its grand towers of pink marble standing tall, looking out across the blue-green waters of Azurite Bay.

As for the southern branch of Dahlia's eastern subcontinent, it is lowly regarded, known for its unbearably hot and barren wastelands. Dominated by Aridana, a vast desert of sand dunes and exposed sandstone steppes—the surface of which could melt the sandals off a traveler's feet—very few people succeed at suffering through life in such expansive and tumultuous terrain.

Hemmed inward by The Hopeless Coast, the desert narrows to a spear-point in the east, and there, at the end of the world, remnants of a great kingdom lie in ruins. Little more than debris, the fallen kingdom's glory has been reduced to skeletal husks among the dried river beds, which once ran with abundance, lending the old world verdure and prosperity. Old Ochre, it is called; the focal point of much history, legend, and myth among the various kingdoms of Dahlia. Devastated by the ravages of time and misfortune, Old Ochre is but a ghost of its former greatness.

But ghosts, as some may claim, rise up from their graves to haunt us.

* * *

Leafe was compelled to walk away. He dropped his wicker basket filled with fruit and wandered beyond the orange grove. Behind him, tidy rows tallied the shallow valley, each tree speckled with bright citrus. The view was inspiring, but faded away with a sudden mist that had seized the clear, sunny day. The world around him melted into shadow, a featureless gloom that now occupied reality.

"Hello, Leafe."

There it was. That same, familiar voice. Leafe had heard it countless times before in a recurring dream that had long troubled his sleep.

"Hear me, Leafe, for your destiny cannot be shirked any longer."

The same old, tired message. The same exact words. Yet, somehow, they seemed more urgent, more demanding. And the visions, like the voices, had become more vivid these last months. The man who came each night loomed larger, appearing clearer in the dream visions plaguing Leafe's sleep.

Right on cue, he emerged from the mist: the strangest man Leafe had ever known."There you are, Leafe." The man stepped out from the shadows on the fringes. As he approached, the incandescent glow that seemed to emanate from within him highlighted his image. "I come to you with counsel, my friend. Counsel you mustn't ignore."

Again, the same old trite. Again, the same stale message. Why, for goodness sake, couldn't this apparition leave Leafe alone? Why, for the love of Garden, couldn't Leafe win a single night of uneventful sleep? This is what Leafe wondered, and indeed, this is what Leafe voiced in vexation: "Why can't you leave me alone? Must you invade my sleep each time I close my eyes?"

"Your destiny cannot be shirked any longer."

"Gods above!" Leafe would have pulled at his hair had he not gone bald years ago. Instead, he slammed his fist into his thigh, hoping it may wake him up—it did not. "The morning cock call is less repetitive than you, and with more to say, besides."

For a long time, Leafe was fearful of the stranger who visited his dreams. But the man's nightly appearances became too frequent, too predictable. As the weeks matured to months, ripened to seasons, spoiling into rot among many sleep-deprived years, the stranger's repetitious visits dulled all fear and intrigue, thus reshaping Leafe's emotional response into nothing but boredom and contempt.

"Do you wish for me to say more, Leafe?"

Leafe was about to shout that he wished for the man, or ghost—whatever he was—to say nothing at all, to finally shut his mouth and go away. He was *about* to say these things, when he realized that the man, or ghost—whatever he was—had deviated from the script.

The robed figure stepped toward Leafe, asking again: "Do you wish for me to say more?"

Leafe's curiosity outweighed his irritation. "Yes," he answered. "Yes, tell me more."

Once again, the dream wraith stepped closer, drawing nearer to Leafe than he ever had in any of his previous hallucinatory invasions. Leafe saw in greater detail the strange visitor that plagued his dreams, and this is what he saw:

A stooped figure, tall and powerful, wizened yet ageless. Shrouded in black robes, silken layers of midnight and ink, no hint to its sex was made visually clear, yet its voice determined it was male. His face was veiled by the wide brim of a comically large, purple hat, and though he had never deigned to remove it before, just then, he took it off.

For the first time, Leafe witnessed the man's face, or, more precisely, his lack thereof. Where eyes, nose, and mouth should have been—all the hallmark features of a human face—there was only smooth, unbroken skin.

No, not skin, but *stone.*

In place of a head, there was a perfect, polished sphere. It sat on the robed man's shoulders, divided neatly into halves, one side the deepest of black, the other the purest of white.

Leafe stared, afflicted by stupor. Not afraid, but simply amazed, he remained silent for several moments, transfixed by awe. "Who… *what*… are you?"

The dream wraith cocked his crystal head, searching for words, perhaps, before announcing them out loud. Without a mouth, no tongue to fashion his message, he issued it telepathically, directly in Leafe's mind. *I am all and everything, and nothing… I am alabaster and onyx, white starlight and the great black void between.*

Leafe knew the sound of a riddle, and knew, too, that wizards tend to speak in them more than others. He determined at that moment that the apparition was not a ghost, but a wizard. He could not know it, but he felt it, and then, as if in answer to his unspoken thoughts, he was *told* it.

Yes, a wizard. One who can see the future.

"My future?"

Yours and mine and everyone's. You just happen to be at the center.

"The center of what?"

Importance.

More riddles? Leafe would rather speak plainly. "Please," he begged, "if you are to raid my dreams every night, and rob me of my sleep, then tell me in words clearer than these countless visits have determined: why do you come to me as you do? And what would you have of me?"

The robed figure took a step backward. Retreating to the shadows, it replaced its ungainly, purple hat to cover its uncanny, crystal head. Then, urging Leafe as he always did, the wizard repeated words he had said one thousand times before in one thousand identical dreams: *Head eastward, and brave the great wastelands of Aridana. Cross its unforgiving, fiery dunes, and seek the fallen kingdom. Go to Old Ochre. Walk among its ruined towers. Do this, and they will rise, brick by brick, to soar up to their former glory. Do this, and you will rise along with them.*

Leafe blinked away the bright light of day as he lay among the dry, dead grass between two rows of sickly orange trees. Beside him, his wicker basket was empty. Hoping to escape the heat, he had sought shade, and lay down at the base of one of his many trees, allowing sleep to take him. Now awake, he recalled his dream, the same dream he had each time he slept—although this one was a little different.

Go to Old Ochre. Walk among its ruined towers.

Leafe shook his head, willing away the echo of his dream. He did not want to linger on nightmares. Unable to find any fruit, he took up his empty basket and walked back home between the rows of unladen citrus trees. All around him, their boughs sagged to the cracked and dusty earth. Their leaves were yellow, migrating to brown.

His father had tended the orchard, his grandfather before him, and at the beginning of it all, his great grandfather, who planted the trees from seed; specimens which have stood more than three generations, the reigns of six different kings.

Never before had the oranges failed to grow. Never before had they skipped a season. Yet now, the trees bore no fruit. They clung to life by roots that were far-reaching and tenacious with age. But they would not endure much longer. Never before had the orange grove seen such hardship. Never before was his family's land so thoroughly cursed by drought.

And never before had Leafe sensed the impending doom that seemed to cast a shadow over all he had ever known. From his twenty-acre orange grove, to his village, to the kingdom of Southstone… to the South Savanna, and beyond to The Summerwood—to all of Dahlia and all other lands across Garden. Far and wide, an unnamed darkness seemed to manifest with invisible dread. And to the east, ever beckoning, Old Ochre, and something ancient beneath its crumbled foundations.

* * *

Aster was busy in the kitchen when her husband walked through the door. She turned away from the orange slices simmering on the pan, to see Leafe standing in the doorway, and the empty wicker basket he carried.

"No oranges?"

Leafe set down his basket and sniffed the air. "Candied oranges." He sat at the table that dominated the center of their small cottage. "When will they be ready?"

Aster let out a long, slow sigh. "No oranges."

"It's worse than no fruit." Leafe echoed his wife's sigh. "The trees… they are dying."

Aster returned to her cooking, flipping the orange slices to sizzle on their opposite sides. Then, after removing the pan from the open flame, she sat down with her husband. She reached across the table's old, pockmarked surface and took his hand in hers. "Tell me true, Leafe. Are we doomed?"

Leafe squeezed Aster's hand in reassurance, but when he began to speak, he stopped short, realizing that he had no assurances to give. None that were true, in any case.

The dream wraith's words resonated in Leafe's mind. *Head eastward, and brave the great wastelands of Aridana.* A wizard's cryptic counsel. *Cross its unforgiving, fiery dunes, and seek the fallen kingdom. Go to Old Ochre. Walk among its ruined towers.*

Will I ever be free of these phantom omens? Leafe asked

himself.

"Leafe?" Aster tugged at his hand. "Will the trees survive another week of this drought? Tell me, husband, will we be okay?"

Go to Old Ochre. Go to Old Ochre. GO TO OLD OCHRE.

"I have to go." Leafe pulled free his hand.

"Go?" She frowned, furrowing her brow. "Go where?"

"I have to go," Leafe repeated, rising.

"But you've only just arrived. You've been out in the orchard all afternoon. Stay here. Stay home." She reached out for his hand again. "Pacing the trees won't save them, you know? You'll be wasting your time. Unless, that is, you've learned to command the rain to fall at your whim?" Aster was joking, but something about what she said struck a chord in Leafe.

"Command the rain to fall..." he whispered. "Now wouldn't that be something?" He marched over to the door and reached for his hat hanging on a hook, took up his travelling pack and walking stick, carved from the wood of one his own orange trees.

Now Aster was up on her feet, and, walking toward the door, closed it firmly before Leafe had a chance to run off. Leafe looked at his wife reproachfully, but her own worried look withered his resolve to hurry off without proper explanation.

"I have to go," he pleaded weakly.

"For the love of Garden! Go *where*?"

"To Old Ochre. To walk among its ruined towers."

* * *

Two days later, as Leafe ate the last of his wife's candied oranges, he recalled the long, frenzied conversation they shared—it had not been easy breaking the news to her: "Honey, I've been having these dreams lately. How often? Every single night. How long? Let's see... about twelve or thirteen years."

As it turned out, sharing the details of his dreams proved no less complicated: Wizard riddles and prophecy… faceless crystal heads… incessant beckoning that strongly urged him to *Go to Old Ochre*.

It was no easy feat to convince a headstrong woman like Aster to allow her husband to face the hazards of a realm known specifically for its outrageous dangers. Such a task becomes even more difficult when the basis for said perilous adventure hinges on the content of dreams.

"I think you are unwell," Aster suggested.

"For the last thirteen years?"

"Thirteen years, you say? I shouldn't think you'd need reminding; we have been married longer than that." Aster prodded Leafe with an accusing finger. "Dreams are dreams, Leafe —nothing more!— but you and I, this farm… that's all *real*. Thirteen years or three hundred years… dreams are visions, Leafe, but life is material." Aster barred the door and crossed her arms. "You will not walk out on me, Leafe. You will not leave me to go chasing *dreams!*"

"Aster, my love, hear me out…" Leafe paced the room, stating his case.

In the end, despite her strong and very understandable misgivings, Aster agreed to endorse her husband's crazy idea. When she had added to the argument that his absence would leave the orange grove free from the expertise of his care. Leafe had reminded Aster that the orange grove was dying with or without his expert care. He added that his absence may lead him to true opportunity, a chance that might aid in the orchard's return to health and prosperity.

But it wasn't anything Leafe had said or argued that convinced Aster by the end of their long discussion. *That* came independent of her husband's desperately stated case. What convinced Aster was the sudden intrusion of a stranger who inexplicably manifested atop their dining table.

The robed figure's presence was both alarming and confounding, but it was his face, or lack thereof, that seized Aster's attention. In her own cottage, sitting at her own table, a man with no mouth to speak transmitted messages directly to her mind. With no eyes to scrutinize, she stared only at a smooth, crystal sphere resting upon his shoulders. Divided in perfect halves, she alternated her gaze between perfect black and pristine white.

The man, or wizard, or "dream wraith," as Leafe had named it, stated its case, explaining to Aster that her husband holds an important key.

"A key to what?"

"A better future for Garden."

Hoping for clarification, Aster turned from the faceless wizard to Leafe, who shrugged. "He speaks in riddles," he explained. "How do you think I feel? I've been listening to this for years."

Aster turned back to the crystal-headed figure, whose image began to fade. "Who… *what*... are you?" She asked.

I am all and everything, and nothing… I am alabaster and onyx, white starlight and the great black void between. The wizard's words faded with the passing of his image. The dream wraith had faded from reality. In their humble cottage, Aster and Leafe sat alone.

* * *

Leafe already missed his wife, his thoughts consumed by fleeting images of Aster as he savored the last of her candied oranges. He sucked on the leathery rind until all traces of its sweetness had dissipated like morning mist ushered away by the rising sun.

Even now, he faced a misty morning, vapors rising to unveil the horizon before him. He took one step closer toward the land he was reluctant to visit. He did not know it, but that step carried him beyond the bounds of Southstone, the only home he had ever known. From there, it was unknown territory. From that moment on, every step would lead to places unimaginable.

Two days into Leafe's long journey eastward, Leafe

followed the coastline that would eventually become The Hopeless Coast. This far west, it went by a more amicable name, if only just: The Edge of Fire. He walked The Edge, and understood its name. To his right—the south—was a sheer drop into the beautiful blue waters of The Amaranthine Sea, its breath warm and briny, carrying the smell of salt on the breeze.

To his left—the north—an arid world without end. Leafe gazed into a sun-scorched void blurred by mirage. Each dune folded over into the next, spreading out like a disheveled quilt well beyond the horizon.

Though the steady sea breeze blowing northward kept the worst of the desert heat at bay, if Leafe strayed from the coast, venturing into the dunes, the desert fires would quickly extinguish his life. And so the choice, not being a choice at all, was simple: Leafe would walk the coastline and would not wander from The Edge of Fire.

In those parched, tormented lands, water was a constant concern. One was never far from the body's next demand for hydration, regardless of the quantity of their previous drink. Luckily for Leafe—and any traveler treading The Edge of Fire—settlements dotted the coastal trail. Mostly, such places were humble fishing villages, never nearing the status required to be called a town, but they had food, shade, beds—and most importantly, water. They bore names like Drymouth, Bonecliff, Fishside, and Drabstone. Needless to say, they lacked the distinction of places like Glyndor, Two Harbors, or Russet; kingdoms north of The Sienna Steps, which divided Aridana from The Roanwood in the north. Even so, modest as they were, Drabstone, Fishside, Bonecliff, and Drymouth were all godsends.

After all, a parched man does not balk when water is on offer. Not when a chance to sate a deadly thirst presents itself. There is a common saying among places like Drymouth, Bonecliff, Fishside, and Drabstone: *Where there is a well, there is a way*. After having his fill of fresh, cold water, Leafe saw the wisdom hidden within the sentiment.

Even bloody Drabstone becomes paradise when one is handed a glass of cool water.

And so, in towns poor in refinement, but rich in water, Leafe made his way southeast along The Edge of Fire, never comfortable, but always alive. Within a fortnight, he was weary, suntanned, and had become a connoisseur of grilled bonefish, the local cuisine of many villages along The Edge.

After a fortnight, these small, coastal villages were well behind him, and as the trail turned away from the coast, guiding Leafe northward, he arrived at a large, urban settlement, his first taste of a proper Aridanan city.

On the morning of his fifteenth day of travel, he picked his bonefish breakfast from his teeth and looked out from the peak of a tall dune. Rounded spires silhouetted the rising sun, scattered across the sands. Distant, but clear, he heard the droning din of horns announcing the new day. It seemed to Leafe a lifetime since he laid eyes on anything close to civilization.

Thus concluded the first leg of Leafe's journey, which spread out behind him all the way home to Southstone, where he began.

Ahead, a new phase to his quest, Sinopia, City of Dogs and Men.

* * *

Sinopia offered quite the contrast to small villages like Drymouth and Bonecliff. It was a world apart from pesky settlements like Fishside. To be perfectly frank, it bore no resemblance to no-horse towns like Drabstone. And truly, Sinpoia was *anything* but drab.

When Leafe crossed the last stretch of desert to enter the city's dust-laden gates, he was greeted from within by a profusion of color, a vibrancy that sprang out from the featureless parched earth surrounding the city for untold miles. From each rising tower's peak, across all the many gilded parapets of palace walls, flags ruffled in the wind and banners draped in bright displays.

Town square was mad with activity: bustling bodies and loud noises, rich, pungent smells to entice one's hunger or tempt their craving for spice. Streets and alleyways, narrow and wide, sprawled in a complicated maze of frenzied activity. Market stalls clogged the endless bazaar, and voices called out among music, argument, and laughter.

Sinopia was smaller than Southstone, Leafe's homeland kingdom, and yet it seemed to have several times the amount of people, dozens of times more activity. Indeed, he was not prepared for the stimulation that assaulted his senses. And though he had heard of the dogs of Sinopia, who lived in harmony among humans, he had always pictured them more dog-like, and less human-like. Yet all around him, Leafe observed the strange canine faces of the Jackali, the dog-people who crowded the streets as much, or more, as the human men and women who lived among them.

It was all very exciting—perhaps *too* exciting—and Leafe found that his fascination quickly led to his exhaustion. As the morning became afternoon, and rising heat joined the intense hysteria around him, Leafe determined some downtime was warranted. He found an inn and rented a room to rest in before he ventured out into the city for a more thorough investigation of its wonders.

Later that night, in the relative quiet of his modest lodgings at The Prickly Pear, Leafe studied a book he had borrowed from The Sinpoia Library, hoping to learn more about the desert dogmen who both intrigued and repelled him. Sipping his cactus blossom wine, he poured over the pages of *Sinopia, and Its People*, focusing mainly on its chapter regarding the Jackali.

This is what he learned:

Sinopia was inhabited in equal numbers by the Aridanan humans and the Jackali dogmen, whose ancestry hailed from the coastal desert tribes in the south. Which species was responsible for the original settlement of Sinopia—human or Jackali—remains unknown. Most of the city's extant architecture suggests that humans likely built the city. This unproven facet of Sinopian history is not an active matter of contention, at least in most circles. Scholars viciously debate the matter and have failed to come upon an amicable conclusion. As it stands, the notion of who came first remains unimportant to most humans and Jackali alike. Sinopians, be they of human or Jackali descent, are happy to coexist, for the most part; disinterested in claims of outdated birthrights or ownership. It is owing to this harmony between man and dog that travelers like Leafe can visit Sinopia without undue prejudice or risk of belligerent harm.

Most racism, the book explained, comes from visiting outsiders, humans who are unaccustomed to living among dogs. Typically, it is not a problem, but occasionally fights break out and, very occasionally, murder occurs. There is a rule of thumb, which applies to any would-be bigoted travelers to Sinopia. Leafe read this rule aloud as he finished the last of his cactus blossom wine.

"It is not required for travelers to love the Jackali, or even like them, when passing through Sinopia. But it is required that these travelers respect the Jackali, or, in failing that, pretend to. If you hate our people, we do not want to know about it. If you let us know you hate our people, we will let you know how we feel about you."

Though nothing else was written about it in the book, there was an illustration beside the motto depicting many arms—paws and hands alike—pushing a man through the Sinopian gates into the desert beyond.

Though the foreign wine was making him drowsy, Leafe read a bit more about the Jackali before crawling into his bed to call it a night. He read about the basics of dogman anatomy, physiognomy, and genetics, simple lessons revealing mostly facts he already knew—the Jackali are a mix of hominidae and caninidae (man and dog); they are bipedal, though are capable of running on all fours as comfortably as their genetic cousin, the wolf. Though each

Jackali bears some semblance to both man and dog, there is a wide physical diversity among them; sometimes they look like men, sometimes like dogs, and sometimes, most strange of all, Leafe thought, an unattractive blend of the two.

Most interesting to Leafe — more so than elementary lists of physical features—was the descriptions of Jackali culture, religion, and custom. Though he was far too tired to read through the entire book on his very first night in Sinopia, he was intrigued to learn that the Jackali alone were responsible for operation and flight of the desert dirigibles, ballooned aircraft that used the heat of Aridana's sand to rise into the cloudless skies to safely cross the scorched wasteland. As masters of aerial engineering, the Jackali act as flying ferrymen, offering transport across the otherwise untraversable expanse of the Aridana.

This is how I will travel north, Leafe thought. *By this method, I will cross the fire, the wide desert of Aridana. By dirigible, I will fly to Old Ochre. By balloon, I will soar to meet my destiny... led by dogs, it would seem.*

This was Leafe's final thought as his borrowed copy of *Sinopia, and its People*, drifted open and face down over his lap, the chapters on Jackali religion yet unread. This was Leafe's final cogent musing of the day as his eyes fell heavy with sleep, fast taking hold of him. And what sleep it was! How Leafe snoozed on the cozy mattress and comfy lodgings of The Prickly Pear. What sleep it was, indeed, further improved by the absence of a spectral-wizard-dream-wraith, which failed to manifest and preach adventure and quests throughout the night. After all, there was little need for further visitation...

Leafe was already in thrall to the ghost that haunted his dreams.

* * *

The next morning, Leafe ate his breakfast in The Prickly Pear's common room. He wasn't overly fond of the grilled cuts of sand skink, but he was startled to discover that the orange juice on tap was every bit as fresh and delicious as his own back home: a perfect balance of tart and sweet that conjured nostalgic memories of his orchard in Southstone. He wondered if the trees still clung to life, and if they would continue to do so until he returned home. Leafe thought of Aster, too, wishing he could stroke her long, dark tresses. Suddenly, he became aware of how solitary his weeks of travel had been, and though unexpectedly peaceful, they had also been lonely. If Aster was there with him right then, Leafe thought, he would march back up to his bedroom and make love to her with gusto and tireless passion to match the early days of their blossoming romance... so many years ago.

A gecko the size of an alley cat crawled up the leg of his table, and just like that, Leafe was brought back to the here and now. He finished his orange juice, savoring every drop. Leaving the dregs of grilled skink and loose pomegranate seeds to the gecko reaving his breakfast, Leafe absconded from The Prickly Pear, walking out into the bright, hot streets of Sinopia.

He made his way to Balloon Town, the northern district that housed dirigible factories and aerial ferrying services. It was quite a trek, but there were plenty of distractions along the way to fill the hours. One could spend a whole day in the labyrinthine bazaar and still only scratch the surface of its outermost layer. But shopping wasn't something that Leafe was drawn to—quite frankly, it wasn't something he could afford. And so, without much purpose beyond getting from one end of the city to another, Leafe simply took in the sights as he sauntered along the bustling streets. Riding the edge of overstimulation, he delighted, nonetheless, in the many sights, sounds, and plethora of stimuli that seemed to exude from every brick and stone of the desert metropolis.

Among all the colors, bright banners, and vibrant wares all around him, Leafe nearly overlooked one curious detail: the Jackali's uniform clothing. Well, *nearly* uniform. The dogmen wore robes of identical style, and near-identical color. Tied at the waist, their loose-fitting garments terminated just above their ankles, each one dyed in colors that seemed to mimic the Aridanan region from which they hailed. Leafe marked the limited distinction of their hues: shades of umber, orange, and tan. Then, after losing interest in their conformity, he witnessed a robe worn by a Jackali that stood out among all the others. He only saw it for a moment—bright, vivid green, as loud and unreserved as the feathers of a parrot. In an instant, the tall, distinguished Jackali vanished within the throng of people and dogs; a flash of verdure in a sea of sand.

It was nearing afternoon when Leafe finally made his way to the edge of Balloon Town. In this far northern corner of the city, many of the festive elements and boisterous activity closer to its center had ebbed into sedation. Without all the bright colors, all the hustle-and-bustle to lend its ample distraction, the heat of Sinopia took center stage.

It was too much to bear.

Grateful to have reached his destination, Leafe entered the shaded, canvas-covered domes of Balloon Town. Inside, a world of its own awaited him; a palm-laden district muted by the filtered light of the fabric domes high overhead. There, in this indoor-outdoor zone dedicated to aerial engineering and manufacture, humans were scarce. Everywhere Leafe looked there were dogs dressed in shades of desert sand.

He wandered the palm-lined avenues, brushing shoulders with passing Jackali who went about their business with sterile efficiency. Though crowded, Balloon Town was orderly—quiet in comparison to other sectors of Sinopia. *Who knew*, Leafe mused, *that a pack of dogs could be so.... civilized?*

"Lost, are we?"

"I'm sorry?" Leafe turned to come face-to-face into the golden-brown eyes of a stranger who looked *almost* human, but his paws and pronounced canines marked him as Jackali. The dogman wore sienna robes in the traditional Jackali style, yet he also sported a pendant, a small, silver jewel in the shape of a balloon over his breast.

"You seem to be searching for something. Do you need direction?" The dog followed Leafe's eyes to the ornament that he wore, and smiled wide and wolfish. "Do you seek passage across the desert?"

"How did you know?" Leafe wondered if the Jackali, like wizards, were capable of reading minds.

The Jackali tapped the pendant pinned at his chest. "Your eyes are fixed to this like a young pup for a bitch's six bared breasts." He allowed a soft chuckle to fall out of his mouth along with his long, lolling tongue.

Six breasts... Imagine that. Leafe blushed, and muttered an apology. "Yes, you guessed it," he told the dogman. "I seek passage across the desert. And between you and me, my need to do so is imperative. Tell me, can you help me?"

Once again, the Jackali smiled in a rather wolfish manner—or was that simply how all dogs smile?

"Come with me." He waved for Leafe to follow. "I will help you cross the desert myself."

* * *

The Jackali airman introduced himself as Husky, leading Leafe to the far end of Balloon Town where its overhead shelter receded in favor of clear skies. Beyond the shade, the direct sunlight was overbearing, and uncomfortably hot.

"Here she is," Husky announced proudly, gesturing to a long row of flying machines that glinted in the searing sunshine. Which dirigible, balloon, blimp, or airship Husky had referred to was unclear to Leafe, who only stared at his guide.

"Which one? I can see you are dying to know. Why, the best one of them all, of course!" Husky laughed jovially, but seeing Leafe squint against the sun without a hint of humor over his human face, the dogman cleared his throat to elaborate for his hopeful client. "The red one, yonder." He thrust his paw in the direction of a non-profound but respectable dirigible whose name Leafe could only just make out against the gleam of desert sun.

"*The Crimson Wind...*"

"That's the one," Husky declared. "Most dependable balloon in the entire Sinopian fleet—and one of the fastest, too." He winked. "Now, shall we discuss the small matter of airfare?"

"Airfare?" Leafe's gaze shot from *The Crimson Wind* to her captain, who seemed like he was on the verge of salivating.

"Well, of course," Husky barked. "You won't find an airman in all of Sinopia that will fly you across Aridana in donation to your 'imperative' business."

"Yes, of course. How much?"

Husky looked away from Leafe to study his long claws. "Sixteen dunes," he said. "A bargain."

Leafe allowed his jaw to fall to the floor. "Sixteen dunes? You must be joking!"

"When it comes to money and flying, I never joke. Sixteen dunes is my price."

"If you're not joking, then you must be crazy." Leafe removed his hat to pull at nonexistent hair, a habit he had not outgrown, even after he had gone bald. "Sixteen dunes? A *bargain*? More like a fortune!"

Husky spread out his paws in a wide shrug. "Sixteen dunes, my human friend. It is the standard ferryman's price. It is the cost of crossing the desert."

"I am an orange farmer, not a prince!" Leafe grew red in the face and, for once, it was not because of the heat.

"Sixteen dunes," Husky repeated. "It is the cost of passage to Tawny."

"Tawny?" Leafe frowned. "I do not wish to travel to Tawny."

Then it was Husky who was frowning. "You wish to go north of the desert, no?"

Leafe nodded. "To Old Ochre."

"Old Ochre?" Husky was caught between amusement and irritation. "You wish to go to Old Ochre?"

"Yes," Leafe was not caught between amusement and irritation. He was *only* irritated.

"And you ask me if *I* am joking? You accuse *me* of being crazy?" Husky spat in the sand. "I would not fly to Old Ochre for *thirty* dunes. I would not fly there for all the dunes an orange farmer could scrape together in a lifetime."

Agitated and perplexed, Leafe threw his hat to the ground. "But I *must* go there! It is of the utmost importance that I go to Old Ochre as soon as I might."

Husky dragged a paw over his face and sighed. "Why?" He asked. "Why must you go to Old Ochre as soon as you might? What business could a human from—where are you from?"

"Southstone."

"What business could a human from Southstone possibly have visiting that old, ruinous graveyard? Don't you know? There's nothing there. Nothing, I tell you!"

Leafe shook his head, working himself up as he stated his case, pleading to Husky to fly him to the ancient, ruinous kingdom of Old Ochre. When asked about specifics to his quest, Leafe had nothing to offer, nothing at all. He admitted that his reasoning was unclear, the precise nature of his business unknown even to himself.

"But destiny calls me to Old Ochre," he concluded. "Where I will awaken the power to bring the rain!" His own proclamation startled him, but as soon as Leafe shouted those words, he felt them to be true.

Husky waved his paws to ward away additional folly. The Jackali airman dismissed what he considered to be ravings, telling Leafe that Old Ochre is too far out into the desert, too isolated beyond any inhabited settlement, and well outside the Jackali trade routes.

"I will take you to Tawny," the airman concluded. "It's the closest settlement to Old Ochre. From Tawny, you can pursue whatever wild whim takes hold of you. From there, you can attempt to reach the forsaken ruins by whatever means."

Dejected, Leafe slumped down in the sand.

"Well?" Husky badgered him. "Will you be wanting passage to Tawny or not? If you do, you know what it'll cost you."

"Sixteen dunes..." Leafe moaned.

"An exorbitant price," a newcomer announced, "but one I am willing to pay for a good cause." Leafe looked up to a trio of Jackali who emerged from the shadowed peripherals of the balloon yard.

"Who are you?" Husky demanded.

"We are your clients," the Jackali stranger smiled. "And we have heard this human's case, wishing to endorse his cause as our own."

If Husky was mildly surprised, then Leafe was flat-out shocked.

"My name is Aardwolf, and these are my companions, Dober Man and Collie." The two Jackali in his train bowed respectively. "We will fly to Tanwy in your *Crimson Wind*," he told Husky. "We will pay the price you require, each of us to a dog—and man."

Leafe stared up at the mysterious and confident Jackali named Aardwolf. In a blend of confusion and gratitude, he accepted the paw that helped him rise from the sand.

"That's right." Aardwolf did not flinch from Husky's suspicious glare. "Sixteen dunes. It is no problem. We will pay on behalf of the human."

"Okay," Husky nodded, and received the burden of coins that Aardwolf extended to him. "Okay," he repeated. "Let's go then. Across the desert to Tawny… Let's fly."

And while no explanation was offered at that particular moment, Leafe accepted the unexpected stroke of fortune riding on the back of a Jackali stranger's generosity. He had his questions, but for now, they could wait. He boarded *Crimson Wind* with Husky at the helm, and with three mysterious Jackali who had, for their own reasons, serendipitously paid his way.

It's just as well, Leafe thought, as the dirigible took him high into the air. *Sixteen dunes is more than two year's wages selling oranges at the Southstone markets. And it's more, besides, than I currently claim to my name.*

* * *

Leaning over the gunwale of *Crimson Wind*, Leafe gazed in wonder across untold leagues of volatile wasteland, the great expanse of Aridana. Even at an altitude of over two thousand feet, he could feel the heat radiating off the sand below.

High up in the dirigible, he felt secure… sort of… kind of… In truth, he had no idea if he was safe at all. Broodingly, he tallied the dangers: fire below, falling two thousand feet into it, and the potential menace of dogmen he did not know beyond the names they gave him. All it would take is a gentle nudge. A push from behind. And so, the question remained… *Am I truly safe*?

"It's perfectly safe," Husky announced, wearing his familiar, wolfish grin. His expression did not inspire confidence in Leafe. "I've crossed The Aridana hundreds of times. Made the journey to Tawny more than I can count."

Leafe smiled politely, reserving his comment: *If "hundreds of times" is "more than you can count," then your ability to tally numbers caps somewhere below one thousand.* He understood, of course, the Jackali pilot was using turns of phrase to explain his experiences—still—recieving Husky's words as literal made Leafe's smile come much easier.

"It's true, you know?" Aardwolf approached from the stern of *Crimson Wind,* joining Leafe at its starboard gunwale. "Flying by dirigible is the safest way to travel across The Aridana."

"It's the *only* way," Husky shouted from the helm.

"Well," Aardwolf shrugged, "the only sensible way."

Dober Man nodded, and Collie signaled she agreed. They both smiled at Leafe when he met their gaze, then returned their attention to far horizons over the opposite side of the boat.

"It's beautiful, isn't it?" Aardwolf made a wide sweep with his paw to indicate the desert stretching endlessly beneath them. "Deadly, of course. But undeniably beautiful."

Leafe could not refute Aardwolf's claim: The Aridana *was* beautiful. And though he preferred the greener, more arable lands of Southstone, there was something uncanny about the desert's bleak, hostile landscape that augmented its beauty. It wasn't that its golden dunes, in their innumerable miles of sameness, were visually pleasing. Nor was it that any of the sights were especially *pretty*... but staring within the infinite desolation, the endless undulating sea of sand, inspired—demanded—a sense of otherworldly awe. The beauty of The Aridana did not manifest in gentle brushstrokes and subtle touches, but in a bold, singular color spread across a continent-sized canvas.

"Why did you help me?" Leafe suddenly asked Aardwolf.

"Help you?" The Jackali did not avert his gaze from the western expanse of desert.

"You paid for my passage," Leafe said. "I'm asking you why. And don't tell me that generosity alone swayed you to act on my behalf—or that pity moved you to come to my aid." Leafe leaned in closer to Aardwolf, who still only had eyes for the arid panorama before him. "I saw you sulking on the edge of the balloon yard. I saw your ears perk up when I arrived, led by Husky, who never meant to offer me a fair deal. I do not believe you are in cahoots with the airman… that doesn't make sense... But I saw the light in your eyes, Aardwolf, as you thought yourself unobserved in the shadows. Something I said motivated you to spend sixteen dunes on my behalf. Do not mistake me, I am grateful for your magnanimity. Even so, I would like to know why… why, Aardwolf, did you help me?"

Grinning, Aardwolf finally looked Leafe in the eye, turning away from the view of The Aridana below. Eye-to-eye, the Jackali addressed the human eagerly awaiting his answer. "You are very perceptive, Leafe," he began. "For a humble orange farmer, you have the eye of a trained assassin."

"I have never killed a soul in my life!" Leafe protested.

"Relax, my friend. I was merely making a comparison. I was *complimenting* you. Your senses are sharp. Your wit has an edge. This is good."

"Okay..."

"So you'd like to know why I helped you?" He looked over his shoulder to Husky and, determining the pilot was uninterested in their quiet discussion, carried on talking to Leafe. "You'd like to know what sparked that 'light in my eye?'"

Leafe nodded. "I think I deserve an explanation, yes."

Aardwolf visibly relaxed, giving in, perhaps, to the inevitable. He took a deep breath before speaking. "What you were saying back in the balloon yard," he said, "when you were arguing with Husky about prices, but more to the point, about Old Ochre, and the imperative business you had there..." he trailed off, pointing over the side of the gunwale in a northwesterly direction. "Well, Leafe, some of the proclamations you made... some of the words you used to state your case—'destiny,' and 'bringing the rain'—indeed, even the disclosure regarding your 'unknown business,' it all closely echos the prophecies of The Hopeful Return."

"The Hopeful Return?"

"The name we have given our religion. Though in our own tongue, we would say *Groen Aarde*."

"Green Earth?"

Aardwolf beamed. "There it is again: the scholarly mind of an orange farmer." He nudged the human at his side.

"It's all so strange to me..."

"What's strange, Leafe?"

"That your religion is named Green Earth, what with the desert where you live, and its complete lack of green."

"Very astute," Aardwolf nodded. "And yet..."

"Its other name," Leafe blurted. "The Hopeful Return."

"And..." Aardwolf prompted.

"And you, the Jackali, are hopeful of the desert's return

to green earth?"

Aardwolf applauded Leafe before speaking. "Very much so, Leafe." The dogman gestured to the vast desert below. "Once, not so very long ago, the desert was much smaller. The Aridana was but a quarter of the landmass that has now inherited its name and desolation. The desert is the heart of the Jackali, and the land whence we hail. Where once ran rivers, only dry canyons remain, bearing the scars of their lost geography. Deep lakes have become nothing more than craters. And the trees, Leafe, the *trees*. Not even their stumps remain. The Aridana is not something we wish to overthrow, to slay like a monster that threatens our existence. We would live in harmony with the desert, and honor it as a fundamental keystone of Jackali culture. So too, do we wish to see the land return to the way it was, when desert and oasis and river valley were one. This is the desire of the Jackali: our 'Hopeful Return' to a green earth."

Leafe chewed on that for a while. Then, suddenly, he made a connection. "The robes you wear," Leafe said, patterns fitting together in his mind, "the Jackali bear colors to match the desert, and yet I saw one of your people wearing green."

"A priestess of our order. A holy woman. A leader."

"Always a priestess? Always a woman?"

Aardwolf nodded. "Disciples of Mother Earth. Those who can bear life."

Leafe fell silent, lost in his thoughts. As the sun began to set, the dunes on the horizon grew darker, taking on a reddish hue. The heat, if anything, was hotter than before. The land looked and felt like a raging furnace.

"You spoke of prophecy..." Leafe said, finding his voice. "You said my words closely echoed your religion. What part, I wonder, does a human—an orange farmer from Southstone—play in the Jackali's Hopeful Return to a green earth?"

Looking out across the endless vermilion dunes of The Aridana, Aardwolf laid a paw on Leafe's shoulder. "I quote from The Holy Text of Hope: *an outsider will come. He will arrive, ignorant to his own cause, and bear the fruits of the Jackali's deepest hope.* You said it yourself, my friend. You will bring the rain."

* * *

At night, The Aridanan sky was deep blue, and the dunes gleamed like silver under the moon. The heat lingered for an hour or so after the light of day faded into evening shadow, after which, much to Leafe's surprise, the desert air became uncomfortably cold.

"She's an entirely different beast in the nighttime," Collie said as she joined Leafe at the prow.

"She?"

"Aridana. The desert. In the heat of the day, her fangs are fire. At night, under the stars, her claws are ice."

"Jackali poetry?"

"Something like that," Collie playfully winked, and when she did, Leafe finally noticed her handsome face. She was vaguely human, though more dog than man… and yet, despite this, he understood the allure of the female Jackali. Under the cold, spectral light of the moon, he discovered that Collie, observed at certain angles, reminded him of Aster.

For a moment, he was almost tempted to reach out and touch her, to stroke Collie's brown fur behind her pointed ears. But then she turned to him and smiled, and when she did, the moonlight caught her pronounced, yellow fangs. And that was that… Whatever ghost of attraction had risen from the tomb of Leafe's loneliness had been dispelled, dust scattered on the cold, desert wind.

"Look!" Collie leaned across the prow and pointed. "Manticores! A dozen, at least."

On the ground, a pride of manticores prowled across the sand. They appeared as lions at first glance; a second look determined that the animals had long, spiked scorpion tails, and disturbingly human-like faces, which looked up to *The Crimson Wind* with interest. One of them roared, and Leafe shivered at its haunting call. Like so many other aspects of The Aridana, the strange desert predators were both majestic and terrifying.

* * *

The Crimson Wind set down at the balloon yard in Tawny, where, amid tall palms and wide acacias, the land was green. Nestled in the southeast foothills of The Sienna Steps, the city was split by an unremarkable river—but a river, nonetheless—that flowed anemically from the high, northern slopes of the barren mountains. *The Trickle*—an apt name, Leafe thought—branched into narrow, shallow streams, which divided into a complex web of finger-width rivulets before terminating into nothing at Tawny's western edge.

The Trickle's modest waterways were more than made up for by the vibrant greenery that festooned its banks: date palms, papyrus, sycamore fig trees, poppy, and marshmallow plants. A profusion of agapanthus lined the water's edge, and, undisturbed by its languorous flow, lotus flowers blanketed the water's surface. Dragonflies danced in erratic, spastic flight from one blushing bloom to the next. Great herons and graceful egrets waded the waters, ever on the hunt with their speared bills and focused, beady eyes. Through the gaps between great leafy pads that shadowed the shallow depths beneath them, variable species of fish maneuvered in the emerald gloom. And frogs. Everywhere, frogs. Their music was tireless and monotonous, an endless, cacophonous anthem to the river.

Though less than half the size of Sinopia, Tawny possessed a dozen times the biomass. Despite its hefty population of Jackali and men, Sinopia paled in comparison to the modest settlement of Tawny regarding life at large.

Who knew, Leafe thought, *that such a small waterway can*

provide so very much.

"There is more life in Tawny than I expected to see," Leafe said as he shielded his eyes from the rising sun to watch *The Crimson Wind* return south across The Aridana.

"Water is life," Dober Man remarked. "The river bears its blessing."

Leafe studied him for a time; Dober Man had been the least talkative amongst his party. He was a head taller than Aardwolf, and twice as wide as Collie. His lean muscle was pronounced beneath his short black and brown fur.

"It is paradise, is it not?" Dober Man said, looking out over the shallow river with its great, green offerings.

Leafe joined Dober Man in his river-gazing, and agreed with the strong and silent Jackali. *The Trickle*, with its abundance of life, was indeed a veritable paradise. From his vantage on the riverbank while surveying Tanwy, Leafe imagined that this green cityscape was an accurate glimpse of the "Green Earth" of the Jackali "Hopeful Return."

"I don't understand," Leafe said. "Why aren't there more people living here? More Jackali. Why are there so many in Sinopia—dogs and men scratching their livings off nothing but dust and sand?"

Dober Man turned his attention from the green river to the human who unwittingly slandered his homeland. "Be gentle with your words," he urged. "Sinopia is my home, and the land of my people."

Leafe blushed. "I did not mean to…"

Dober Man disbanded the tension with a kind smile—though it did reveal a set of razor fangs, which could efficiently dismember Leafe should the dogman so desire. "Not long ago—no more than a pawful of generations past—Sinopia was every bit as green as Tawny. More so, in fact. It was an oasis, Leafe. A hub of life and beauty. A vivid ember. An emerald jewel among the sand. The dead river, Zoisite, once coiled through the city like a great, green water snake. It would shed its liquid along the banks and gift the parched earth with tall grasses, floriferous blooms, grain, and ripe fruit. It was not so long ago, Leafe, that Sinopia was paradise on Garden. It was the good, Green Earth—the cradle of the Jackali."

Leafe saw the tears in Dober Man's eyes. "It is my conviction," he said, "that The Aridana will once again grow green." He did not know why he said it, but his words came unbidden, as if directed from a will beyond his own. "I shall bring the rain, my Jackali friend. I shall open the heavens to fill the rivers and lakes. You will have your oasis, Dober Man. Your people will walk once again among paradise on Garden."

* * *

They did not linger in Tawny. The trio of Jackali travel-guides-turned-acolytes and the orange-farmer-turned-prophet did not even opt to stay for a single night among the city's river-enriched comforts. The company was on a quest, after all, not a holiday. They purchased mounts—strange, flightless birds called fire moa—that were capable of running at great speed. The creatures stood on two powerful legs that elevated them to heights of twelve feet, sometimes more. And though they could not breathe fire, as their name may have suggested, the fire moa were well-equipped to handle heavy loads in the intense desert heat, and their wide, razor-sharp beaks were the bright color of flame.

Leafe and the three Jackali set out from Tawny before sunrise, taking advantage of the light offered by Garden's moon, Opal, that shone brightly in its waxing gibbous phase. Without the sun assaulting the sands from above, the desert was cool and comfortable. Under a black canvas peppered by copious stars, they rode east toward Old Ochre. The fire moa provided transport nearly as fast as flight by dirigible, and as the leagues fell behind them on their tireless, long strides, Aridana was painted silver by the moon as it voyaged across the sky.

They rested during the day, erecting crude shelters in the

low points between dunes for what meager shade they could manage. Unburdening their mounts from their heavy loads was hard work, but the rest that followed was well worth it, and necessary besides. Their supply of water made up more than half the weight they carried, and more than half of that went to the fire moa, who drank greedily before dozing off to sleep, still standing.

Despite the daylight, sleep came surprisingly easy for Leafe—riding fire moa all night tires a man out! The Jackali also slept, but they seemed to need very little, talking amongst themselves after waking, or privately meditating. At dusk, when the sun reclined hazily on the western horizon, the travelers prepared their mounts to ride the length of the night once again.

For three nights they rode, and three days they rested in what shadows they could find or affect, and on the fourth night, the company came upon the moonlit remnants of an ancient, fallen kingdom.

"Behold," Aardwolf called out, pulling his fire moa to a halt. "Old Ochre! The crumbled bones of Garden's greatest empire."

In truth, there was not much to see. Just as Aardwolf had described, these were merely the eroding vestiges of what had once been a great empire. What Old Ochre may have been like, before the great calamity had reduced it to the husk that now remained, no one alive could know. Still, despite its dilapidated state, the old ruins resonated with ancient import, a palpable energy that hinted at more than former glory.

As they approached its broken structure, the "old bones" of Old Ochre revealed themselves to be rather large—massive, in fact—stones the size of elephants, fabled creatures that were said to once roam The Aridana in large herds. Among the fallen towers that lay in the sand, one spire rose skyward, largely unbroken, eclipsing the moon. Its serrated edge knifed upward into the sky, casting a long, dark shadow across the desert sand. Swallowed by the dark smear that reached out like a phantom arm to seize him, Leafe shivered in the shadow of the tower that obscured the menace that had been stalking his party.

"Manticores!" Dober Man shouted, and, as if prepared for ambush, all three Jackali flipped aside their robes to reveal the pronged spears they had been concealing for days.

"I count five," Aardwolf shouted, jumping down from the high vantage of a crumbled tower.

"Six!" Collie corrected her leader. "Behind you!" She warned Aardwolf of the manticore he had overlooked, the same one that was poised to pounce upon his back.

Aardwolf turned around in time to intercept the beast's lunging attack, planting his five-pronged spear into the open mouth of the manticore. Roaring in agony, it fell upon the sand, writhing in the blood pooling around the base of ancient stones. Its suffering was acute, but did not last long. Aardwolf drove his spear into the heart of the monster, then called out to announce the new total:

"Five!"

All around him, Leafe watched in wonder at the martial dominance of the Jackali who had become his companions. Collie danced among the ruins and twirled as if carried by the wind, side-stepping the mighty clawed paw of a manticore swipe powerful enough to decapitate a battle ogre. She dipped down to evade the speedy strike of its scorpion tail, its venomous barb dripping in the air where it missed its target. Effortlessly—or so it seemed to Leafe, who gazed, detached, as if watching a choreographed performance—Collie avoided one deadly blow after the next, timing her counterattack in an artful thrust that sent her four-pronged spear to waylay the manticore.

"Four!"

Dober Man jumped high into the air, dodging the savage bullrush of a manticore whose attack, had it landed, would have resulted in the dogman's broken legs. He swung his three-pronged spear, slamming its blunt end into the leg of his assailant, then, having caused the beast to stumble upon the sand, drove his weapon's sharp end into the manticore's neck, killing the creature instantly.

"Three!"

After that, the remainder of the skirmish happened so fast that all Leafe could remember was a flurry of silver moonlight glinting off the tips of many-pronged spears, and dwindling numbers announced in the dark:

"Two!"

"One!"

"Zero!"

The Jackali cleaned the blood from their spears, weapons bearing a number of prongs to reflect the rank of the warrior priests who wielded them. Each pointed tip corresponded to the five stages of devotional advancement in The Hopeful Return. Collie explained this to Leafe as she checked him for wounds. Searching his body with exploratory paws, prodding her prophet to ensure he was unharmed, Collie met the human's eyes with affection. Leafe became aware, once again, of his attraction to her, to female dogmen, who he could not bring himself to call bitches, as was the colloquial, Jackali term for the gentler sex of their species.

Lost in the moonlight within her doe-brown, doggy eyes, Leafe was about to lean in and kiss Collie across her muzzle. But, for better or worse, this romanticism was interrupted by her sudden offer of an object, a bejeweled blade wedged between them.

"A dagger?" Leafe asked.

"A jambiya," Collie told him. "A treasured blade among our people."

Leafe looked at the blade laying flat across Collie's paws. "Beautiful," he told her, and while it *was* exactly that—beautiful—it was Collie whom he had praised, not the jambiya.

"For your protection," she explained, then slowly unsheathed the weapon to reveal its magnificent, curved blade.

Dober Man approached them. "There is a legend among

our people..."

"A prophecy that speaks of a man." Aardwolf stepped into view. "A human from a western land." He paused to clear his throat. "And I quote from the holy text of Hope: *He will raise up the jambiya given to him by the Jackali. He will thrust its blade into the sky. He will pierce the heavens...*"

"*...And the rain will fall,*" the four of them said in unison, Jackali, human, and all.

* * *

The fire moa had scattered during the skirmish, leaving Leafe and the Jackali to endure the desert on foot. The loss of their transport was disheartening, but the loss of their water was far worse—it was fatal.

"We will die within the day," faced with death, Dober Man lowered the veil of his stoicism, "should we not find water."

"Have faith," Aardwolf calmly counseled. "We sit on the edge of destiny."

Dober Man shook his head. "I would place my faith in chance, in finding an oasis. I would leave these empty ruins to wander the desert. I would rather do that than sit here idly and await my death."

"Faith, Dober Man!" Leafe's voice issued like a command, and indeed, his own voice seemed to command himself. Often, during those days, his words and thoughts had seemed to come from a source outside of himself. And just then, another message came to him from the core of his inner mind. *At the base of the tallest tower. The stone with the scar.* Leafe shook his head to free himself of the voice that echoed in his ears. Even so, he heeded the ghostly words, though they provoked a sense of insanity. He walked to the base of the tallest tower and sought the stone with the scar.

There it was, unremarkable but clear, a stone with a shallow, diagonal gash across its wide surface.

Trace it with the blade. Again, that invading, inner voice.

The scar… Draw your jambiya, and run its edge across the stone.

Leafe recognized the voice of the wizard, the dream wraith who long haunted his sleep. *Draw the blade. Trace the scar with your jambiya.* He heard the voice, and saw the visage to match its faceless speaker… A smooth crystal, divided black and white, alabaster and onyx.

Now… the voice beckoned.

NOW! the wizard commanded.

Leafe drew his jambiya. He traced its blade across the scar in the stone. Behind him, the Jackali priests beheld his actions with utmost reverence as the stone sank slowly into the sand, its huge bulk falling back to reveal a sheltered tomb, and a sarcophagus within. Descending its steps, Leafe entered the tomb and, pushing with all his strength, removed the heavy, stone lid from the coffin.

Inside, a mummified corpse lay in the throes of eternal slumber. The ancient linens that framed its face and body revealed that its wasted shape was Jackali, not human. The petrified body rested with its withered arms folded over its sunken chest, its spider-husk paws clutching at a stone—a bright jewel of amber. Somehow, the eons of dust had not diminished the brilliant luster of the shard. It was so radiant, so dazzling, that it almost seemed to glow among the gloom of the tomb.

Take up the shard.

If the Jackali behind Leafe heard the voice, they did not indicate in any way that they had.

Take up the shard.

Leafe obeyed the command, and, holding the amber stone, felt its power leach out into his hands, up his arms, and into his heart—the very core of his being, igniting his soul with a power he could never have imagined.

Exiting the tomb, Leafe held up the amber shard to show the Jackali faithful. Aardwolf fell to his knees. Beside him, Collie and Dober Man followed his example. Kneeling in the sand, the dogmen watched the human raise the amber shard high above him. They waited, expectant and hopeful, but the minutes unfolded to reveal nothing had changed, nothing was happening.

Leafe strained to unleash the power that seemed just beyond the reach of his grasp. He could feel it, a font of relentless force waiting to take form in the manifestation of his will.

Blood… The dream wraith whispered on the desert wind.

Life… The apparition called out from the deepest chamber of Leafe's mind.

Souls… The wizard flatly stated.

And then it became apparent. Leafe knew what he had to do to unlock the power of the demon amber shard.

"Dober Man," he called to the Jackali priest of the third rank. "Assist me, if you will."

Dober Man looked to his companions kneeling upon the sand. He searched Aardwolf's face for approval, awaiting his leader's command. Finding none, and receiving neither, he rose up to meet the request of the human prophet.

"How may I serve you?" Dober Man asked Leafe as he crossed the sand to meet him.

Leafe turned to Dober Man, and, smiling pleasantly, plunged the jambiya into the dogman's heart. "You need only to die, my friend." Clutching at his chest, Dober Man fell to the sand.

A commotion stirred behind Leafe, behind the Jackali priest who lay dying at his feet. Collie stood up in alarm, shouting in protest, before Aardwolf pulled her back down to her knees. Then, without any interruption, Leafe took the amber shard in his bloodstained hands. He thrust his blood-slick jambiya high to the sky above him, willing the power of the crystal to take the form of his whim.

Dawn lit the world in hues of lilac and rose. Then, among the black, billowing clouds, the heavens ruptured. The desert filled with the sound of rumbling thunder, and the sky erupted in a deluge of rain.

IV

ZINNIA

He won her in a bet—a log-splitting contest that showcased his raw and terrible strength. Fair and square, Rolph inherited the rights to a young girl. The bet was ill-placed. The contest, not even close. It ended with a regretful father, and the utter dismay of his daughter, Aisling, who had suddenly become Rolph's prized acquisition.

As Aisling grew, maturing to an adult, she became easily the tallest woman in the small town of Harveston, and stronger than most of its men. She was often chastised for her mannish nature, her wiry muscles, and her plain face. Among the ladies, she was the only one who, without the aid of a ladder, could gather the apples from the high branches in the orchards. Among the gentlemen, she was one of the few who could split a twenty-inch log of ironwood with a single swing of her axe.

Yes, Aisling was strong. Indeed, she was tall, if spare. But Rolph, who owned her, was stronger still, taller by a clean six inches. And Rolph, to the discontent of Aisling, was a mean, rough bastard with an appetite to match his ample dimension. Many was the night—or day—that Rolph imposed his heavy-handed lust upon his "wife." Many was the evening—or afternoon—that Rolph demanded Aisling's body, if not her heart.

Often bruised, always disgusted, Aisling would leave the

bed as soon as she was allowed. It was her custom, in darkness or light, to run through the woods until her lungs burned, until the sweat oozed from her pores and the toxins bled free from the wounds festering in her heart. Then, totally spent, she would dive among the icy pools and wade in the muddy streams clotted by logs and leafy debris. Away from Harveston, across The Gold Belt of The Meadowlands, miles away to the edge of The Autumnwood, Aisling would bathe in the frigid water until her skin was blue and wrinkled. Afterwards, with a semblance of feeling marginally clean, she would seek the nulliparous berry. One handful, two, she would gorge until she felt as if she might die; relieved in the certainty that if Rolph's child grew within her, it certainly would.

On these ventures, her jaunts into the wild to cleanse herself of Rolph's lingering stench, Aisling was accompanied by a bird, a single magpie, which trailed her far-off wanderings. Though she thought it was strange, uncanny even, that a lone bird—the same exact one, as far as she could tell—would follow her so far and so wide, Aisling was not troubled by the magpie's presence. Quite the contrary, she became fond of the black and white bird that flew with her wherever she ran. She named it Seren, meaning "star" in the ancient language.

"For you are a bright and cheerful thing in this dark and dismal world," she explained to the magpie after announcing the name she had assigned to it. "And like a star, Seren, you are white on black, a beacon in the night."

In response, Seren sang to Aisling as it often did, sweet birdsong to fill The Meadowlands and The Autumnwood where they roamed. It was just a bird, Aisling reasoned, but in all of Zinnia, or any other continent across Garden, it was the thing she cherished most.

Her only love in a world that offered her none.

* * *

"Bed. Now. I need love."

Rolph was no poet. Though he *did* have a way with words—the emphasis he put into them. When Rolph made his wants known, they were met, and met quickly. What Rolph wants, Rolph gets, and he always wanted Aisling.

"Undress. Come."

"Yes, Rolph."

Reedy as a willow, hard as iron, Aisling undressed, athletic and long of leg, but far from feminine, with an androgynous, shapeless body. Pale as bone, she'd walk naked to the bed, arranging her white-blonde hair to fall over her small breasts and cover her nakedness where it may. Forlorn, but resolved to her fate, she'd crawl over the hulking, swarthy mass of her "husband" who had won her in a game. Their intercourse was coarse, often rough. Aisling gave only what was required to sate Rolph's daily pleasure.

On one particular evening, no different from any other, Aisling answered Rolph's curt summons as she always did. Outside their bedroom, perched upon a window that looked out to the muddy streets of Harveston, a magpie gazed through the smokey panes of glass, its beady eyes trained on Aisling as she undressed for her husband.

"Seren..." Aisling croaked longingly. Rolph followed her dreamy stare, hurrying from the bed to glare out the window, assuming his wife was in communication with some secret lover. Enraged by the thought—despite that his suspicions were immediately shown to be unfounded—Rolph took up Aisling and hurled her to the bed. What followed was so heinous and invasive that Aisling, even as Rolph's rightful property, raised a hand against her husband, demonstrating the strength of a woman.

Roplh's teeth landed on the pillow, even if his head had not. Spitting out globs of blood, cradling his broken jaw that hung loose from his battered face, he reached for his axe which rested against the wall by the hearth in their bedroom.

"You belong to me, Aisling..." Rolph swore in oaths that would make a pirate blush; blood and broken teeth spilling from his lips upon every foul word he spat. "I will have you, Aisling," he told her, raising up his axe, "You are mine."

There was a tap on the glass, the sound of a little beak clacking against the window. When Rolph turned to investigate, Aisling put all of her weight into a downward kick, right into his knee. Hearing the mighty *crack* before the fury of screams that came afterward, Aisling gathered her clothes and ran out into the night.

With Seren flying by her side, Aisling ran and ran, then ran some more. She left the sound of Rolph's agonizing screams and the town of Harveston behind her. As she often did, she ran beyond The Gold Belt of The Meadowlands, entering the fringes of The Autumnwood far to the east. Then, for the first time ever, she ran even further into lands unknown to her.

* * *

The night was still young when Aisling's boiling rage reduced to a simmer, when all her anguish, disgust, and fear began to cool. The adrenaline conjured by her violent act, the elation that she felt after striking that *bastard*, leaving him behind, began to ebb as the hours and miles disappeared behind her.

Suddenly, soberly, Aisling became aware of her present predicament. Shifting focus from the domestic hell of her life back in Harveston, she considered a new, immediate threat: exposure to the elements, darkness, and hunger. Clinging to the few garments she had managed to collect during her hasty retreat, Aisling shivered in the midnight chill. Among the darkness of The Autumnwood, her optimism was swallowed up in the gloom. And in every shadow, a new anxiety budded into pitch-black blossoms, each one foretelling her doom.

Daylight, she knew, would dispel her worries. But then the thought came to her: *Will I last the night? Will I see another dawn?*

Then, rather timely, Seren swooped down from the deep obscurity of the canopy, clacking away as magpies do, his avian noise somehow reassuring Aisling that she was not alone, but with a friend. The bird's presence, on its own, was comfort in itself. But the way the creature flew off into the distance, returned to Aisling, then repeated this—coming and going, coming and going—suggested motivation beyond that of birdbrain antics. To Aisling, it seemed as if the bird intended to guide her.

And indeed, having nowhere else to go, she followed Seren, who led her to a shallow cave. Buttressed by towering pines whose low branches provided a thick curtain of needles like a doorway over its entrance, the cave provided excellent shelter from the wind, and adequate lodging for the night.

It was no feather bed—the rock and moss and carpet of pine needles—but it was better than the bed she shared with Rolph back at home, mainly, *exclusively*, because it lacked Rolph himself. Though she did not sleep very well—or at all, for that matter—Aisling *did* feel better in the morning. Nonetheless, as she rose from bed, she understood that her situation was not a bed of roses.

Aisling knew there were still plenty of concerns to address, and actions to take. The concern was food. The action… hunting? Without her bow, or even a knife, there was little chance of any success in *that*. She would forage, Aisling ultimately decided, knowing enough about the local fungi of The Autumnwood to pick the edible mushrooms, and avoid the ones that would cause her intestines to implode. It dawned on her then: deadly mushrooms would have offered a convenient method to killing Rolph in the form of mushroom pie, or cream of mushroom soup. It was an opportunity lost—she could not return to Rolph now, let alone prepare his meal (which was just as well, because it was the very last thing she wished to do). If Aisling showed her face, Rolph would smash it in, just as she had done to his knee.

With that last lovely image framed and hanging on

the walls of her inner thoughts, Aisling smiled, ready to embrace whatever adventures lay ahead. Full of nonlethal mushrooms to sustain her, she turned away from the west, where Harveston and her husband languished well beyond the horizon.

"Take the lead," Aisling said to Seren. She had no expectations the magpie would actually do anything, but the bird sprung to action as if it understood her every word. Taking flight, careful not to lose the human who trailed it, Seren flew back to Aisling, then away again, back, and away, leading her—randomly or by design—southeast...

Always southeast.

* * *

As the hours ate away at the day, and Aisling, in turn, ate benign mushrooms —and pocketing one she knew to be toxic— the forest began to change. The wet moss and soft, rich earth underfoot became drier, harder, more rocky; the trees more coniferous, more brooding, somehow. The shadows that the tall pines cast from the hem of their branches was pervasive, oppressive. Even the noon day sun had trouble penetrating the eerie gloom consuming Aisling's surroundings.

It was as if something sucked dry the life from The Autumnwood itself.

That observation led to revelation—Aisling was no longer in The Autumnwood. Those familiar woods with their familiar routes were long behind her, scattering northwest. Though she possessed no map among her scant belongings, and hadn't gazed upon one in many years, she could see vivid maps of Garden in her mind; the artful, gorgeous scrolls from her forays in the limited, but adequate library in Harveston. She closed her eyes, bringing those beautifully inked geographies to the forefront of her mind, recalling the many names of kingdoms and their borders, like so many pieces fitting together to form an entire world.

In her imagination, she traced a finger from Harveston, her home, southeast to…

"Mistvale," she said aloud, before clamping her hand over her mouth. She recalled all that she had heard of the region. The Mistvale was known for its bandits, rogues, and zealots that worshiped false gods, freaks, cannibals, and worse... The shadows of the pines around her at once seemed unnatural, full of hidden menace. Aisling became terribly frightened.

"It's just a forest," she reasoned, speaking in defiance of her paranoia. "A wood like any other," she determined. "Except darker… and very much… *unknown*." Aisling recalled the things she knew very well, like her life in Harveston—which brought her musings back to Rolph—and quickly determined that mystery is preferable to misery.

"Besides," she said, forcing cheer into her timbre as she addressed the magpie perched on her shoulder, "I have you, Seren. I am not alone."

"No," an unfamiliar voice agreed with her. "You are not alone."

Aisling's blood ran cold. She froze, then willed herself to turn around to witness the owner of that gravely voice that seemed to sweep in from the depths of the gloom behind her.

Who's there? She may have asked.

Friend or foe? She may have inquired.

A simple *Hello*, she may have ventured.

But Aisling had no voice. It was caught in her throat, closing with trepidation

"Sadly, for you, it is just as you say..." A man with the girth of a mountain stepped from behind a clot of close-growing pines. "My lady," He looked Aisling up and down. "…that is, if you *are* a lady. My goodness! You are as tall and tough as a titan pine!"

Aisling studied the stranger just as he had studied her. The man was more than large; he was monstrous. And though he was *decidedly human*, he bore many tattoos and body modifications—markings and augmentations that hinted at self-mutilation. When he spoke, his forked tongue, scarred from its ritual splitting, flickered serpentine, almost demonic. Every inch of his skin was green, and his ears had been cut off, making his shaved head look smooth and featureless beyond the green ink that stained it.

"My lady," he said again. "If I were capable of pity, I would surely reserve some for you. You will certainly need it." He hefted an axe that looked about the size and weight of Rolph. "But you will not receive it." He brought two fingers to his green lips and issued a whistle that cut high and shrill through the forest.

"Nor any mercy," the green man added as the pine trees came to life, or appeared to in the murk as a large band of unwholesome rogues emerged from their shadows. Each face, to a man, was disfigured and vandalized, the human qualities removed or tainted. With personalities to match, the unsavory group proudly displayed their maimed and tortured bodies. Mean faces grinned at Aisling with filed teeth, shark-tooth smiles on boys that were not yet men, and old, hoary bastards with their beards dyed green, hanging like moss from gaunt, tattooed faces, scarred with deliberate, dehumanizing markings.

Aisling reached for her bow, for her knife, for *something*, and though she came up empty, she raised up her fists, poised like a leopard to take down one or more of her aggressors until their inevitable brutality engulfed her.

"My, oh my, would you look at this!" Laughed the big, green one, presumably the leader. "She's not going down easy." The gruesome, reptilian faces of boys and old men alike licked their lips and joined the laughter. "Well, I'm not one to play with my food... not usually… but why not? We can give her some sport, can't we, lads? We can play with the tough girl for a while… before we eat her."

And then Aisling dropped her fists, the fight falling from her, sinking like a lead weight dropped into a river. Of the many terrifying stories she had been told as a child regarding the Mistvale and its menaces, she recalled one that had disturbed her most of all: a tale of pagan cultists, dragon worshipers and cannibals, self-mutilated and tattooed to mimic the mythical lizards whose devotion they assigned to their would-be reptilian hearts. They lived in a dreaded castle, a doomed stronghold by the name of the Drayke Fort. There, in its dingy stone towers in the cheerless hills of Mistvale, they tortured countless victims, which for them, was a scholarly form of art. It was said that after years of inflicting the worst of abuses, heinous torments that left their prisoners alive but thoroughly mad, they would finally feed their "pets" to their fabled drake living in the depths of their castle.

"The Varanus..." Aisling whispered, trembling to her knees.

The mammoth bastard who she first encountered grunted his approval. "Hear that, Greenmen?" He called out to the rabble. "She's heard of us. Now ain't that flattering?" The lizard faces around Aisling grinned and nodded and closed in on her.

Crying in spite of herself, Aisling looked up to Seren, who had flown high above her to perch in a branch of a looming pine. Even with the magpie close, and the dozens of men descending inward to seize her, Aisling felt very much alone. As many pairs of rough, taloned hands took hold of her, she felt as if she had stumbled from real life into a genuine, material nightmare.

* * *

If Aisling's life in Harveston with Rolph was unpleasant at best, and most often miserable, then her life in the Drayke Fort dungeons among the rats, lice, and bones was hellish even among the best of times. Each day passed with the expedited rush of an era, each week a veritable eon, and not a single second of these days and weeks, adding up to so many months, could be regarded as worth living. Pain came frequently, such monstrous pain as only torture can achieve. Discomfort was a fixed condition, presenting mostly in hunger and cold, but also in aches, injury, and sorrow—and fear, always fear.

Terror was her sole companion, a wretched roommate in her tiny cell of stone.

And then, like a blessed angel appearing to alleviate the plague that was Aisling's life, apathy came over her like a tranquilizing tide. Dissociation fell upon her like a heavy drape of relief. No, not relief—not exactly. A release, perhaps. The bliss and tragic sadness that comes with giving up. Total despondency. The death of all of Aisling's hopes. The demise of her will to take another breath.

Aisling's gaolers at once noticed the change in her demeanor. With whip and hook and needle, with fist and fiery brand, their efforts were ineffectual; they grieved her screams and pleading that she no longer bothered to exert among her suffering. Everything had been dampened, softened, *muted.* Mind and body, Aisling was going blank, fading away. Tragically, she was becoming a ghost even before dying, and really, it shouldn't come as a surprise—her internment in the dreaded Drayke Fort dungeons had stretched on for nearly a year. Had Aisling remembered she carried a fatal mushroom, a ticket to her final destination of death, she would have swallowed it down with her gruel many months before.

* * *

When she heard the tapping on the bars high above her, Aisling assumed it was one of the Varanus kids playing outside, teasing her from the world beyond, where the sun still warmed all it touched. When the tapping persisted, she assumed the kids were up to no good, goading her to look upward, and, once she turned her face to the dim light above, she assumed to be rewarded with a golden stream of reeking piss pouring buckets upon her face. Resolved to get it over with—whatever foul jest the cannibal kids had in mind—Aisling looked up to the tiny aperture and prepared for the shit, piss, or fetid remains of Gods-know-what to rain down upon her.

When she deigned to appease the snot-nosed brats, finally looking up to investigate the tapping from above, she did not witness the sneering, tattooed faces that she had expected. For the first time in what seemed an eternity, she did not look upon someone unwelcome, something unpleasant, but the happy visage of a godsend. Aisling stared in disbelief, slapping her face to be sure what she saw was no dream of hallucination. High above, looking down, was a familiar face—a magpie's face—as Seren tapped its beak upon the grating of the barred window.

Aisling's malaise departed in a blink of the magpie's beady eye. Like a drop of water upon a searing pan, it evaporated into scattered molecules, a ghost among the ether. With the return of her hopes came the return of her fears. Aspirations of living came with a price: anxiety and dread. Giving up came with certain comforts: a sense of invulnerability, knowing there is nothing to lose. But Aisling was glad to feel the old agitation and familiar dread. She was glad to once again have something to lose.

"Seren!" Aisling tried to shout, but only a whisper escaped her cracked, bleeding lips. "Seren! My friend! You have returned to me." She wept with an unrestrained melange of emotions, her parched throat protesting with fire. "Seren, my love. You have come to save me!"

All at once, relief, sorrow, joy, and fright washed over her.

How could a magpie save me from my terrible plight? She thought. *Only an army, perhaps a dragon, could storm the Drayke Fort and scour the filth of Varanus in hopes to deliver me from its dungeons.* And then, as if in harmony with her thoughts, the Greenmen's drake roared from within its cavernous holdings somewhere deep beneath the dreaded stronghold. *To think such a creature exists!* It made Aisling shiver, not least because her eventual fate was to be fed to the monster.

Drakes were not dragons—which are believed to be extinct—but they are close cousins; only marginally smaller and without wings. In the absence of an army to rescue her, Aisling would settle for the aid of an angry drake. An idle thought, and a foolish one besides. She did not have a drake at her disposal. She had only a magpie.

But a magpie was better than nothing. The presence of Seren was, for that matter, *everything* to Aisling. Even if the bird could not save her life, it had saved Aisling's heart, which had laid cold and dormant for many months, and once again pumped warm, tender blood.

"Come to me, Seren," Aisling called up to her feathered friend, who squeezed through the bars of the high window and swooped down to perch upon her bony shoulder. The bird's touch was a balm, its mere presence a lifeline. Overwhelmed, Aisling wept for a while, then smiled for the first time in a year. She would have been content to cuddle the magpie for hours, happy to linger in the joy of reunion with her friend. But Seren flew away from Aisling, retreating to the darkest corner of her cell. Ignoring Aisling's command to return to her, the magpie tapped upon the wall, tracing the mortared edge of a large stone with its beak.

Seren's odd behavior persisted. The magpie tapped upon the stone—always the same one—then dragged its beak along the mortared edge. Seren paused to look at Aisling on occasion, tapping the stone, tracing its edge, repeating the sequence, meeting Aisling's gaze with its own, almost as if trying to show her something vital.

It was only after Aisling noticed the crumbs of mortar piling up at Seren's feet that she determined what the bird was doing, and understood what it was trying to tell her.

"The stone!" she gasped. "It's loose!" Prematurely, Aisling had visions of escape, excitedly divining her freedom. But then she fell back to earth, fell down to reality at the bottom of a deep, dank dungeon.

"We are underground," she told Seren. "If I remove the stone, it will lead nowhere. It will lead to black earth, or rock. One stone removed, it may lead to yet another. At best, it will open up to my neighbor's cell. And at worst, that neighbor will not be happy to see me." Aisling sighed. "It was a good idea, Seren, if a little bit birdbrained."

Seren was limited to the expressions available to a bird—not many to speak of—but the magpie managed to offer Aisling a look that suggested annoyance and, above all, insistence. What it failed to achieve with its demonstration, and failed to communicate in its limited retinue of expression, Seren did not mean to fail a third time, or to mince words. When the magpie *spoke* to Aisling, it commanded her with a voice far from birdsong or sweet twittering: "Remove the stone, Aisling. Pry it free. Crawl forth into the darkness that lies beyond. Take up the sword, and brandish your talons. Remove the stone, and fly free, no longer a bird in a cage."

Seren's words echoed in the small cell, deep and resounding as thunder. Aisling did not move, did not even breathe, as the bird cocked its head at her before taking flight to perch high above on the window that led to the outside world. "Remove the stone," the magpie said one final time. Then it flew away, and Aisling was left alone to contemplate the tenuousness of her sanity.

* * *

Aisling's gaolers came sporadically, about once a day, sometimes more and sometimes less. They came with food—if the slop that they brought could, in fact, be called food—usually at night, sometime after the meager light from the tiny window high above faded to nothing. The Greenmen would come, hooded and tattooed, and Aisling would accept their offering of food, or torture, sometimes both, and often neither. The torches that they carried were harshly bright amid the darkness, revealing the nuance of her dismal, little world.

The gaolers knew Aisling well, having long grown bored of repeating the same old slurs after the first few weeks of her "stopover" in the Drayke Fort. And so, when they paid their visits, they often did so silently, or with wordless grunts to communicate the bare minimum, the base acknowledgement that both gaoler and prisoner still existed in their respective roles. When they would leave her, Aisling's cell returned to a black and lightless void. Then, when her eyes adjusted, she would see through the lens of a nocturnal animal, guided by distant torchlight flickering around the ascending spiral of the stairwell beyond the locked door.

That night, Aisling had no stomach for the swill that was left to her. In her emaciated state, she hardly had a stomach at all. She pushed away her "food" and got straight to work. With the gaoler having come and gone, she knew that she had a full day to work with. One more day in hell... But on this day, Aisling had purpose.

She found the stone that Seren had started chipping away at. She traced its mortared groove with her brittle fingernails and scraped away what she could. It was slow work, painful work, and within the hour each one of her fingers was bloody at the tips, two of her nails having cleanly popped off. The pain was what she may have once described as excruciating—once, but no longer. A seasoned guinea pig on the wrong end of torture, Aisling had redefined "excruciating," and this was *not* that. Still, the task was far from pleasant, and, working up an appetite, she soon suffered the slop that was left to her.

Refueled, reinvigorated, and regretful, too, for not thinking of it sooner, Aisling picked up the bony fragment of an ex-prisoner's rib and chiseled away at the mortar with increased efficiency, and less pain. In an hour, two, maybe three, the mindless work was complete, allowing Aisling to find a fingerhold deep enough in the grooves she had carved to wiggle the stone loose, eventually pulling it free.

With a sense of dread, Aisling hazarded a glimpse into the gap that was left in place of the stone. She feared to find what she expected: more rock, another stone, or the endless black earth of Garden, bearing no hope of freedom. When she found the courage to peer inside the hole, she was startled to find a crude, yet unmistakable, staircase beyond. And what was more, an eerie glow that resonated in the bowels of… *What is that?* Aisling wondered. *More dungeons? A crypt? A tunnel to the outside world? Hell?*

There was only one way to find out.

Aisling crawled on all fours, her belly scraping against the cold stone floor. Then, wiggling back and forth, she squeezed through the hole in the wall of her cell, leaving it behind.

* * *

The unearthly glow filling the cavernous space was foreboding, and very offputting. Despite this, Aisling reveled in its uncanny light, for the illumination was just enough to notice the bottomless abyss a few paces to her right. As it was, with the gentle lustre unveiling the deepest of shadows, she discerned the cliffedge lining one edge of a staircase, moving quickly to hug the rock wall on its opposite side.

In this careful fashion, Aisling descended the stairway leading deep beneath the Drayke Fort. As she immersed herself in the glow, it did not grow more intense, instead bathing the entirety of her surroundings with even, muted light. This made little sense to Aisling, but she did not dwell on the logic nor mystery of the strange conditions aiding her—she was simply grateful for the gift of sight. As the cliffside tapered to even ground, Aisling quickened. Without the fear of stumbling to her death limiting her speed, she swiftly reached the end of the stairs, which terminated in a wide stone arch, its aperture covered in a spectral gauze like spiderweb woven from light, or…

"Magic!" Aisling's exclamation echoed in the hollow chamber, fading away in a long sequence of her own amazement.

Magic, magic, magic, magic…

The "web" of light was transparent, but opaque enough to cloud whatever wonder (or horror) awaited Aisling on the other side. Unsure which procedure to follow, how to break the magic barrier between her and whatever lay beyond, Aisling lingered, pondering what to do next. A voice called out from above—at the top of the stairs, or back in her cell, she was unsure. *The Greenmen!* Aisling at first panicked, but as the realization dawned that the voice did not originate from the top of the stairs or back within her cell, but from inside her mind, she calmed and reaccessed the situation at hand.

Persimmon. The voice in her head enunciated clearly, and with command.

Persimmon. It repeated.

PERSIMMON.

Once more, and the last was so loud in Aisling's mind that she winced, nearly falling to her knees as the word droning in her came fluttering off her lips unbidden.

"Persimmon!" She cried. "Persimmon!" Her shouts diminished to whispers, then her words ceased altogether as she watched the vaporous barrier fade away, opening to make way to whatever wonder lay in the honey-hued light of the next chamber.

Catching her breath, collecting her wits, mustering whatever courage still resided within her, Aisling stepped through the stone archway into a much smaller, more intimate chamber. Suffused in the bronze light emanating from its center, a stone altar bore an epic weapon. Squinting amid its brilliant glare, she approached the light, identifying its source: a vibrant jewel, a marmalade crystal shard, an amber stone set within the pommel of a greatsword. Its length, standing upright, would rise taller than her own six feet. Its double edged blade, smooth as liquid silver, gleamed like polished glass. The marigold stone—probably amber, assuredly magic—was a beacon in the dark, ablaze with potent energy and evident power. It was the size of Aisling's thumb—so small a thing, and yet there was no doubt of its power, which would dwarf the might of ogres and giants alike.

Aisling leaned over the altar, gazing down at the sword. As large and mighty as it was, there was no way she could wield it, let alone remove it from its place. In her weakened, malnourished state, she doubted she could budge the monolithic weapon a single inch. And yet…

Take up the sword, and brandish your talons.

Aisling recalled the strange words that came forth like a sermon from the beak of a bird.

Take up the sword. Fly free, no longer a bird in a cage.

That was rich, coming from an actual bird. But was it really a bird? Was Seren truly a magpie, as he appeared to be? "*He*," because his voice was distinctly male when he bid Aisling to obey his commands. Maybe it was foolish, all this time, to assume Seren was merely a bird; he had, afterall, always acted more like a human than a magpie.

Take up the sword, and brandish your talons. Fly free, no longer a bird in a cage.

She heard Seren's words echoing in her memory, morphing into the words of a mighty wizard, the words of a magical man taking the form of an animal. She had no time to feel tricked or betrayed. She would do as the magpie-man-wizard had instructed her. And though Aisling doubted she could lift the hulking greatsword off the altar where it lay, she tried, nonetheless, reaching out to grasp it by the hilt.

With the ease of lifting a feathered quill, or the hem of a summer dress, Aisling took up the monstrous weapon and raised it high above her head. So high and so fast did the blade soar into the air, she scraped the blade across the rocky ceiling, showering sparks over her like the stars above, content to tumble earthward.

It didn't make sense. How could a weapon so large and so monstrously proportioned—absurdly, mythically portioned—be so very easy to wield, to lift, to swing, as if it were made of air, or nothing at all? Was it a ghost blade? Did such a thing even exist?

No, that preposterous notion was nonsense, for when the blade struck, it struck *hard*. The sword was nearly weightless, and yet it packed a punch as if it bore all the bulk logic suggested. It was an odd sensation that Aisling quite liked; a stretch of the mind to hold something so large, to swing something so powerful, that yet felt as if she held something as dainty as a dandelion stalk.

When she swung the blade, or even subtly shifted stance, the amber stone reacted, glowing brighter to match the intense motion of the sword.

So it *was* a magical blade. Of course it was. Powering it was the same artifact that lit the chamber—the amber set into the pommel.

Exhilarated by her fortune, Aisling swung the blade wildly, thrilled by the unnatural effortlessness of wielding such a mammoth (and deadly) tool. Carried away, she lost sight of her surroundings, and the greatsword came swinging down into a mighty arc to crash into the stone wall at the back of the chamber, shattering its rocky surface, revealing a separate cavern, and the agitated beast within.

The Drake—the object of the Greenmen's worship—narrowed its bloodshot dinner-plate eyes, crusty at the corners, and issued a forlorn, pathetic growl at Aisling. It opened up its maw, showcasing its razored rows of needle-sharp teeth, sighing away the weight of the world in a gentle breeze blowing out of its great lizard lungs. The Drake, in all its fabled might, was a wretched, despondent creature. Weighed down by the roots of the castle above it, encased in the darkness beneath the weight of the Drayke Fort, the great lizard was crushed by its own apathy—a prisoner, Aisling realized, of the Greenmen that worshiped it.

The drake's malaise was palpable, its depression stronger than its lizard-brain instinct to live on. Aisling had known this feeling first hand, confined beneath the same castle, by the same lawless bastards. She stepped close to the mighty reptile, not for a second fearing for her life. She knew the drake could snap her in half with a whip of its mighty tail, or bite her in two with a clamp of its jaws, but as Aisling looked into the spiritless gaze of the close-cousin to dragons of yore, she knew…

There was no fight remaining in the dejected lizard.

Aisling walked across a mound of bones, a veritable hillock of death that was the remains of the Greenmen's previous prisoners; all fed to the Drake, their glorified pet.

In its meager chamber, the Drake was not kissed by the sun, nor afforded fresh air to sate its mighty lungs. It was living on a bone mound of its spent meals. As it shifted, moving to expose its long neck to Aisling's raised blade, skulls rolled and rib cages clattered, cascading into darkness.

With one last piteous moan, the Drake seemed to offer thanks for the release Aisling provided. At least that's what Aisling told herself, bringing down the greatsword as if it were as light as a beetle's antenna, yet as devastating and fatal as a titan's cleaver. It sliced through the Drake's neck, scales, spine, muscles, and all. The Drake's head rolled to the bottom of the mound of bones, and its body collapsed, finally resting without pain.

With tears in her eyes, and rage in her heart, Aisling took up her giant blade and thrust it to the exposed foundations of the Drayke Fort above her.

"Here I come, you fuckers..." she whispered in the dark. "Here I come!" she yelled at the top of her lungs. "Death and affliction!"

Thus is how Aisling's magic greatsword earned its name, an instrument of death known forevermore as *Affliction.*

* * *

Back in her cell, Aisling looked around, confused by the slurry of unexpected emotions that surfaced upon her return. And though, yes, she was angry, disgusted, and consumed by the all-too-familiar fear she associated with the filthy cell that contained her for the past thirteen months, she also mourned the passing of a familiar. This made little sense to Aisling. But humans are paradoxical by nature, intrinsically complex as magic—and magic, as it never had before, seeped through Aisling as much as any emotion.

Pushing away the twisted grief that crept up on her, she embraced a newly kindled rage, smoldering in her soul. Without any understanding of her newfound strength, Aisling raised *Affliction,* whispering arcane words she had never before heard. Without knowledge of where her power originated, nor the nature of the spells she effortlessly began to weave, Aisling slowed down time... or so it felt, becoming so very—magically—fast. Ignorant that the Drake's blood, life, and soul fueled the potency of her witchcraft, Aisling had become a warrior wizard with a weightless greatsword, now impossibly lethal, and saturated with the power of haste.

Imagine this: a warrior woman, six feet tall and full of anger, wielding a feather-light greatsword with the power of a ton of razor-edged steel behind its zero-gravity swing. Scary stuff. Now add to that daunting image: a formidable woman that is magically enhanced with the cheetah-like speed of haste. This is a fearsome foe in any scenario. Had the Varanus Greenmen known what came for them, they would have run screaming with their artificially attached tails between their legs. They would have spared themselves the pain of slaughter, drawing their rusty dirks from their fetid leather harnesses, and sliding their greasy blades across their unshorn necks.

With one last look at her dismal lodgings, Aisling turned her back to the cell for the last time. With the casual ease of a cat stretching across the carpet, she swung *Affliction* at the oak and iron door, sending it careening down the dark corridor, splintering against the stone wall.

Then all hell broke loose. Glorious, vengeful hell.

Aisling ascended the spiral stairs with impossible swiftness. When she met the wide eyes of her gaolers, she didn't pause to hear their screams. The two who regularly attended her torment fell first. She had never learned their names, instead internally labeling them Short and Tall. Tall slumped to the floor, a head shorter. Short cracked his green, shaven head on the way down, stripped of his feet. Various severed extremities rolled down the spiral stairwell like olives circling down a drain.

At the top of the stairwell there were rooms and wide chambers and hallways that Aisling had only seen once, long ago—a lifetime ago it now seemed—when she was first brought to the Drayke Fort. The Varanus had dragged her through the stronghold by her hair only to leave her languishing in the dungeons below. Seeing these areas again stoked the fire of need for vengeance, her demand for righteous violence.

The Drayke Fort was not overly large, insofar as castles go, and it was easy enough for Aisling to flush out most of the drake worshipers, spilling their red blood from their green bellies and littering the stone floors with their entrails, like coiling serpents writhing at her feet. There were, on occasion, women wandering the dank castle halls. One look at their tattooed faces, patterned scars, and filed teeth sharpened into points, and Aisling let them taste *Affliction* just as she had the rest of the mad zealots. The children she could not bear to murder, but she frightened them with relish, shouting at them to leave, and yelling out loud that dragons are dead among the world of Garden, and so was their religion.

Some of the Greenmen escaped. Aisling did not care so much. She had killed their drake, delivering their living totem from a living hell. The mass slaughter of the lizard-hearted bastards was akin to kicking over an anthill, pouring boiling water into its exposed holes. Insects would remain, but their colony would be in shambles, and the time required for them to rebuild would extend beyond her need to make them suffer. It was enough to do what she had done. Aisling was appeased.

Except…

One fat, lizard fucker remained that she needed—just *needed*—to skewer up his ass.

Aisling's gaolers had been the first order of business. *Check.*

Then the wide-spread flushing out of the scum, the great enema of the Drayke Fort. *Check.*

All that remained was the gorged, reptilian bastard who had mocked her in the Mistvale one thousand years ago, back when Aisling's life was her own. That nameless, green-hued shit pile deserved a special visit. And, since he had clearly been the Varanus chieftain, Aisling thought she knew exactly where he might be found.

Aisling climbed the highest tower of the Drayke Fort in less than half a minute, the magic haste in her legs furiously propelling her up, up, up to the top. Then, kicking down the door, she penetrated the topmost chamber of the stronghold, where a hulking, tattooed mass of a man lay upon his bed with two young boys, naked—inked in green. The fat man removed himself from the entwined limbs of the children and, pushing the boys from his bed, rose naked to intercept his intruder.

"Who the fuck *dares* to enter my chamber unannounced?" The Varanus chieftain reached for an axe by the bedside, a weapon the size of Aisling's *Affliction*, though hundreds of times heavier. Aisling could not abstain from the pleasure of murder and thus uttered no clever final words. She took up her weightless greatsword with a mere flick of her wrist and brought it down in a diagonal slash that split the mammoth man from collarbone to hip. A nest of snakes poured out between the two fillets, soiling the bed and the frozen children with blackened gore.

"Go," Aisling commanded. And as if affected by a spell of haste, the children fled. Theirs was a horrible life, Aisling reflected, but she smiled, knowing their luck began with the death of their abuser, and the demise of the cult that had bred them.

Aisling lowered *Affliction*. She approached the open window of the highest chamber in the highest tower of the Drayke Fort. Leaning out into the cold, autumn air, she gazed out to the northwest, where, beyond the hills and forest and fields, Harveston (and Rolph) awaited, unprepared for her return.

Turning away from the window, away from the lands stretching far below and beyond, Aisling sighed with relief known only to a tortured soul, finally released from wretched limbo.

She looked down at the remains of the fat man sprawled, cloven, and spread upon the bed. *Check.*

She tallied her to-do list before falling back onto the bed. *All that remains is Rolph.* But that would come soon enough. First… rest. Some sleep… in an actual *bed.* Mad with the fever of sated revenge, the comedown following so much murder, Aisling laid her head upon the gore-soaked pillow, and, sprawling among the spilled organs and coiled piles of intestines, she fell asleep, dreaming of magpies flying free from their cages.

* * *

Harveston was just as Aisling remembered it. Thatched roofs over wattle and daub walls. Muddy streets. Apples. So many apples.

She picked a rosy red-green apple from the nearest tree and took a bite. Delicious. She threw the fruit's carcass splashing in the fountain, centering the square.

"Oi! Lady!" A passing townsman called out to her. "Don't be throwin' yer shite this way and that, ye hear?"

Aisling smiled, turning to look at the man as she unsheathed *Affliction* from the drake hide scabbard she had fashioned before leaving the Drayke Fort. The steel gleamed like liquid silver, and a fiery gem radiated at its pommel.

The man gaped at the massive blade that was even longer than the height of the exceedingly formidable woman wielding it. "Of course, 'tis yer own business, my lady. Beggin' yer pardon. A fountain is as good a place for an apple as any other." He scurried off behind the muddy stables of a small home.

With *Affliction* propped over her shoulder, Aisling walked the length of Main Street before taking a casual stroll down the avenue of her old home. Without the flurry of emotions she had expected to feel returning to this place, she knocked on the front door of her and her husband's modest house.

Aisling heard the heavy, labored footsteps within, and saw Rolph through the window, limping on his bad knee. When her husband opened the door, he smiled at Aisling, an alien expression on his face. But upon second glance, Rolph's smile was revealed for what it was, neither one of joy, nor relief to see that Aisling had returned to him. His was a bitter smile, filled with malice, and promises of pain—and *that* particular smile Aisling had seen before, had known all too well.

Aisling had so much to say, so much to tell, so much blame and anguish to unpack and heap upon her husband. But looking into his cruel eyes, even as they stood six inches above her own, Aisling decided it was all beneath her, that Rolph and Harveston were buried miles beneath her contempt.

Walking away, Aisling sheathed *Affliction,* turning her back on Rolph, who stumbled after her on his bad leg.

"Oh, no you don't, bitch! You come here, now. You hear me? You come back here this instant! Your days of running are over, Aisling."

Aisling stopped, turned around, and faced her husband, who was no longer her husband, but just another sad, mean man. She dug into her pocket, where she found the petrified remains of the fatal mushrooms she had picked so very long ago on the edge of The Autumnwood. She studied them sitting on her calloused palm and softly chuckled.

"What in the fuck is so funny, whore?"

Aisling looked at Rolph and shook her head. "Nothing," she said. "Absolutely nothing." Then she turned around once more and, letting the mushrooms fall from her hand to the muddy streets of Harveston, she walked away, never to return.

V

DIANTHUS

Castle Tanzanite rose from a forest of pines. A dozen indigo spires stood darkened by the shadow of a great, black cloud of ash, pluming from the angry head of the volcano to the south. . A warm southerly wind ushered the acrid air northward, where the Tanzanite sentries blinked their watery eyes against the sulfuric sting. Among them, one sentry could stand no more abuse. He left his post, descending from his assigned tower and abandoned his watch. For all he cared, the marauding saurian monsters that routinely flew from their roosts in The Blackmire—a 200-mile wide swamp separating Zinnia to the south from Dianthus in the north—could soar the dark skies, free and wild.

At the base of the tower, free from the current of volcanic pollutant that poisoned the air above, the sentry stepped outside to fill his lungs with fresh air—rather, as fresh as air can be found among the rot of The Blackmire. In the distance, he heard the saurian bastards crying out in shrills that would make a banshee blush for want of more pungent screams. The Tanzanite soldier saw them, too—winged lizards in flight, their wide silhouettes drifting along the western horizon.

"My life is shit," the sentry announced in revelation to the plight of his existence. He did not know it, but his shitty life was about to end.

A basilisk slithered from the depths of the brown-black water of The Blackmire, sifting through the yellow foam at its edge. The creature hissed and coiled and curled toward the sentry, who had seen the monster too late, or rather, too late had he remembered to avert his eyes, for it is well known that a basilisk steals the life from any who dare look into its eyes. And with this terrible power, the basilisk killed the Tanzanite soldier, stopping his beating heart the moment man and monster exchanged appraisals. The basilisk merrily wormed its way under the sentry's armor and broke its fast on warm, fresh manflesh, devouring his hot, silent heart.

If there is one absolute truth in the world of Garden, or any world where preternatural creatures roam, it is this: there is always a bigger fish. Or, in this case, a bigger reptile, for as soon as the basilisk finished its meal, a wide shadow obscured the area and a saurian dreadwing, wisely closing its eyes and following only its sense of smell, descended from the foul air to easily sink its talons into its formerly deadly prey. After filling its belly with dead basilisk filled by a dead Tanzanite soldier, the dreadwing cried out shrill and terrible, riding the tainted air on a wingspan the length of two warhorses. Among the clouds, threading the spires of Castle Tanzanite and drawing the ire of its bowman, the saurian beast swerved to evade the poison-tipped arrows arcing through the sky. The dreadwing swooped in close and savaged a sentry with its sword-like talons, dismembering the poor fellow with its hawk-like beak and alligator jaws. Human limbs fell to the swamp below as more arrows zigzagged high among the heavenward towers.

Most of the poisonous missiles missed their mark, but one of them landed true—right into the dreadwing's asshole. Its woeful ululation echoed all across The Blackmire. The Tanzanite soldiers fell to their knees, cradling their heads in their hands to nurse their ruptured eardrums. Flying off, bleeding from within, coughing and crying blood from each of its orifices, the dreadwing sagged, crumpled, and fell crashing into The Blackmire below.

Dead before it hit the water, the dreadwing splashed among the tar-like mud, ebony depths unknown. The great winged reptile sank to the bottom of a black abyss, where its carcass would remain preserved for millennia untold. And there, beside it, an amber shard, resting at the bottom of The Blackmire, its radiant shimmer buried under a sea of mud.

* * *

At the end of the world, life was but sparsely scattered among the frigid grounds of Moonpearl, a castle of myth overlooking a frozen lake, a frosted wood—and to the north, a barren, ice-bound plain subsumed by uninterrupted permafrost. Beyond that lay the Bay of Opals, where fat, furry seals and giant alabaster bears subsist on glacial islands floating ghostly pale on the horizon. Further north, there was nothing. Nothing save for the unforgiving, angry open waters of Blizzaga.

Dimly lit by a score of silver candelabra and the embers dying in a blackened hearth, a pale woman, a mournful queen, clung to what little hope dangled by a rotting sinew, bereft and hollow.

Her husband, King Clematis, laid upon his bed. He had been dead for twenty-six years.

Lady Wisteria, Queen of Moonpearl, clutched her nephrite shard, the jewel of death. She was a sorceress of legendary power and Garden's only true necromancer, thus she willed the brittle bones of her King husband to rise and meet her kiss. Wisteria remembered his mustache, how it tickled her nose and lips when they leaned in close. Now, his open, yellow grimace clanged against her teeth, and the wide, vacant caverns—where once his lovely gray eyes probed her very being—stared listlessly without expression, devoid of even an ounce of passion in their dark depths... There was nothing where his eyes should be, nothing but cold and hollow holes.

Letting go of her nephrite crystal, her husband's skeletal remains clattered back onto the bed. Wisteria abandoned her bedside vigil, walking across the icy stone floor of Moonpearl's royal chamber. At the far end of the room, she gazed out at a cold, cheerless world from the lofty window of the castle's highest tower. The Queen of Moonpearl sighed, expelling a mournful gauze of mist from her fair, mauve lips. Behind her, the hearth faded, its last embers going cold as the fortress walls became white with frost. A frigid wind stole through the window—just a draft, or perhaps a visiting spirit. Pages of an open book fluttered, a cadre of weak flames flickered, then went out. The candelabra no longer offered any light; only faint columns of smoke, and the smell of melted wax. The room went dark. And everything was cold.

Wisteria could stand it no longer—the life-after-death that she suffered day in and day out—and she took up her nephrite shard and entered a realm not her own. Transported, she walked among the mind of a man who did not welcome her.

* * *

Melorin dreamt that he was sipping lemon verbena tea and munching down oat cakes. In the tea party of his subconscious mind, his many gargoyles served him on fine porcelain plates, wearing bow ties and dapper hats. Dreams are funny things… often random and always strange. In the unchecked reign of one's subconscious mind, the difference between reveries and terror rest upon the whim of a single synapse. In the dreamworld, wonders are multitudinous, a hazy landscape where delight and dread may come, one or the other, or both. In sleep, we are exposed to visions that inspire joy, and to nightmares that maim and scar.

Melorin sipped his tea and flinched. It didn't make sense—dreams rarely do—but his tea had become sour. A nuanced flavor he had not tasted in a very long while. His tea, somehow, tasted just like unwanted company.

"Quaint little dreams you have, old man."

Melorin looked up at a handsome, horrible woman he had not seen in over twenty-six years. She had not aged well, seeming to carry the weight of Garden on each wrinkle of her dour expression. Her hair had gone completely gray, her hands thin and bony. And yet her eyes were more alive and as youthful as they ever had been, when life seemed a long, exciting journey rather than a dismal tribulation soon to run its course. All circumstances considered, the Queen of Moonpearl remained a beautiful woman.

As Melorin studied his former student, he determined that the many woes and boundless grief Wisteria endured had somehow made her all the *more* beautiful. Time had not been kind, but regret, in its cruelty, had sculpted her into a very attractive sorceress, indeed.

"Lemon verbena?" Melorin offered, uncertain if this was still his dream or something more, something *malign*. "As I recall, liquorice was your favorite? Alas, I am restricted to my dreams… Lemon verbena is all I can offer you. But I do have oat cakes, if you'd like to try one."

Wisteria fixed Melorin with a stare that made his tea go cold, his oat cakes crumble. Hanging from a silver chain around her neck, a green crystal splinter rested against her pale throat. It lit up, dimly at first, then blindingly bright. The jewel was jade fire, noxious flame, filling the dreamworld with nephrite fog.

"I do not invade the mind of wizards casually. I did not come to reminisce, Melorin, nor to partake in tea and oatcakes." Wisteria's dark eyes became netherworld beacons of emerald flame. Reaching out, her arm extended across the dreamscape toward Melorin, extending from her shoulder like a python unfurling from a tight coil. Then, like a spider, her thin hands finger-walked up Merlorin's shoulder and neck, burrowing into his ears, tearing his mind asunder.

Melorin howled in pain as Wisteria clawed at his brain. "The demon shards," she said, now looming over him, warped like a ghoul. "You know where they lie. Your books have revealed their hidden places."

There had been a great shift in the material plane—a magical infusion introduced among the ether—and like a strong scent, its residual power led Wisteria to Melorin. The Queen of Moonpearl did not know the extent of Melorin's plans, nor the depth of his knowledge regarding the amber shards. But by invading his dreams, covertly at first, she had read the wizard's subconscious thoughts to confirm he indeed held the secret locations to the artifacts of power. Wisteria wanted them for herself, but first she would need to extract the information. The time for subtlety was over. Wisteria began her excavation of Melorin's inner mind.

"Get out of my head!" Melorin screamed, coughing up chunks of oatcake. It was only a dream, but the pain was real, and the invasion, magically orchestrated, was potentially fatal.

"The demon shards, Melorin," Wisteria insisted. "You will reveal their hidden whereabouts."

"I shall not!" Even within the dream that Wisteria controlled, Melorin was not a sitting duck. He was a powerful magician, after all, and if Wisteria were an eagle, then he might be an owl. "Hoo! Hoo!" Melorin did his best to mock and irritate the Queen of Moonpearl, who sunk her talons further into his mind.

"You have discovered the locations of the shards, Melorin. But you cannot retrieve them. You cannot abandon your tower… I have seen to that!"

Melorin strained against the searing pain. "I am bound by your curse. But I can, and *have* recovered the shards, you dire witch! By my hand, I have moved pieces from afar. I am still a wizard, you fool! My reach is as long as yours, you heartless, frosty wench."

Wisteria fingered the folds of Melorin's mind, prodding each recess of his brain. "You have recovered three of them, I see… but not the Dianthus shard. You must divulge its whereabouts, Melorin. You must do so now!" That final word thundered through the molested halls of his psyche as she scraped at the pink pâté of his thinking organ. Melorin keeled over, writhing on the ground.

"You shall never have it!" He screamed in defiance. "Its location is safely hidden. I guard it with my life!"

"Which is exactly what you'll lose should you withhold this information from me."

"So be it!"

Wisteria scowled, digging deeper, up to her elbow in Melorin's skull. "The shards… their locations… you have seen them in a book! You have this book. Show it to me!"

"The book is destroyed." Through his anguish, Melorin managed to laugh. "My apprentice brought it to me, revealing what was under my nose all this time. I read it. I committed every page to memory. Then I set it aflame. The text exists only in the archive of my mind. And I promise you this, Wistera… you shall never have it!"

Melorin summoned every ounce of power he could muster beneath the hold of his captor, and the tenuousness of the dreamworld.

"I am alabaster and onyx, white starlight and the great black void between," Melorin intoned. "Now *begone*, pythoness! Retreat to your icy hole in hell!"

* * *

Sitting beside the window, panes opaque and frosted over, Wisteria caught her breath and slumped in her chair. Her gray hair was wildly dishevelled, and she tasted blood from where she had bit through her lip. A trickle of sweat trailed down from her forehead to fall into the corner of her mouth.

"Salty," she said to no one but herself and the bones of her dead husband eternally sleeping on their sullied marriage bed. "Salty, like the ocean, like the cruel Blackbite Sea." She cradled her crystal shard and, raising it to her lips, kissed it tenderly. "I have become powerful by finding one of the great crystal shards. Nephrite is a lovely stone. Green, a color these cold, bland lands see little enough of. But amber… *amber*… the color of fire, of warm flame and vibrant embers. With amber, I would not feel so cold. With amber, I could warm my bones... and my heart." She sighed, and like always, a ghostly vapor floated from her lips across the room. "With amber—*and* nephrite—I would wake the dead. I could end all life if I wished for it. With amber, I could set the world on fire… I could burn every inch of Garden."

Wisteria wiped away the frost from her window and, gazing southwest, envisioned the tower of her former master. Though she knew the wizard's glorified prison lay well beyond the horizon, she knew too that Melorin could not run from her. "I will have the demon shards, Melorin. Sometime soon, you must sleep. And when you do… I will see you again."

* * *

Wisteria stoked the dying fire, throwing pine cones and twigs into the hearth to feed its meager flames. The bedchamber was cold—always cold. More pine cones. More twigs. Finally, after working up a decent blaze, Wisteria added larger branches that she hoped would burn for long hours and last the night.

It had been many days since Wisteria's psionic assault upon her former master. Since then, she had languished in the disappointment of her failure. She had been close, so very close, to extracting the whereabouts of the Dianthus amber shard, which would lend her the power to bring back her husband from his twenty-six-year sojourn in the afterlife.

Recounting her missed opportunity on the battlefield of Melorin's dreams had done nothing to elevate Wisteria's frame of mind. Seeing her husband's skeleton splayed on the bed sheets did nothing to bolster her heart. But now, many days later, still cold, but well rested, Wisteria was ready. She was prepared for another invasion of the wizard's dreams.

But first, a walk down memory lane, a cold, dark avenue slick with ice and pitfalls.

"Do you remember?" Wisteria sat at the foot of her husband's bed, at the feet of her husband, which lay in scattered pieces; so many metatarsals and phalanges. "Do you remember, sweet husband, when the fires in every hearth, in every room, roared throughout the short days, and the long, long nights? Do you remember when we needn't even *think* of the cold? Do you recall when Moonpearl was warm? When the outside world, frozen and black, felt so far away? I remember it… When we were cozy behind our walls, the warmth of a healthy fire always near. Do you remember, my darling husband, before everyone died? Maybe I'd overreacted… But at the time, killing them all seemed the only just way."

Wisteria lay down beside the bones of King Clematis, leaning into the yellowed ribcage of the dead king, nuzzling against his hollow carcass where once the pulse of his love organ beat fiercely for her. For her, yes… and another, too. It was the one thing to spoil the memory of their shared past—an interloper that formed a triangle of the King's affection. There was his death, too. That was the worst of all. But before Clematis' demise there was the blight of another lover, a lover outside the bonds of marriage. It was this lover—this blight—that slayed the king, unraveling every strand of Wisteria's happiness, which led to the mass murder of her people.

"But before all of that…" Wisteria kissed Clematis on his cracked orbital socket. "Before the doom and gloom and the death of a kingdom… before the great rupturing of Moonpearl… before rivers of blood poured from her splintered gates…" Wisteria's words died on a forlorn sigh. Moaning, she leaned over her dead husband to stick her tongue down his wide-pried mandibles. When she pulled away, she studied Clematis' gumless grin, his smile that forever spread across his skull.

"Do you remember, my love, when our hearts beat as one? Do you remember when I was but a girl, and how, in my youth, I came to steal your heart, all those many years ago?"

In fact, Clematis remembered nothing. He had no brain left to him to store memories, or to access them—it had rotted twenty-six winters past. And if there was a time when his and Wisteria's heart beat as one, it was a distant dream, long before the nightmare took hold of Moonpearl.

"Do you remember?" She asked again, tears and smiles warping her pale face. "The origins of our coupling…" She wiped her lipstick from the hard surface of Clematis' fossilized face. "Allow me to pass the hours by recounting those sweet, glorious days…"

* * *

The Queen of Moonpearl, second wife to King Clematis, had risen from humble origins. She began life in the village of Rimehold, a mining settlement hemmed in by The Frost Thorns, the tallest, cruelest mountain range in all of Garden. When the clouds were not amassed to clot the frozen valley, as they usually were, and the snow was not falling, as it often did, Demon's Peak cleaved the white sky in two like a purple dagger impaling the heavens above. The vista held a furtive beauty, but was arresting in its own right.

Most days were obscured by fog and clouds and chill, injured or frozen miners. Yet the promise of silver affixed the Rimehold citizens in place, never to seek a warmer, more comfortable life. Women did not often venture into the mines. Such was man's work, or so the Rimehold motto declared. But women were not wasted in Rimehold; more than bed-warmers and mothers to squabbling children, more than a pair of tits to plug the crying mouths of babes, or be fondled after a hard day's work in the mines—women were healers, herbalists and nurses and thus earned their keep beside the coal-dusted men.

Among the Rimehold healers had been a particularly skilled woman—a young girl, rather—whose talents exceeded that of any other. Her name was Wisteria, and there were none among the Rimehold nurses who could match her skill with bandage, poultice, or bedside manner. Nor could they hope to compete with her repertoire of herbal knowledge, which was exceptional.

Such was her value among the miners, such was her skill, that Wisteria's local fame budded, and, over the years, sprawled like stranglevines towards the awareness of the court of Moonpearl. Wisteria, who was already in contention to join the royal court, was a favored prospect thought soon to be invited—summoned, really, as no commoner such as she would be granted the luxury of choice. But the honored invite had come sooner than Wisteria expected. Her role in the castle was expedited when the Queen of Moonpearl, Her Grace Delphinium, fell ill to the Blackbite Scourge, a dreadful disease that had arrived with sailors who contracted the illness sailing the Blackbite Sea.

Wisteria was called to Moonpearl to serve the Queen, to save her from the malady that besieged her health. As a renowned healer, Wisteria was whisked away from small town origins to rise high among the court of Queen Delphinium. The risk of contracting the Blackbite Scourge did not even enter Wisteria's mind. Hers was a chance in a lifetime, and it was worth seizing that chance, even at the risk of death. And so, Wisteria left the cold, gray village of Rimehold. At the tender age of twenty-two, she had become a lady of the court.

The castle of Moonpearl was more beautiful—and balmy!—than Wisteria could ever have imagined. The blue and white marble floors, though cold to look upon, were warm underfoot, heated by the raging fires that never died in the many, mighty hearths in each room, hall, and chamber. Water reserves were held in great, stone tanks, heated by flames, endlessly ablaze. The hot water was funneled beneath the lower levels, and even throughout some of the castle walls, radiating warmth that rose gently upward to abate the worst of cold even among the highest of Moonpearl's towers. Wisteria was grateful for the comforts of her new home, having never felt such bountiful warmth while living in Rimehold.

But where beauty and warmth rose to the surface within her grand lodgings, the dire signs of disease were a literal plague to life at Moonpearl. The Blackbite Scourge turned the extremities of those who carried it into black, bloodless appendages. Cold and crippled fingers, toes, and tips of noses—and other intimate extremeties—blackened, withered, rotted, to eventually fall off. But Queen Delphinium did not suffer these most gruesome symptoms. After all, she had Wisteria, the most talented healer and gifted herbalist in all of Dianthus, who tended to the Queen's every care.

And indeed, it was Wisteria's ministrations that kept the worst of Delphinium's afflictions at bay. There is no doubting it… It was Wisteria's curative efforts that allowed the Queen to live as long as she had. But it cannot be ignored… It was Wisteria's careful applications, too, that caused Her Grace's steady recovery to end in her sudden death. By her healing hand, Wisteria had saved the Queen. And when the time was right, after Wisteria's station in court solidified, she killed Delphinium. All it took was a pinch of powdered harpy horn added to her patient's juniper and rosemary tonic.

The Queen is dead. Long live the Queen.

The bells at Delphinium's funeral sang more bright and cheerful in Wisteria's ears than heaven's own chorus of singing angels. Queen Delphinium was a good woman, and serving her had been Wisteria's pleasure. But there were reasons the Queen's death led to Wisteria's elevation of joy. In her own mind, Wisteria was justified in her killing of Delphinium.

After all, she did it in the name of love.

Long had Wisteria loved King Clematis. Long had she

hoped to catch Clematis' eye. She was assigned to nurse the King once, after he had fallen from his horse on a hunt. At the time, she had just arrived at Moonpearl, and had never before known a man to be so gentle, so forward with his gratitude. The king was old, but handsome, and tender of heart. Wisteria fell in love as she tended his broken bones and bruises. And one time—a shining jewel among her precious memories—the king lay in his bed after taking his valerian and feverfew, and, as he drifted off to sleep, Wisteria leaned in to kiss him on the lips.

He did not deny her advance—what's more, he returned it in full. As their lips came apart, the king was fast asleep, but Wisteria swore that she heard him whisper: "I love you, my Queen."

Opportunistic to the King's grief after the death of Delphinium, Wisteria wormed her way into Clematis' heart. Through the aid of love potions and subtle incantations, whispers, kisses, and deep intimacies, she wooed her way onto the throne, becoming the Queen of Moonpearl. But her motivation was never one of power—that was a mere bonus—instead, her motivation stemmed from genuine affection, as Wisteria loved, and still loves, her husband, Clematis—even now, twenty-six years after his death.

* * *

"So long ago," Wisteria sighed, expelling a plume into the cold room, the walls crusted with creeping frost. "Our first kiss," she swooned against the skeleton at her side. "How you seized my heart right then and there. To think… you called for me as a nurse to mend your broken bones after a hunt. Yet the hunt for my heart began in your bedchamber, bandaged and bedridden." Wisteria nuzzled into the collection of Clematis' vertebrae to kiss the ancient ruins of his neck. "Well, my dearest King, where you may have failed to fell the woodland hart, you certainly aimed true with your love arrows upon my own." Giggling, Wisteria placed her thin hands over her chest.

"Oh, how I love you, sweet Clematis. I will always love you. And even now, I love you more than I ever have before. I remember how perfect our love had become… In the days after Delphinium had died and before that dreadful wizard invaded our lives. Had he never come here… that terrible man… you would still be alive, my love. And I would be lying with you, like this, in the arms of a man whose embrace is warm, and not cold." Wisteria shivered. "Always so cold."

"Tell me, do you remember when our perfect love began to sour? Do you remember when the ripeness of our affection spoiled to rot? I do. It began with *him*. With that vile man. That loathsome fucking wizard."

* * *

Wisteria refined her proficiency in healing, herb lore, and potions, so much so that during her first full year as the Queen of Moonpearl her craft transcended from medical to magical. Such could scarcely be denied, nor ignored, when she first resurrected a dead animal.

Truly, she was a woman destined for sorcery.

The poor cardinal, vivid red, looked like a small splatter of blood on the pure white snow. It had collided with the window pane, thinking to fly through the transparency of a barrier it did know was there. Stunned, the crimson songbird fell into soft drift. Within the hour, it lay dead, frozen through from its tiny heart to its brittle, porous bones.

Walking through the courtyard, Wisteria had rushed to what she thought was the bloom of a miracle flower, a rose erupting in midwinter to pierce the snow. When she saw the bird, its apparent death did nothing to dissuade her. Instinctively, she picked it up and held it to her lips, breathing hot air carried by the whispered incantation of strange, foreign words she could not fathom.

Had she gone mad? Wisteria wondered. Was she

deranged? But at the core of her strange behavior, Wisteria knew that she was returning life to the cardinal, a creature that in that very moment blinked its black, beady eyes and sang its sweet music as it took to the air and zipped like a vibrant dart through the cold, white sky.

Above, from the very same window that the songbird had dashed itself against, King Clematis watched Wisteria. The king had witnessed the queen's miracle, her offering of life to a dead and inanimate thing. He decided then and there that her inborn talents must be honored with proper education. And so, Clematis called for a great wizard to teach Wisteria the art of magic. Seeking the very best for his wife and queen, the king made a summons to a magician of unrivaled power, a tried-and-true sorcerer hailing from Birchwood Isle off the eastern coast of Zinnia. His name was Melorin, weaver of starlight, master of the night sky, and wielder of alabaster and onyx. When the legendary wizard arrived at the court of Moonpearl, Wisteria's power quickly grew under his guidance. And so too, much like her magical abilities, did her problems grow, and grow, and grow.

Melorin had been a fantastic tutor, and if teaching had been the extent of his role, Wisteria would never have had reason to resent him. But in addition to being Wisteria's educator of magic, Melorin, in his evident wisdom, swiftly advanced in the court and became chief advisor to the king. The time the wizard spent with King Clematis outstripped his devotion to Wisteria, who began to feel disregarded by both her tutor and her husband alike. Melorin and Clematis became close—indeed, their professional relationship played second fiddle to the blossoming warmth of their friendship, which escalated into intimacy beyond the platonic.

Wisteria had not known the extent of it—at first. But soon enough she watched them holding hands, leaning in close with a mutual twinkle in their eyes. She had tried to approach covertly, to observe more closely, but Melorin and Clematis abruptly broke away from each other as they heard her careful approach. The surreptitious grins they shared and the flushed cheeks they wore on their faces was enough for Wisteria to assume what she would soon find out.

Her husband and her tutor were lovers.

But nothing cut Wisteria so deeply as the moment she confirmed what she had already suspected in her heart. Deciding to expose the truth, Wisteria took action; visiting the castle rookery, using the very techniques her master had taught her, she took the life of a messenger raven, using its blood and soul to fuel the incantation that allowed her consciousness to enter a second bird. Then, abandoning her own body upon the cold floor of the rookery, Wisteria took to the wing in the possessed body of a raven.

She knew where to fly, where to scope out the secret intimacies of her husband and teacher. She had been tracing their movements, and had noticed their frequent sojourns to the storehouse, which was an odd place, indeed, for a king and his chief advisor to hold intercourse. Unless, that is, the nature of their intercourse was sexual... Through the eyes of a raven, Wisteria confirmed as much, perched upon the rafters of the storehouse. Below, among the stacks of grain, naked and powdered in flour, Melorin and Clematis, her tutor and her husband, were engaged in passionate, physical love such as Wisteria and the king had never shared.

Wisteria's raven heart nearly burst from the black feathered breast she inhabited. Cawing, crying, flapping, pecking exposed, soft flesh, she assaulted Melorin, who she assigned full blame for the love affair with her husband. Deep in her heart—her human heart, back in the rookery—Wisteria knew that the blame was two-fold... Clematis, too, was at fault for breaking her love organ, which bled freely amid her grief. Raking her claws into the intimate regions of a wizard who had woven a curse into the seams of her marriage by the force of his mere presence in her life, Wisteria flew away from the storehouse to sulk, to rage, and to fester.

Back in her body, Wisteria dismantled the wings and feathers of the raven whose eyes had transmitted her great tragedy. And she did not stop there… she killed every last messenger bird, leaving the rookery a blood-soaked ruin of beaks, talons, and black feathers.

* * *

"Why did you abandon our perfect love?" Wisteria asked the bones of her husband, the collection of human scaffolding that had remained lifeless for over twenty-six years. "Why did you seek the pleasures of an old man when you had a young woman, a wife, who loved you more than the sun and moon and all the facets of Garden touched by their blessed light?" She struck her husband over his bony brow, then recoiled her hand to suck her bleeding knuckle. "Why did you betray me, my love? Why, Clematis? Why?!"

Wisteria pounded her fists down onto the ribcage of King Clematis' remains, which splintered under the impact.

"Oh, no. No, no, no!"

Panicked, Wisteria collected the fragments of her husband that had scattered across the stone floor. Gathering them all up, she tossed the bone shards back onto the bed. Then, combing a hand through her mussed up hair, she cleared her throat and composed herself. "Forgive me, my lord husband. It is my own distress that betrays me—not you. But Melorin… surely *he* is to blame for all that happened between us."

Wisteria spent many minutes mumbling and groaning under her breath. Once she had expelled her involuntary babbling, she at long last took a deep, controlled breath.

"What is past is past," she declared. "It is only a shame, I suppose, that the past has so much sway on the present." She leaned over and kissed Clematis across the exposed cavern of his nasal bones. "My dearest love… Our future awaits. I will see to it that you rise, alive, to rule Moonpearl and my heart once again. What is past is past… even so, it haunts me to this day."

Wisteria pet her husband on his cold, yellow brow.

Leaving the bedside to stoke the fire, which was always threatening to die out, she warmed her thin, pale hands over its suffocating flames. Staring into the hearth, its bright, bewitching embers, Wisteria was lost in old, stale memories.

"The past is a scourge on the present," she whispered into the fire. "I must confess, I dwell on it far too often..."

* * *

Wisteria's relationship with Melorin became strained—as tends to happen when one discovers their husband is having sexual relations with an interloper. The king and the magician's love affair was kept quiet, only the two men entangled in their passions knew of it; and Wisteria, of course, the Queen who had been scorned, the wife whose heart had been torn out and ripped in two. In light of Melorin's betrayal, speaking nothing of King Clematis' breach of faith, the dynamic between student and teacher had shifted. And even when they converged for their lessons —private lessons, close enough to touch—a great rift had opened between them, a mighty chasm that neither one could ever hope to leap. Bridges had been burned, dismantled and tossed into an abyss, dark as sin. On one side of a gulf, Wisteria stood, hoping only ever to cross it to throttle the man languishing on its opposite side. As for Melorin, he was not without his guilt, nor a measure of regret. But his love for King Clematis was greater than his sympathy for Wisteria. And so, in silent bitterness, the two of them continued their joint pursuit and study of magic.

"Silent" is one way to describe the bitterness plaguing Wisteria and Melorin's meetings, though not an entirely accurate descriptor. Telepathically in tune, the two of them could not help the occasional, accidental slip of their various thoughts, emotions, and, for Wisteria's part, a frequent venomous curse. They shared glances, too. And though wordless, the looks exchanged between teacher and student spoke volumes, with full chapters of jealousy, rage, apology, and grief. They may have never spoken out loud about everything that went on between them, but it was as clear as a cold, mountain lake: Melorin was fucking the King, and Wisteria knew it.

What's more, Melorin knew that Wisteria knew—he knew that she had seen him making love to her husband in the storehouse; that she was the raven who attempted to dismember his sex, and shovel out his eyes with her razor, black beak.

Melorin knew. Wisteria knew. Clematis, blessed fool, might have known, but probably did not. No one ever put him to blame.

At some point, the anger and heartache had become too much, and when it did, it was imperative for Wisteria to escape the court of Moonpearl—her sanity depended on it.

Wisteria bore no great love for the mining village she came from. In no way was she sentimental about her childhood, parents, or the paltry charms of the cold, hard place she had spent the majority of her years. Even so, Rimehold beckoned her heart. Almost against her will, Wisteria planned a trip to visit her hometown, whose bland streets and ramshackle homes would provide a much needed break from the trauma and heartache of all her dramas at Moonpearl.

It was a cold, hard road to a cold, hard town. Almost at once, Wisteria regretted coming back to Rimehold. Her parents, she had learned, had fallen ill, but even with the knowledge to save them, she could not be bothered to apply the proper ministrations. Wisteria felt nothing for her mother, who had raised her, or her father, who had worked the mines to support her. She made them herbal teas and burned mountain flower incense. They needed more. They needed time, for one. And magic. Wisteria could not spare the weeks it would take to see her parents to recovery. Or rather, she would not parcel her heart to accommodate their needs. Hers was a focused misery that devoured her conscious mind. Jealousy and rage spiraled in her thoughts, an endless loop.

And so, Wisteria allowed her parents to die.

It was then, as her mother and father's bodies turned blue and cold as ice, that the heart of the mountain called to Wisteria. Something beneath the immensity of The Frost Thorns demanded her attendance. Leaving behind the aging corpses of her parents to ferment in the cottage she grew up in, Wisteria approached the tooth-like snarl of the snow-capped mountains, entering the Rimehold mines, which beckoned her into their deep, dark chambers.

In the mines, the sconces that lined the rock walls had gone cold. With no light to speak of, Wisteria summoned an ember of starlight upon her palm and, holding it before her, lit her way with its pale, ethereal brilliance. The first thing she noticed was a lack of activity, the absence of sound, of echoing pickaxes against the rock, or the footsteps of tired miners trudging along in the daily grind of their dismal existence. Next, she noticed the bodies. Not one, nor two, but dozens of Rimehold villagers who had collapsed while they worked, as if taken to their deaths suddenly, without awareness of their own demise.

Wisteria had heard of gases in caves that could kill those who entered them, toxic fumes that were odorless—a silent assassin in the mountains. But she wove a canary from nothing, a guinea pig of residual magic that lingered from her mass slaughtering in the rookery. With the lives she had taken, she formed a pseudo-life, a delicate animal to test the quality of the air. The pathetic creature, designed to be weak, did not seem to struggle breathing in the dusty, mineshaft air. And so it was determined… The cave was safe enough for Wisteria to proceed. Recycling its power, Wisteria throttled the feeble animal she had woven from the raven souls she had stolen. Remorseless against its piteous protest, she walked on, deeper into the mines.

As Wisteria ventured further into the depths of the mountain, the bodies of Rimehold miners continued to tally. Among the corpses, there was no blood, no signs of any struggle. Just clean, efficient death. Where fear should have filled Wisteria, there was none, no apprehension whatsoever. On the contrary, Wisteria was compelled to carry on, pulled in by a strong, seductive urge—not a voice, per se, but an intoxicating pull. *Deeper. Deeper.* It seemed to suggest.

After a time, several hours marching down into the narrowing chambers tunneled under the roots of Demon's Peak, Wisteria came upon a glow that did not come from her own source of starlight, nor from the torches that remained unlit throughout the mine. Its radiance was subtle, uniquely green. And despite its understated glow, it was hard to look away. As Wisteria crept closer, the eerie light drew her in. Like gravity, Wisteria was bound to obey its laws. She could not escape the light even if she had wanted to.

But that's just it... She did not want to.

When Wisteria turned the corner to stand point-blank beside the source of the strange radiance emanating from the mountain, she saw a pickaxe embedded in the rock, a crack extending from its blade revealing a shining light in the stone. At her feet lay the body of the miner who had gouged the mountain and unearthed a demon-tainted crystal. It was a live ember pulsing in the dead rock, its green glow glinting across the shimmering silver embedded among the granite. Wisteria reached out to touch it, shuddering in ecstasy as its power coursed through her, body and soul.

Wisteria knew little of crystallography, and was largely ignorant of geological science. And though she was born and bred in a mining town, she was also born a woman, and as the Rimehold motto decreed: mining was man's work. As such, her mastery befell the arts of healing and herbology. Despite this, Wisteria knew the stone for what it was.

"Nephrite," she said aloud, and the crystal confirmed that she was correct.

Yes. The green shard somehow voiced. *That is correct, Queen Wisteria. I am nephrite, it's true. But I am more. So much more.*

Wisteria pressed in closer to the shard embedded in the side of the mountain. She savored its smooth, cold touch and the immense power that it seemed to lend to her upon contact. "What are you? Apart from nephrite, the stone, what are you, really?"

I am two souls, deeply tarnished, bound as one.

Wisteria opened up her cloak and unbuttoned her shirt. She leaned into the green stone so that it lay against her heart. Moaning at the height of pleasure, enraptured by the power that hatched in her core, she asked of the crystal: "What do you mean? Tell me all about you, your two souls. Although I cannot believe you are tarnished… You feel too good, too pure."

Sin feels good. Nothing better. And we are, indeed, pure—pure evil. We are tarnished, my queen. We are so vilely tarnished.

"But who are you?" Wisteria stood over the corpse of the miner to press in closer, harder, against the stone. "What are you? Tell me everything."

Free us from this rock. We will not kill you as we have the miners. We have been waiting for you, Wisteria. Free us from the rock, and we shall tell you all. We shall empower you, become you, thus becoming three… becoming whole. Free us. Embrace us. Together, we will wake the dead. We will take hold of Garden…

…We will seize it for ourselves.

Wisteria could have been told anything at that moment, the promise of her death and a lifetime of torture, and still she would have obeyed. Such was the intoxicating pleasure and power offered by the nephrite stone. And so, wiggling free the dead miner's pickaxe that remained lodged in the rock, Wistera struck the mountain wall repeatedly, freeing the nephrite shard from whatever force or circumstance had put it there.

Indeed, what was the origin of this dreadful, powerful stone? There are some things even the gods do not know. There are mysteries untold, and Wisteria wondered at many of them. Where did the nephrite come from? Wisteria pondered. How and why did those two, tarnished souls become trapped in the crystal?

And that is something she would never know, for the nephrite shard stopped talking to Wisteria after divulging one last piece of information: *We are Blemish, Lord of Rot, and Goreah, Queen of Anguish. We have come to your world through the power of the crystal. Take up the nephrite shard, my Queen, and complete our transition to this realm. In your soul, we will take shelter. Through you, together, we will rule the land of Garden.*

Wisteria did not pause to weigh the consequence of her actions. Without a second thought, she took up the shard. She placed it over her heart, and when she did, the chunk of nephrite pressed against her, as if gravity had recentered to Wisteria's body. Even without a chain or cord to hold it in place around her neck, the gemstone stayed with Wisteria, secure against her heart.

Wisteria called to the crystal, speaking to the voices that had lulled her into the heart of the mountain. She called out, over and over again, but no one answered her. There was nothing but silence to fill the void in the darkness; no more ecstasy to fill the vacancy of joy. Wisteria felt nothing beyond the familiar aches and pains, the jealousy, rage, and grief that she had come to know all too well.

And above it all, beyond her ability to contain, was the terrible power she had inherited, the demon essence of the nephrite shard. The taint was in Wisteria's blood, now and forever a part of her life. It enveloped her, through and through, to the core of her very soul.

* * *

Upon returning to Moonpearl, Wisteria held back any details alluding to the deaths of the miners. She said very little of her trip, neglecting any reports of the mysterious illness that had swept through the village of Rimehold. In fact, so strong was her will to keep the secret of the nephrite shard—and the pair of demons housed within it—that Wisteria did not even announce the loss of her parents.

With the aid of the power that the crystal provided her, she blocked the telepathic channels in her mind. As such, Wisteria's thoughts were shielded from Melorin's mental scrutiny. Her secrets were safe, and with them, all outside knowledge of the shard.

Wisteria's lessons with Melorin proceeded with alacrity, her focus vastly heightened by the concealed talisman resting at her breast. Her true emotions—disgust, disregard, hate—were also kept hidden, and, without the telepathic leak to suggest them, Melorin could not begin to guess at the reservoir of resentment held in Wisteria's watertight mind. Bolt spells, charms, enchantments, potions, summons, demonology (oh, if only Melorin knew), and curses—any and all facets of magic and the lessons that came with them—Wisteria absorbed, practiced, and promptly mastered. In a year and a half, Melorin had produced a student nearly as powerful as himself. He had seen nothing like it, only read of such easy mastery in old texts, the histories of ancient magicians of yore, wizards whose power elevated to godlike status, legends like Persimmon the Great, or his tainted scion, Tamarillo the Bitter Seed. If Wisteria's trajectory of advancement continued, there was no telling what magic she might wield, what miracles, or calamities she might unleash upon the world of Garden.

The year and a half had not only seen the development of Melorin's student, Wisteria, the Queen of Moonpearl, but so too the vast maturation of his relationship with Clematis, her husband, the king. What had started as an exchange of philosophical ideas, shared wisdom, and friendship seeded in mutual hopes to see Moonpearl prosper under the reign and influence of King Clematis, had quickly shifted to physical intimacies, thus transcending into love.

During his long life, Melorin had known many lovers, many men and women with whom he had shared his affection. He had pledged his heart to princes and queens, stable boys and barmaids, troll-kin half-breeds and dryads of the oak. On one occasion, Melorin had loved a ghost, happily haunted by the spectral visits of a witch under the moon. Melorin was a man whose passions were diverse, whose love never came in half measures. But in all his time, in all of his many lusty liaisons and private passions, he had never known love so true as his love for Clematis. Melorin's love for the king was founded on infinite angles and bottomless depths; a relationship founded in laughter, academic musing, and, yes, physical lust. Although it was wrong—betraying his student and his Queen—never had a connection felt so right. With Clematis, Melorin found that his soul had expanded. By loving Clematis, the renowned wizard had redefined the very meaning of magic.

And so it was made worse—far worse—when the day came that everything fell to ruin, when Melorin and Clematis' love crashed to splinters upon the ground. The termination of their love was succinct, its decimation, severe, like a crystal urn filled to the brim with goodness, one day catching the sunlight in prismatic glory, then tumbling down in spoiled fragments, spilled contents, never to be mended, nothing left to be salvaged.

Wisteria, who was herself a bubbling vat, a black cauldron filled with noxious rot, allowed her resentment to simmer over the edge of her vessel, and in so doing, thwart the wizard who enchanted her husband with his so-called love.

Metaphors are fine things, but urns and cauldrons aside, these are people, human beings, and lives, not receptacles, who were soon destroyed.

During one of their lessons, after it seemed Wisteria had long swept her ire under the rug, Melorin found himself at the wrong end of one of her bolts. The conjured starlight, made into a spear, shot from Wisteria's palm to pierce Melorin through his shoulder, above the collarbone. Had he not ducked in the nick of time, the projectile would have ruptured his heart.

It was evident from the onset: this was no accidental misfire.

Melorin healed his wound with golden light borrowed from far-off planets, and erected a luminous, white shield, harnessed from the energies lent by the moon. With his defenses up, killing Melorin would be almost impossible… But Wisteria had her nephrite shard.

"I see you have not yet come to terms with my betrayal," Melorin said to Wisteria. "Or perhaps you have, and those terms clearly state that you wish to see me dead. Well, I cannot say I blame you, my apprentice—my Queen. And though you are a gifted magician—gifted beyond even me—I am half a lifetime further into my study. And where you have your trinket," he gestured to the nephrite shard that slipped free from her neckline during her attack, "I have two!" For a split second, Melorin's head manifested as a crystal orb, one half pearly white, the other, inky black.

"With my nephrite, I will end you, old man." Wisteria levitated an inch off the stone where she stood, her body charged with a flickering of erratic, green light.

"With my alabaster, I shall defend," Melorin declared. "With my onyx, I shall end you, if I must. But do not force my hand, young apprentice. I would not like to kill the wife of the man I love, nor would I willingly commit regicide, my Queen."

Wisteria did not wish to battle with words, but with potent, deadly magic. And so, reserving any would-be retort, she refrained from shouting some ugly curse. And then it came to her, just before she attempted to serve Melorin his fatal end… a curse was the surest way to victory. Not a direct, physical attack, but a curse that would remove Melorin from Moonpearl, cutting him away like cancer from the life she had made for herself, from the heart of Clematis which rightfully belonged to her.

There was no way Wisteria could penetrate the shields of Melorin, not with his guard up and magic poised for a volley of harsh retribution. She may have killed her master while he remained unaware of her intentions, but the chance had slipped through her fingers; Wisteria had not committed to her full power.

Now, while Melorin was expecting an attack, there was only one chance…

Strike hard, she thought on her feet. *But not with a sword… not with an arrow…*

Poison and traps… How else to deal with a rat?

And so, like a fox dressed as a bear, Wisteria made herself look big before applying her subtle cunning. She formed a massive cloud of acrid smoke, molding it into the likeness of a serpent, a titan reptile with the girth of a castle tower and fangs as long as knight's lance. It was all pomp, all illusion. An image, and little more. But Wisteria had infused her mirage with fraudulent magic, coating its image in energies that wizards were sensitive to, a counterfeit potency to falsely advertise the image, and in effect, selling her illusion as a demonic summons. Her trickery was akin to serving spoiled food with the smell of succulent freshness. It would not take long for Melorin to see through Wisteria's deception, but she did not require long to do what she did next.

Ignorant that he had been hoodwinked, Melorin prepared for the onslaught of what he believed was a giant demon snake. His lunar shield would have stopped the assault of an entire nest of such snakes, but its application was fruitless against the shedding of its skin, which sloughed from its image like a discarded sock, slinking across the earth unobserved among the distraction of the dummy serpent. When Melorin realized the snake he defended against was merely an illusion, it was too late to stop the real threat, the worm-like embodiment of the curse that entangled around his leg, crawling up his waist, and around his neck. At once, he knew he had lost the battle, that his mistake was assuming it was a battle in the first place. This was a capturing, a caging, a trap.

And Melorin was in it… At the mercy of whatever curse his apprentice had prepared.

Wisteria met Melorin's eye as he floated away in the air, faster and faster, far, far away. For hours, the wizard was whisked away in a torrent across the sky. Below him, kingdoms scrolled into vision, then passed on distant horizons. Whole continents, oceans, mountain ranges came and went like playing cards flung by a cheating dealer. For hours, Melorin flew across Garden, from one side to the other, knowing he would never see King Clematis again. When finally he crashed to a halt within a forest glade, he fell to his knees, exhausted and drained, emptied of everything he had. Melorin knew what curse had been laid upon him, and knew, too, he would not be leaving the glade anytime soon, if ever.

The misery of Melorin's dilemma may have been too much for him to bear had it not been for one blessed mercy to dampen his tragic fate. Just before he was swept away to his exile, he had managed to cast one last enchantment, a spell that bound his many books in the Moonpearl library to his body, causing his copious collection to be transported with him. Though Melorin could not break Wisteria's curse that bound him to the forest glade, his books would provide him with knowledge and references to serve his hopeful, eventual escape. Maybe, just maybe, the thousands of books, their millions of pages, would lead Melorin to his freedom.

Until then, he would remain cursed.

Melorin's curse was manifold, for he was bound to a forest a world away from his home, but worse, his dearest love. His curse came in the form of banishment, of isolation among a gilded cage. But he was cursed by Wisteria's parting look, too. He could see it in his mind as clear as if she stood among the glade where he was bound to stay. There was more than victory reflecting in Wisteria's eyes. There was hate, and malice, and more anguish than Melorin had ever known. But still, there was something else, something more. In Wisteria's glare, Melorin had seen evil. Not from one pair of eyes, but from three. In those many eyes he had seen the fall of Garden, the end of all life in this realm.

* * *

"And with the rat in its trap, everything should have fallen back into place." Wisteria's eyes stung from staring into the bright bed of embers, which were once again beginning to fade. The room was growing chilly, frosty even, with nothing to keep Wisteria warm, not even a single, living body to hold beyond her own.

"Why, dearest husband, why did you do it? Why did you sully our love? And then, when I worked to mend what had become broken, finally rebuilding what had collapsed into ruin... Why did you do it again? Why did you throw away the perfect affection that we shared?"

King Clematis, two hundred and six bones without a drop of blood or a fiber of flesh, did not answer his wife, who awaited his response.

"Must you take something beautiful, Clematis, something precious, and fuck it all up?" Wisteria pulled at her hair, which was as pale and gray as a snowstorm cloud. "Why did you do it, my love? Why did you jump to your death?"

Wisteria crossed the room to the window and, pushing open its frost-covered frames, leaned out to look below. She did not know the height of the tallest tower of Moonpearl, but sitting at its top, looking down, she could sum it by saying it was a *long* way down. She wondered what it might feel like to allow herself to slip out into the open air, to free fall for ten or twenty or thirty seconds before splattering upon the stones, ending all her pain and memory, ending her life full stop. She wondered what she might think in those final seconds before her life ended, what her husband had thought as he plummeted to the cold earth below. Wisteria hoped Clematis would have been thinking of her, the love that they shared... But it was not so. She could never know it, but Clematis had been thinking of Melorin, his truest love, hoping that in death he might join the man he believed to be dead.

The air through the open window carried the viscous bite of winter. Wisteria shivered against the cold and came down from the windowsill, latching its frame tightly. She stoked the fire, then stopped, giving up any hopes of building it back to life. Returning to the bedside where her husband lay, twenty-six years into his slumber, Wisteria shook her head and endured silent tears. She took up Clematis' hand, which fell into a dozen pieces across her palm.

She had tried to bring him back. Using the nephrite shard, Wisteria was sure she could return the broken body of her husband back to one piece, back to life. But even after Wisteria had killed every single person in Moonpearl, each member of court, each handmaiden, each soldier, each scullion, each stablehad, each prisoner among the dungeons and the vermin that lived among them… Even after all of their murders, all of that blood, those lives, those precious souls… Even after all of that, Wisteria failed to resurrect Clematis from the finality of his mortal end.

She could animate her husband, move him like a puppet, command him to rise, or, in his devastated state, tremble upon the bed like a sack of bones being shaken. But Clematis remained dead. And Wisteria remained miserable, and alone.

"If I can manage to acquire the amber shard," she whispered. "I am certain I can bridge the netherworld to retrieve your soul. If I can draw upon the information that Melorin, that detestable goblin shit of a man, has accumulated; well, I am almost positive I can mend what he, and you, have broken." Wisteria rose from her husband's bed, letting go of his "hand" to fall in many pieces to thud upon the mattress.

"If you'll excuse me, dear husband, I have business with a rat."

* * *

Melorin was dreaming of hibiscus wine and teacakes. Little goblin women in grass skirts served him on bamboo platters laid out upon banana leaves. The sun was shining on his little picnic, and all was well in the dreamworld, until…

"Quaint dreams you have, old man."

Melorin winced, setting down his wine and pushing back the platter of teacakes. "Run along," he ushered out the little goblin waitresses. "Believe me, you do not want to be here in a minute's time. Now go."

Wisteria watched as the line of goblin servers waddled off among the trees, which were hazy on the dream horizon.

"Melorin," she said in a flat, cheerless greeting.

"Wisteria," Melorin answered back. "Or should I say *Wisteria and company*? For I detect in your eyes the same vile presence I had seen the day we squared off in Moonpearl… You are not one, but three. You carry demons in your heart, Wisteria. Sadly, my apprentice, you are a host to vermin."

"Ha!" Wisteria spat. "*You* would call *me* vermin? You? The fattest rat of all? That is rich, coming from a thief and bandit and defiler of true love."

Melorin stood, brushing the teacake crumbs from his robes. "I am not a defiler of love, Wisteria. I am a practitioner of it. I am sorry that I hurt you—that *we* hurt you—but what Clematis and I had was nothing but the truest love of all. You might not wish to hear it, but facts are facts."

Wisteria fumed, making fists at her sides and gnashing her teeth. "The *facts* are this: you killed my husband. You drove Clematis to his death."

"On the contrary, Wisteria. It is you who drove Clematis to his death. I know it was never your intention, but in making Clematis believe I had disappeared, run away without a word, or died… It was a dagger in your husband's heart. And even though you grieve as I do for his death, I will never forgive you for it."

Wisteria frothed at the mouth, crackled with unrestrained magical power. "You, forgive me? *YOU,* forgive *ME*?! Enough of this goading and nonsense! You are a perversion of the worst kind, Melorin. A befouler of love and a king killer. A rat, Melorin. You are a plague-ridden rat!"

And then Melorin's dream warped into a nightmare.

Wisteria crashed upon him like a tsunami of molten lead, pouring herself into his mind with such force as to sear his brain, nearly causing his head to explode. "You will give me the whereabouts of the amber shard, rat. You will offer up your finest cheese. No more gentle Wisteria, vermin scum. No more gentle rat-catcher."

Melorin made a show of defiance, but he could feel his mind fraying like the blackened edges of burned paper. "I will not reveal the shard to you, foul woman. I am alabaster and onyx, white starlight and—"

"Oh, shut up, old man!"

Wisteria reached into Melorin's deepest chasm of the darkest recess in his mind. She pulled apart his will to retrain his secret. And then she had it, the location of the Dianthus demon shard.

"Oh, that is lovely. How good that feels to hurt you and take what is rightfully mine." Wisteria gloated in her victory. "How does it feel, old man? Shall I kill you here and now? Shall I put you out of your misery? No, I think not. You stay, little rat. Stay in your gilded cage and have your petty picnics, your floral wines and teacakes. Stay here and rot, for all I care. But know that I'll have it now, the choicest morsel of your cheese. The amber shard is mine!"

Wisteria blew away like smoke on strong wind, and Melorin woke in his bed, his pillow covered in blood and his sheets soaked with sweat. In his bedroom in his tower, there were no obvious signs of the end of the world. But Melorin knew it was coming.

The death of Garden was near.

* * *

Wisteria stood at the edge of The Blackmire, its tar-black surface bubbling in wafts of sulphur. She ignored the arrows of the Tanzanite sentries that harmlessly deflected off her energetic shield. Their weapons were ineffectual, like dragonflies trying to break down a fortress door. A basilisk emerged from the water, which Wisteria promptly destroyed, melting its organs from within and leaving a pulpy mass to seep into the mud. Closing her eyes, she reached out with her mind for the shard she knew lay in the depths of the horrid swamp of this dismal region of Garden. It did not take long for her to find it, down deep where Wisteria, herself, could not hope to dive and retrieve.

The obstacle was small, no problem whatsoever. A 200-mile swamp and its poisonous depths… what of it? Wisteria scanned the region with her all-seeing eye, and she found it: the perfect body to retrieve her precious amber shard. Conveniently, almost as if planned, a perfectly preserved corpse of a saurian dreadwing lay at the bottom of the swamp, so close to the amber stone that its leathern wings almost touched it.

It was no difficult thing for a talented sorcerer aided by the power of two royal demons; Wisteria animated the dreadwing to "life," clutching the amber shard in its taloned feet, moving its limbs in unnatural ways it could not achieve when it remained alive, propelling its legs and wings to plough upward through the mud and out into the toxic air among The Blackmire. The grotesque, dead, winged thing half flew, half crashed to the shore at her feet. Then Wisteria kicked the amber shard loose from its grip, picked up the bright, luminous shard of power, and joined it to the nephrite hanging by her heart.

She inhaled sharply. She shuddered. Then Wisteria smiled. "So this is what it's like… This is how it feels to become a goddess."

* * *

But even a goddess, it seemed, could not return life to the dead. Back in Moonpearl, when she failed to restore the body and soul of King Clematis, Wisteria lay on the bed among the collection of his useless, scattered bones. Then, with her two shards—nephrite and amber—she walked to the window where her husband had willingly fallen to his death. She opened up its frames and allowed the cold air to assail her. Wisteria looked out over Garden as far as its gray horizon.

"You will know my pain," she spoke to no one in particular, and yet to all.

"You will feel my grief," she somberly promised.

"You will suffer the cold," she calmly stated.

"You will cower amid my wrath, and all shall be intimate with dread."

VI

GARDEN

Melorin knocked on Wrenna's door. "Apprentice? Are you there?" Before Lady Raynewald answered, he heard her stifle a giggle, followed by an exchange of whispers.

"I am here, Master Melorin. How may I help?"

"Hawthorn is with you?" It *was* a question, but he knew its answer.

"He is," Wrenna said.

"I am," Hawthorn confirmed.

"Fine. Good." Melorin smiled on one side of the door, knowing well the joys of young love blossoming on the other. "When you are finished… *talking*… come see me in the solar. Both of you."

"We will be there in half an hour," Wrenna said.

"Make that an hour," Hawthorn called beyond the closed door.

Melorin was happy for his apprentice, The Princess of Raynewood; and for Hawthorn, The Azurite Knight. He only hoped that their own happiness would last. All things, he feared, were soon coming to an end.

"An hour will be fine," he said. "See you then."

Alone in the solar, Melorin gazed out the window over the glade that he both loved and loathed. He would love it more, and loathe it less, if he could wander beyond the five or six miles of forest that Wisteria, his former apprentice, had bound him to when she placed upon him her curse.

Still, it could be worse. He could have been confined to the Blackmire, or the fiery sands of Aridana, to the arctic shores of Permafrost, or harsher, harder places—the Scowlands, Woeworre, or The Hopeless Coast. All told, a tranquil glade in the beautiful, temperate forest of Raynewood was not so bad. Besides, he had his gargoyles, which he had created from nearby boulders, and his tower, which had taken him a decade to build while harnessing the utmost of his magical talents and focus. But that was not all... He had Hawthorn, The Azurite knight, who was the sword to his magic, and his eyes as well; his vision among lands he could no longer travel. And Melorin had Wrenna, his apprentice, who had become to him almost like a daughter, the child he never had.

His gilded cage remained a cage. But it *was* gilded. And for now, Melorin was not alone. Soon, in fact, there would be a crowd among the solar in his tower. The thought was a strange one, that his pawns would assemble like so many pieces on a game board. To think of them all in the same room, there, among his tower, in person...

Leafe, with his Jackali acolytes, the orange-farmer-turned-prophet, the bringer of rain. Aisling, the silent, somber lady who was taller and stronger than most men, and now faster than a dreadwing flying with a gale at its back. Leafe, with his jambiya, and lightning at his beck and call. Aisling, with her greatsword, which she called *Affliction,* and the grace with which she wields its paradoxical, feather-light mass.

Hawthorn, whose eyes of azurite are an extension of Melorin's own power. Wrenna, wielder of the Hyacinth demon shard who scoffed at marriage to become a goblin king killer and sorceress of might. Such a motley crew, a varied bunch of misfits, warriors, farmers, dogmen, and wayward princesses. And one wizard, Melorin himself. He, too, if he was being fair, would assess himself as unusual as any of the rest. A motley crew, indeed. And soon, within the hour, they would converge in one room. They would sit within the solar and, among other things, have themselves a chat.

* * *

Leafe sat at the table in Melorin's solar with a perfectly ripe orange in his hand. He had been sitting at his own table back in his home in Southstone with his wife, Aster, and his Jackali acolytes, Aardwolf and Collie. They had been discussing the end of the drought, and the beginning of The Hopeful Return, when the crystal-faced dream wraith who had long haunted Leafe's sleep came to him through a portal to disturb him in his wakefulness.

"Follow me," the dream wraith told Leafe, nodding to his acolytes, indicating the Jackali could join their prophet. "You stay," he instructed Aster. "I'm sorry, my dear." His forlorn glance lingered on the orange farmer's wife before he stepped back through the portal.

When Leafe, with Aardwolf and Collie, stepped through to follow the dream wraith, Melorin awaited them on the other side, greeting his guests in his fully human form. "Welcome to my home, Leafe. I am glad to see that your orchard has sprung back to health. The oranges look fantastic!" Then, as an afterthought, he added, "Oh, yes. My name is Melorin. It is nice to meet you in the flesh."

* * *

Aisling did not bother burying the pirates. Digging the graves of three-dozen men would be hard work, and besides, the bastards didn't deserve the dignity of proper burial. Aisling had been hired by the lordling of Old Oak to rid the kingdom's coasts of the buccaneers who routinely marauded its seaside villages. From the west, in Zoisite Bay, the Dreadkin came on schooners with black sails, and the pale face of death. From the south, across The Salzar Sea, the Sons of Flame came with fire, burning as they pillaged, raped, and blah, blah blah… all the familiar, by-the-book pirate sort of atrocity.

It was easy enough for Aisling to meet these marauders as they took to the shore, to brandish her greatsword, *Affliction*, which by conventional physics should have weighed a ton, and effortlessly swing the heads free from the Dreadkin and Sons of Flame, on one coast or the other. The villagers were more than grateful, some believing Aisling to be some goddess of mercy, a paragon of retribution. And the lordling, known as The Acorn King, was well appeased. Since meeting Aisling, his coffers had become lighter, but his coastline was much cleaner, far more safe.

Aisling cleaned her massive, weightless sword from the pirate blood and buccaneer brains staining its blade. Returning *Affliction* to rest in its drake-skin backsheath, she looked beyond the many corpses strewn across the gore-stained beach to the forest beyond, where a magpie flew towards her to join the ravens amassing to feast on the dead.

"Seren." Aisling recognized the bird right away, even if it looked like all other birds of its type, even if it had been half a year since she had last seen it.

"Aisling," Seren said without opening its beak to issue noise. "Do you enjoy killing pirates?" The bird asked in the voice of a man.

"It is fine sport. Very easy." Aisling told the magpie. "And it pays well."

"Well, if you enjoy killing pirates, yet find that its challenge is lacking, then you are going to *love* trying to kill a sorceress. I promise you: it will not be easy." Seren opened up his wings, flapping a portal into existence there on the beach. "A wound in space and time," the magpie announced. "Step through it, and I shall join you on the other side."

Aisling looked at the rent in the fabric of reality, the wide gash in the open air. Through it, she could see nothing. Only darkness.

"Why should I?" She asked, placing a hand on the hilt of

Affliction over her shoulder.

The magpie didn't smile—its beak did not allow for it—but something in its beady eyes made up for its lack of amused expression. "Because you will be paid well, Aisling. Killing evil necromancers pays far better than killing pirates."

Seren flew through the portal, leaving Aisling alone on the beach. She looked around at the thirty odd rabid sea dogs, their limbs and heads scattered like servings at a banquet for the crabs and crows. The tide was coming in, and would claim their corpses, returning the men to the sea. It really was boring work, Aisling reflected, before stepping into the open wound of space and time.

* * *

Wrenna and Hawthorn entered the solar with dishevelled hair, their robes in disarray. They had been holding hands, but disengaged from one another when they saw among them unfamiliar faces, none of which were smiling.

Melorin, for one, wore a pleasant expression. "Ah, there they are! The love birds have arrived." He gestured to the table where a bald man holding a sumptuous orange sat beside two Jackali dogmen, and further down its length, a sullen woman, who at first glance looked almost like a man, so large and hard and grim was her appearance, and the sword that leaned high against her chair—if indeed the monstrous object *was* a sword—looked more like a monolith with a hilt.

"Please," Melorin continued, "take a seat. Join us in discussion."

Among the bewildered pair, Hawthorn was the first to speak. "Discussion? Can those puppy dogs even talk?" He nodded in the direction of the Jackali. "I see they've been trained to sit at the table like men. That's a cute trick. Who's this?" He pointed at Leafe. "The dog trainer? And what's with the orange? Is that the mutt's reward for being good, little doggies?"

He was not done. "And who, what, is that—*a woman?*" He scowled at Aisling. "What is that *thing?*" He motioned toward *Affliction*. "A prop for some play? Is that what this is? Dog costumes and makeup? Props and… fresh citrus?" Hawthorne threw up his hands. "Actually, you know what? Fuck it. Just tell me, old man," he said to Melorin, taking a seat at the table. "I am out of guesses. Just tell me what this is. If it's not the circus, then I'll be damned if I know what else it may be."

Melorin blinked in the gap of silence that lingered after Hawthorn's tirade, though his pleasant smile never left his face. "Please," he focused on Wrenna, who remained standing in the entrance to the solar, quite taken aback. "Please, my apprentice. Take a seat. We are among friends, I assure you."

"Friends?" Hawthorn glowered. "Two dogs and a fruit vendor? A brooding troll-kin with a sword that could cleave mountains? Friends? I think not."

"Shut up, Hawthorn." Wrenna found her voice, and her composure. "If master Melorin says they are friends, then they are friends. And do not debase yourself by flaunting your ignorance."

"Ignorance? How's that?" Hawthorn asked, greatly subdued by his lover's dominant stance.

"These '*puppies*' and '*mutts*' you speak of are Jackali, a noble race that dwell in the desert of the southern continent. They are as intelligent and cultured as you or I. Well, me, anyways, but perhaps not you… *You* have a long way to go."

Hawthorn grinned, accepting his lover's insult with grace.

"The Jackali are masters of the sky," Wrenna continued. "Engineers who have built flying machines to cross the desert. They are deeply attuned to nature, to the elements, and harbor great knowledge in their religious and spiritual ways. You would do well to honor them with respect, and your apology, too."

"Yes, Lady Raynewald," Hawthorn bowed mockingly,

but *did* apologize to the Jackali, and their prophet, Leafe, and to Aisling, too, when Wrenna insisted that friends who come to sit at one's table are never to be dishonored, even if the weapons they bring with them are well beyond the size and scope of what anyone might consider normal.

"Goodness me," Melorin chimed in to address his guests. "Without needing to explain the difference between my two colleagues, Hawthorn and Wrenna, you see for yourselves their separate natures. I assure you, despite appearances, and first impressions, they are both very good people to have on your side, with richness of character and warmth in their hearts."

"Thank you, Master," Wrenna said.

"Thanks, old man," Hawthorn added.

"Now," Melorin took a long, deep breath. "There is much to discuss. There are introductions to make, explanations, and apologies, too."

"Appologies?" Aisling asked.

"Oh, yes." Melorin said. "Deep, sincere ones." Again, he took a deep breath. "Now, where to begin…"

* * *

Melorin made the introductions, explained who everyone was, and what they carried. Among those converged in the solar, he explained, were three amber shards—all but one. He detailed the history of his life, his past in Moonpearl as chief wizard and counselor to the king, Clematis, who was also his lover. He explained the troubled, noxious relationship he had with his former student, Wisteria, The Queen of Moonpearl, and how she had taken the information of the final amber shard's whereabouts forcefully from his mind.

"She now wields its power," Melorin explained. "Along with the nephrite shard she had already obtained—from what hell, I do not know."

"Nephrite shard?" The company asked as one.

Melorin continued his explanations, accounting

Wisteria's history, or what he knew of it; how their feud had festered over time, and how the strife that developed between them was his own fault as much as hers—perhaps more so—speaking nothing of King Clematis and his own blame. Though his last was a moot point, for Clematis was long dead, his soul drifting in the netherworld for over twenty-six years.

"I don't understand," Leafe said. "If you knew where the amber shards lay hidden, why didn't you get them yourself? Why have you haunted me in my dreams for over two years?"

"Why did you come to me as a bird?" Aisling finally broke her sullen silence. "Why did you guide me from one ill fate to another? Why did you lead me into the Mistvale to endure a year of torture? A life among the bowels of The Drayke Fort, the dungeons of cannibal, lizard-worshiping bastards?"

Melorin spread his hands. "My explanations have only just begun. My apologies await, and they are many. I can only offer them to you, but I have no expectation they will be accepted."

Melorin proceeded with his deluge of information, backstory, explanation, and apology. He started by announcing he was cursed. He divulged a secret he had told no one before, allowing his greatest weakness to become exposed. "I am bound to my home, the glade where this tower stands. I may venture a few short miles into the forest, but that is the end of my tether. With each step I take away from the glade—this tower that is my gilded cage—an agonizing pain compounds within me. If I were to bear this pain and travel as many as ten miles from where I stand now, I would drop dead. And this, my good people, is my curse."

"Wisteria?" Wrenna asked?

"None other," Melorin smiled bitterly. "For there truly is none other; no one else who possesses power sufficient to curse me as she has done."

"Which explains why you could not retrieve the amber

shard yourself," Aardwolf said.

"And why you used us like pawns," Aisling added. "To do your dirty work in the name of what? Revenge?"

Melorin shot Aisling with a glare that was unbecoming on his otherwise kind and gentle face. "I can take the form of a magpie, my lady. But I can also take the form of a dragon. Do not tempt me to do so here and now, for I would bite your head from your shoulders as easily as a magpie plucks a blackberry from a bush. Do not doubt for a second, young lady… *Affliction* would not be enough to save you from my wrath. So do not wake it from its dormancy within me, yes?"

Melorin huffed and puffed. "Dirty work, you say. Bah! Is it dirty work to snatch up relics of power before the one who would use them to destroy the world of Garden? Is it so repulsive that I used you as I did—my pawns, as you have put it—to safeguard Garden from destruction? I offer you apologies, Aisling, and all the rest of you, too, because I owe them to you. But I do not offer my regrets. I did what I did for the safety of our world. I used you, yes, but in so doing, I just may have spared this realm from the ruin that Wisteria may yet inflict upon it."

Aisling shrugged. Leafe nodded. Aardwolf and Collie mimicked their prophet. Wrenna squinted, deep in thought. And Hawthorn laughed—laughed long and loud and bitterly.

"The balance of Garden, its very existence, is a laughing matter to you, Sir Hawthorn?" Melorin shifted his glare from one insubordinate warrior to another. "Tell me, Sir Hawthorn, Azurite Knight, what is so funny about the fragile fate of our world?"

"Our world be stuffed!" Hawthorn cackled. "I am not laughing at Garden, old man. I am laughing at you!"

Melorin scowled. "What? Do I have teabiscuit in my beard?"

"You usually do, dotard. But that is not what makes me laugh."

"Well then," Melorin flashed a sardonic smile. "If you must play the jester today, do make us laugh. Share this amusement with the rest of us, if you will. Go on," Melorin urged. "Tell us what is so damned funny."

Hawthorn allowed his laughter to go on for some time before catching his breath and wiping away his tears. "It's just," *Hahahaha*. "It's just," *Hahaha*. "It's just, I finally figured it out."

"Good gods, man! Figured *what* out?"

Again, Hawthorn forced a conclusive guffaw. "Why you need me," he said, suddenly seeming quite angry. "Your curse. Like these poor bastards before you, I am one of your pawns. I already knew this, of course. But now I know *why*. You need me, old man. You say I am the blade to your magic. Your far-seeing eyes. I am your sword slave, as you have called me before. But I see why you truly need me." Hawthorn slammed his fists on the wooden table. "It's because of your curse. The curse that binds you to this tower. You need me, you old, weak fucker! Because, without me, you cannot see the world beyond the walls of your wretched tower, or the measly glade of this damnable forest."

Hawthorn laughed again, but there wasn't the slightest sniff of amusement to it. His laughter was bitter to the point of toxicity, the air from his lungs a noxious gas. "I am a slave to you as long as you are a slave to Wisteria, is that it? Well, fuck you, old man. Fuck you. Fuck your curse. And fuck the fate of Garden, for all I care!"

Melorin raised a finger in reprimand, but fell silent, sagging into his chair. "It is true what you say. And your anger is just. Your hatred for me is reasonable. I have used you, as you have declared. I *need* you, as you have pointed out. In many ways, I *am* weak, as you have called me. But in other ways I am strong, as powerful almost as any other in all of Garden."

"So what?" Hawthorn spat at the wizard from across the table. "What do you want? A medal? A trophy? A fucking tea biscuit? Lord knows you have plenty." He pointed to the perfect orange that Leafe balanced in his palm. "Have an orange, while you're at it. Use everyone in the world at your whim. Collect their lives like trinkets and display them in the curio cabinet to sate your perverse desires. I hate you, Melorin. And while you may be cursed, I am too. My curse is *you.*"

Wrenna put her hand over Hawthorn's arm and leaned into him to whisper placating assurances. The solar fell silent for several minutes, everyone gazing into the grain of the wooden table.

After a time, Hawthorn spoke again. "Still," he began, taking a long, meditative breath. "If Melorin's curse is broken, so is mine. And if I understand things correctly, we are all gathered here, amber shards and all, to end such curses. Not by using our joint power to free Melorin, or me, but to free all of Garden."

Hawthorn nodded, as did the rest of the company gathered among the solar. "Melorin's curse, my curse, and the curse that will befall the fate of everyone, the whole of Garden… If we join forces to kill Wisteria… each and every curse will be lifted. Melorin would be free, and in turn, I would be free of him. But more importantly, Garden will be free, and with it, the rest of its people—peons, princes, noble kings and vagabond bastards."

Melorin smiled. So did the others, even Aisling, whose smiles were as rare as fabled unicorns. "If we join forces…" Wrenna spoke up, taking up Hawthorn's hand in her own.

"If we destroy Wisteria, the necromancer queen…" Aisling touched the hilt of her greatsword, *Affliction*.

"If we end the curse, all and every curse across Garden…" Melorin whispered in the quiet room. "If we join forces…"

Leafe rose from his chair, and with him, his acolytes, Aardwolf and Collie. "We will see it realized," the prophet announced. "*Groen Aarde.* The Hopeful Return."

* * *

The cutting wind blowing off The Blackbite Sea, which had earned the body of water its namesake, whipped into relentless gales, taking chilling bites out of any living creature that stood among its endless tantrum. Even with his thick coat of fur, Aardwolf shivered amid the frigid onslaught of elements. His kind was built for the desert, and while a desert wind is as fierce as any other—the Aridana sandstorms legendary for their wrath—the cold was a new tribulation to the Jackali dogman, and entirely unpleasant.

Aardwolf perched on an outcrop of rock reaching out over the tempestuous, arctic waters below him. He stood watch, squinting against the horrid wind, scanning the violent swells stretching all the way to the angry, gray horizon. The company, which began to call themselves The Lords of Amber, converged on the rocky shoreline on the northwest coast of Hoarfrost. Beneath the skyward towers of Grimgard, a bleak outpost ceaselessly buffeted by the sea, The Amber Lords waited, poised for the ire of the necromancer queen, Wisteria, who Melorin had assured them would come.

It was the wizard's idea to send them to Hoarfrost, Melorin's strategic location to bait Wisteria's attack. "Close enough to draw her attention," he told them. "But not so close to give her the advantage of familiar ground."

"How long will it take?" Aardwolf had asked. "How long before the sorceress emerges?"

Melorin shrugged. "It could take but a moment, mere seconds. Then again, it could take a day, a week, a month. The truth is, Wisteria may never come to meet you. We can only know by trying."

"And what is this place like?" Collie had said. "This… Horse Froth."

"*Hoarfrost*," Melorin corrected her. "I will not lie to you, it is not exactly paradise. But this is the battle for the fate of Garden, not a beach holiday. So toughen up, and endure. It is chilly," he added. "I advise you to bring a hat!"

Aardwolf had no hat, and so the arctic wind of The

Blackbite gnawed on his pointy ears. He could not wait for his watch to end, to be replaced by Collie, who was next to scan the northern horizon. At this rate, he could not wait until Wisteria arrived to meet them. Better a battle for the fate of the world than this mindless, pottering about!

"And when do we leave?" Aisling had asked back in the solar of Melorin's tower.

"*I* do not leave at all," Melorin reminded her. "For as you know, I am bound to stay in this tower. But *you* leave—all of you leave—right *now*." And with that, he had opened up a portal at the far end of the solar. One by one, The Lords of Amber stepped through its blue-black, shimmering hole.

Aardwolf himself stepped through, transported to Hoarfrost. Thinking back on that moment, three long days ago, he was not sure he would do it again. Aardwolf would follow Leafe, The Prophet, anywhere. But Hoarfrost? He looked around at the raging, dark waves, the bleak, cold sky, shielding himself against the never-ending wind. The world is worth saving, surely. But Hoarfrost, he thought, is something he would cast aside as already lost.

Aardwolf's somber thoughts were interrupted by Collie, who approached to replace him in his vigil. Together, they gazed northward across a seascape devoid of hospitality, rife with hostility.

"Looking out there," Collie raised her voice so that she might be heard among the wind. "It's hard to imagine a green world."

Aardwolf nodded. "Without our faith, *Groen Aarde* is but a myth. But you are right, Collie, it is difficult to imagine a green earth when *this*..." he swept his paw out before him, "this frozen wasteland of poisonous water is part of our world."

They stared out over The Blackbite sea, then Collie laid her paw on Aardwolf's shoulder. "Go rest, my friend. I will take over the watch."

"There is no need," Aardwolf said, his ears pointing toward the sky, and drew out his spear, concealed beneath his robes.

Collie took a cautious step back from Aardwolf. “What do you mean?” She asked. “Why do you prepare for battle?”

“Our watch is over, yours and mine,” Aardwolf said. “She is here.”

Collie did not bother to ask Aardwolf who he meant. Instead, she drew her own spear, then running back to the others who huddled by a fire on the shoreline, shouted: “She is here! Wisteria is here!”

* * *

She came riding on the bones and rotting flesh of an undead leviathan. Its lifeless, white eyes were level with the water as its island-like bulk cut through the violent surf. On its back, legs straddled over its exposed vertebrae like a rider in the macabre saddle of an obscene “seahorse,” Wisteria directed the monster toward the shores of Hoarfrost. As the beast came closer, its single tusk, like a great spiraling horn, speared the surface of the water and, crashing into the shallows, provided the narrow bridge from which Wisteria crossed over the tide pools upon the rocky shore beyond.

No longer requiring her ocean steed, Wisteria allowed the leviathan to slump back into inanimate death. So rotten was the creature’s flesh that the turbulent surf cut into what remained of its hide like swords into slabs of butter. The Blackbite continued to blow its ceaseless breath, which now not only carried the cold, but the stench of decay.

The Lords of Amber, a trio of upstarts vaunted by the tremendous power of the relics they had come to possess, stood beside Hawthorn, The Azurite Knight, whose eyes Melorin watched through from afar, and with them, the two Jacakli acolytes, brandishing their many-pronged spears. Together, the company amassed a rather powerful bunch, a disparate team of misfits, mages, princesses, prophets, and dogs. Together they stood, three amber shards in their retinue, and the fate of the world balancing on the outcome of their efforts.

Standing on the icefield across them: Wisteria, necromancer queen of Moonpearl, a woman scorned—a woman turned goddess—wielder of the double-headed snake, the demon nephrite stone, and a quarter portion of its progeny, the demon amber shard. Wisteria did not know it, but between her two jeweled relics, both nephrite and amber, she held in her possession a royal demon family—mother, father, and son… Goreah, Blemish, and Darkstain. With these potent talismans, in addition to her inherent magical abilities, Wisteria stood as the most powerful being the world of Garden had ever known, more powerful even than Persimmon the Great, or his wayward scion, Tamarillo, eons ago, when Garden was new.

The two opposing forces, The Amber Lords and the necromancer queen, stared each other down on the windblown coast of Hoarfrost. Among them, Hawthorn was the first to speak. The Azurite Knight looked on with magical vision, and thus witnessed what the others did not: a terrible power manifested by the simultaneous darkness and light that emanated in great waves around Wisteria. Hawthorn had intended to offer a slur to the opposition, but in the wake of her prowess, he trembled, and only managed to mumble "May the gods be with us..."

Even among the mistrals billowing from the sea, Wisteria caught the words of Hawthorn's weakened whisper. She turned to study The Azurite Knight, and the impudent rabble who decorated themselves as The Lords of Amber. "The gods are dead, boy. I have eaten them whole." Wisteria took a step forward, raising up her thin wrists and bony hands, eerie light manifesting between them. "But still, I hunger. Always hungry. And truly, I must thank you for coming here to call upon me. I will now satiate myself. I will devour your souls." And with no more words exchanged between them, the great battle for Garden began.

* * *

Shapes emerged from the shallows of The Blackbite Sea, its swelling tide sweeping in more than mere water. The skeletal remains of pirates, sailors, fisherman, seamen of all kinds who had lost their lives to their maritime trades, rose from their watery graves to fight alongside Wisteria, who called to their corpses with her dark dirges of necromancy. Mermen rose from the depths, their half-rotten fishtails dragging across the rocky shores as they crawled across the land to assail the enemy that had been assigned to them. Dead animals were summoned from the stagnant grottoes where they moldered: fat seals and hulking walruses with scabrous hides seeping gore, their flippers in threads and eyes reduced to hollow orbs of crimson rot. Seabirds, too, festering on the wing. Flying, falling, throwing themselves in defiance at targets they held no grudge against, no notion that they even existed, simply obeying —obeying the command of the dark magic, which stirred them into motion.

The oceanic, undead army was at the command of the queen, which was bad enough, but then, even worse, was the queen herself. From the start, Wisteria made plain her dominance. In a show of mockery, she blew a kiss to Hawthorn, who had drawn his longsword and charged. The "kiss" darted across the beach upon a spiral of green and orange light, the twined energetic threads of nephrite and amber. The concentrated bolt shot like an arrow, swift and spinning through the air, yet landed with the impact of a war hammer upon Hawthorn's chest. The Azurite Knight went flying, reeling through the air to thrash against the rising cliff at his back. He dropped his sword and groaned on the sharp rocks of the beach, laboring for each breath through his broken ribs.

Aardwolf and Collie danced their artful ballet of death. With their multi-pronged spears, the pair of Jackali dispatched the animated corpses of pirates and sailors, swatting their rusty cutlasses aside and scattering their bones across the shore with mighty spear-swipes and sweeping kicks. At will, Collie struck down the seabirds that clotted the air with their swooping, dead masses. Aardwolf impaled a walrus through its neck, then twisting his spear, beheaded the great beast, quickly turning around to thwart a mermaid who crawled across the rocks, bashing her so soundly that fish pâté was all that seemed to remain of her.

Such was the efficiency of the dogmen's martial dominance, so graceful and impacting their assault with their spears, that Wisteria decided to eliminate them from contention before her undead army was all but depleted. As casually as one might construct a sandwich, the dreadful sorceress summoned from hell a ball of liquid flame, manifesting in the realm of Garden, white-hot and searing, suspended between Wisteria's widespread arms. Then, as effortlessly as if she had applied her thumb to squash the tiny body of a soft insect, Wisteria stomped out the lives of the Jackali, who were engulfed in the torrent of fire that she had thrown in their direction.

The dogmen dead and gone, Hawthorn down and out; all that remained on the battlefield were the crystal bearers, the trio of Amber Lords and the Queen of Death. On the rocky, windswept shores on the north coast of Hoarfrost—a cold, hard isle strangled by the rage of a frigid, violent sea—four wizards stood, three against one, with five demon shards between them.

And as if an afterthought, an insignificant add-on to the main event… The depleted undead army of seamen and ocean-bound animals ambling among the rocks. Aisling was tired of looking at them, sick of *smelling* them, and she wished only to vent her broiling anger. And so, taking up her greatsword, she twirled its monstrous blade, as light as a butterfly's wing, and, with the speed of a gale-force hurricane, swept across the shoreline, dismembering the foul wretches called from the deep by vile black magic.

In less than a minute, the undead army was utterly eradicated by Aisling's frenzied fury and her monolithic sword. Not a single, rotten corpse remained on its legs, flippers, or wings.

Despite herself, Wisteria was impressed. "With that sword, that speed, you could pose a problem."

Aisling did not hear Wisteria—not in the conventional sense. Wisteria's message came to Aisling from the depths of her mind, the sorceress' threats made by telepathic connection.

It was too late for Aisling to dodge the death ray that had been thrown in her direction—too late to outright avoid the astral devastation shot forth to impale her body. But fast as she was, laden with enchantments of haste, she was able to angle *Affliction* and deflect the worst of what hit her, avoiding her death, but losing her arm. And there it lay on the rock, pulsing blood from where the elbow had joined to her now throbbing stump. Aisling stared down at her detached appendage, her right hand still gripping the magical sword she now ventured to wield with her left.

One armed and bleeding out, Aisling looked over her shoulder at Wrenna and Leafe, who were now engaged in a wild struggle just to stay alive. Wrenna fired bolts at Wisteria, projectiles that ineffectually fizzled upon contact with The Queen of Moonpearl's stalwart wards. Leafe summoned storms from the sea, concentrated blasts of wind and forked lightning —powerful displays, but wasted on the defensive might of Wisteria— managing only to buy himself and Wrenna time before Wisteria's own offensive maneuvers annihilated them.

Aisling fell to her knees, dropping *Affliction,* which for the first time had become too heavy for her to lift. The massive blade clattered against the tide pool rocks. Weak with blood loss, she watched as her companions clung to life by a tenuous thread. Struggling against fading consciousness, she watched the beginning of the end of the world.

But just before her heart sank to irretrievable depths of despair, and just before her wounds ushered her away to the afterlife and unknown, Aisling heard a voice—a familiar voice—and saw the magpie heralding its timely message.

Seren, who Aisling now knew to be Melorin, perched on the wet rocks before her. Without opening his beak to speak, the wizard in the form of a bird spoke to Aisling in her mind.

I am not actually with you, dear Aisling. As you know, I am locked in my tower, far, far away. But while I cannot be there with you to aid you directly, know that I am watching, and I am with you in spirit, always, until we see through our mission to the end. Now listen to me, because I would not have our mission end as it is about to—in your death, in Leafe's death, Hawthorn's and Wrenna's death—and the Jackali, who are already dead—as well as my own death, which will happen soon enough, as will the death of all life on Garden. Should we fail today, and our mission comes to an end in defeat, we will have no world left to save tomorrow.

"But we are losing, Seren," Aisling moaned. "We are losing badly. Wisteria is otherworldly. Against her power, we are sure to die as the sun will rise tomorrow."

But that is just it, my dear child. If we lose here today, there may as well be no sunrise tomorrow. There may as well be no tomorrow at all, for I tell you again: this world will only know doom. The power of the crystals have already consumed Wisteria's soul. Should we fail in stopping her, through her, the crystals will consume all of Garden.

"But how, Seren?" Aisling cried, and when she did, Melorin scrutinized her through the eyes of the magpie he embodied. He wasn't sure how he had missed it before, but he witnessed a woman who was startlingly beautiful, despite her overt masculinity—or perhaps because of it. "How, Seren?" she repeated. "How, Melorin, are we to match the might of Wisteria?"

I shall tell you exactly how, and I am sorry I did not think of it sooner. But set aside your fears, for I have been reading like a madman in my library; long days and sleepless nights I have poured over many a tome and scroll. I have determined a way to defeat our dreadful enemy. Now listen, we are nearly out of time!

Melorin shared the secret of defeating Wisteria, quoting

ancient translations from the old tome, "Demon in the Shard," which he had destroyed but not forgotten. "And so you see," he told Aisling, "there *is* a path to victory. Now go! We mustn't squander our one and only chance!"

Aisling once again took up her greatsword in the one hand that remained to her. Then, sprinting across the rocky shoreline as fast as a marlin cuts through open water, Aisling rejoined her companions and the three Amber Lords stood as one.

And that was just it—they must converge together as one.

It was what made their adversary, Wisteria, so powerful… The joint power of her two crystals, the combined potency of nephrite and amber. And so, just as Wisteria had done with her two demon shards, The Amber Lords must replicate with their trio of totems. Above the howling wind, over the crash of waves and drumming thunder, over the explosions of violent, demonic magic, Aisling yelled as loudly as she could, shouting the instructions that were imperative to their victory.

"Join the shards!" Aisling screamed at the top of her lungs. "Join the amber shards!" She howled against the raging elements. "Join the shards!" She called again and again. Then, weak as she had become with blood loss, Aisling managed to ululate louder than the limit of her body, using her magic to impart her message: "May three become one. Join the shards NOW!"

They may have asked questions if they had the luxury of time. They may have balked at Aisling's command had they not been in the throes of a deadly duel with the world's most powerful magician. But as it was, out of time and nearing their demise, Leafe and Wrenna heeded Aisling's instruction, taking up their amber shards to touch and join as one.

The power that emanated from the joint crystals was staggering, unearthly in scope. The beach, with its rocky tide pools, ruptured and reformed, crumbling to ruin before instantly being remade. The entire island of Hoarfrost shook, its landmass rising higher out of The Blackbite sea. The Lords of Amber were bewildered by the power that surged through their bodies, and the trio of wizards, each grasping their own shard, laughed hysterically at the unfathomable pleasure vibrating through their souls, which had melded to become one.

Too late was Wisteria, who only moments ago had been the most powerful entity Garden had ever known, past or present. She looked across the beach at her enemy, a three-headed god aglow with amber radiance, a divine being whose power would wash away her own like a crashing wave upon a smear of snot. Although she did not like her chances, indeed, she had written herself off as dead, Wisteria would not idly bow to the lickspittle of Melorin, even if they had become the very manifestation of omnipotence.

Wisteria watched the golden light coalesce among the converged soul of her enemy; across the beach, she no longer faced three weak opponents, but one, indomitable foe. In response, as a matter of dignity more than any true sense of defiance, Wisteria gathered her own powers, blending a heady cocktail of nephrite and amber, mixing their two essences as one, and from its combined whole, brandished a demon sword forged from the souls of the tormented dead. Wisteria held the doom-forged weapon high and, shrieking out with the collective woe of twenty-six years of accumulated misery, shouted her husband's name, "Clematis!" before thrusting her evil blade into the shaft of amber radiance that her enemies launched at her.

And then the beach, the isle of Hoarfrost, the whole of The Blackbite Sea, and the four continents of Garden erupted in unfathomable light. The world was baptized in amber—with a dash of nephrite.

Nothing, ever again, would be the same.

* * *

Melorin breathed the arctic air with relish. Long had he missed the sensation of a cold sea wind ruffling through his shaggy hair and his long beard. The gore and bones painting the rocky beach red and black were unsightly, but Melorin did not let it bother him. For the first time in twenty-six years he had left his tower and the Raynewood glade behind him, not as a bird, or a crystal-headed dream wraith, but as a man, a wizard... *Melorin*. He savored it all; the bloody tide pools, the walrus corpses, the icy teeth of the Blackbite gale.

Melorin savored it all. He was finally free.

When the exhilaration of his newfound liberation settled, Melorin calmly cataloged the damage to Hoarfrost. Above him, the towers of Grimgard had crumbled halfway to their bases. High up on the cliffs, great stones of the stronghold lay like a child's bricks in disarray. The conifers beyond the rocky shore lay flattened by a force greater than any torrential storm the island had ever known. The beach itself looked as if a month-long hurricane had wracked its shores; great clots of seaweed mounded in heaps against the base of the cliff; deposits of rock and sand from the ocean depths washed up in disorganized piles; thousands of fish lay motionless, or flapped haphazardly in their final throes, far removed from the water. Hoarfrost was never a desirable island. Now it was a wasteland.

But what of the casualties? Where was Wrenna? Aisling? Hawthorn and Leafe? Where were The Amber Lords? Then Melorin remembered... They are The Amber Lords no longer.

He saw it all through the eyes of a magpie, a bird whose body was now reduced to dust. When the combined powers of The Amber Lords clashed with Wisteria's, when the fiery golden lance struck hard against the hell-forged scimitar, the world was made anew. The five crystal shards—and three demons within—absorbed the impact of their exchanged blows, and, unable to contain the explosive force, exploded themselves, luminous dust carried away on the Blackbite wind.

When the dust and debris finally settled back down onto the earth, and the sun could once again be seen through the mushroom cloud that had bombarded the heavens, Garden was revealed whole, but *changed*—a grub that emerged from the soil, now a beetle spreading its iridescent wings.

The magic of the shards was no longer concentrated into crystals, but diluted, spread evenly throughout the lands. Where magic could once be identified, harnessed, observed as a tangible force, now it had become something different, something altogether subtle, less potent but more widespread. And it was the very last gesture of the old magic that protected The Amber Lords from becoming ashen stains on the rocks where they laid. It was the vestige of the demon shard's mighty power that preserved them in the wake of the doom, the cataclysmic rebirth they had forged. They lay together on the beach. Hawthorn, whose ribs were magically mended, his flesh-and-blood eyes returned to him, and Aisling, whose gaping wound had sealed with new skin over her elbow, lay sprawled next to Leafe and Wrenna, curled up on the rocks. They were all alive, the former Amber Lords and the erstwhile Azurite Knight.

Melorin had seen it all from the eyes of a magpie that had once been given the name Seren. He had seen it all through eyes that were not his own. But now, free as a bird, he was able to see the aftermath with his own human eyes. And Melorin was glad of what he saw: his apprentice, alive and well, and the men and women he had used as pawns, they too were living and breathing, now free from the stranglehold that he had forced upon them.

Yes, the world had changed. The world was new.

Melorin did not say goodbye to Wrenna, nor did he offer a final apology to Hawthorn for the terrible deeds he had inflicted upon to him. He did not wake The Amber Lords from their slumber, but he did cast a bubble over them, a protective blanket from the cold and wind.

With his newfound freedom, Melorin did not wish to be bound by entanglement. He wished only to travel, to walk long roads. To seek new horizons, and cherish every moment, mundane or thrilling. He sought to dive head first into the unknown. Before he left Wrenna and the others, he opened a portal for them, and inscribed a message of farewell on a wide, flat rock. His message was simple…

The portal leads home, whoever may enter.

Lastly, Melorin walked to the cloven rock where last Wisteria had lived and breathed among the world of Garden. At his feet, in the vague shape of a human being, an ashen smear spread out across the rock. Wisteria, the Necromancer Queen of Moonpearl, was no more—her long grief finally ended. Melorin kissed his hand and placed it against the rock. "Farewell, my apprentice."

Drawing from the magic of his alabaster and onyx, Melorin constructed his own portal. Then, stepping through the rift in time and space, he disappeared through the void.

* * *

"I don't know if I'll ever get used to it," Hawthorn said, looking out the high window of the castle.

"Being a king?" Wrenna asked, reclining on her plump mattress in the royal bedchamber.

"That too," Hawthorn laughed, adjusting his golden crown. "But I was referring to my sight… Seeing with my own eyes." He turned away from the window and smiled at Wrenna, gazing at his wife—his queen—with his *actual* eyes.

To Wrenna, they shone as blue and beautifully as they had when they were enchanted gemstones. Wrenna motioned Hawthorn over to the bed. "The crown suits you, my love. As do your new—I mean old—eyes."

Hawthorn jumped into bed with his wife, the very same bed where once the bones of King Clematis had lain for twenty-six years. It had been strange… discarding the fragments of an old corpse that had never been buried, the broken pieces of a king that lay exposed, year after year after year. It was most unusual, having inherited the bedroom of their enemy, the castle and crown that belonged to Wisteria, Queen of the Dead.

But fate does not balk at the strange, nor bat its eyelash at the unusual. It comes how it will, and when it does, one takes it. They take it because they must, because there is no option to refuse.

It had been over a year since their battle with Wisteria, when Wrenna and Hawthorn had walked through the portal that Melorin had left for them on Hoarfrost. Stepping through its shimmering rift, they left the decimated coastline behind them, and emerged in the royal bedchamber of Moonpearl.

The portal leads home, whoever may enter. That was the inscription that Melorin had written on the rock beside the magical gateway. For Wrenna, home did not lead south to Raynewood, but north, to Moonpearl. With the castle and a kingdom bereft of any living souls, nobles and peasants alike killed by their former queen, Moonpearl was left vacant, ripe for the plucking. "Home," it would seem, was an unoccupied throne in an arctic kingdom. And Wrenna, being of royal blood, albeit from the far off kingdom of Raynewood, took up the mantle and crown.

Unchallenged, she had become Moonpearl's new queen.

After all this time, in the end, Lady Raynewald finally consented to marriage. Choosing a partner, as it turned out, could not have been easier for her. Hawthorn had also been transported to Moonpearl when he walked through Melorin's portal, and when he arrived at his new home, seeing Wrenna standing before him, he discovered that, for him, home is where the heart is. When he claimed Wrenna's offered hand in marriage, he also took up the crown. And so it was, a humble rogue had risen to become a king.

In time, when news and messages made their way to Wrenna's brother, King Waldorf in Raynewood, he sent his congratulations, as well as a retinue of knights, nobles, and peasants to make the long journey to aid his sister in the rebuilding of Moonpearl. Among the hundreds who made the journey was Twigg, Wrenna's old handmaiden. When they finally saw each other in Moonpearl, their embrace was so warm it could have melted the ice caps of the Alabaster Ridge, even the snow-top summit of Demon's peak.

All was well in Moonpearl. All was well in the north.

And elsewhere, it would seem…

Leafe and Aster enjoyed the literal fruits of a healthy orange orchard. The long droughts were a concern of the past, as rainfall came steadily to their lands, and all throughout the southern continent. Though Leafe could no longer summon the rains at will, and no longer held the status or desire of being the Jackali prophet, he had heard from passing travelers of a change in the east, of a return to green among the Aridana dunes.

Northwest, here and there among the wild ranges of Zinnia and the vast Autumnwood forest, a one-armed warrior woman wielded a sword. Her weapon was not so great, nor as light, as the fabled greatsword, *Affliction*, but it still clove through goblin skulls as easily as a headsman's axe through a rotten pumpkin. Aisling took up the name Banshee, and under that moniker scoured the central continent, tormenting its pirates, raiders, goblins, ogres, and heavy-handed husbands.

As for Melorin, the last great wizard, the only crystal-bearer left in Garden…

No longer bound to his tower, the mighty magician wandered where he willed. He sought the tiny shards of amber, the infinitesimal slivers of nephrite scattered across Garden. If Melorin collected enough crystal dust, crumbs of amber and nephrite to add to his alabaster and onyx, he too might one day become as mighty as the legendary wizards of old—men like Persimmon the Great, who in the days of yore, when the old strong sorcery was more than myth…

Ah, yes, that old tale…

…At the end of every story is the beginning of another…

And so Melorin began his search.

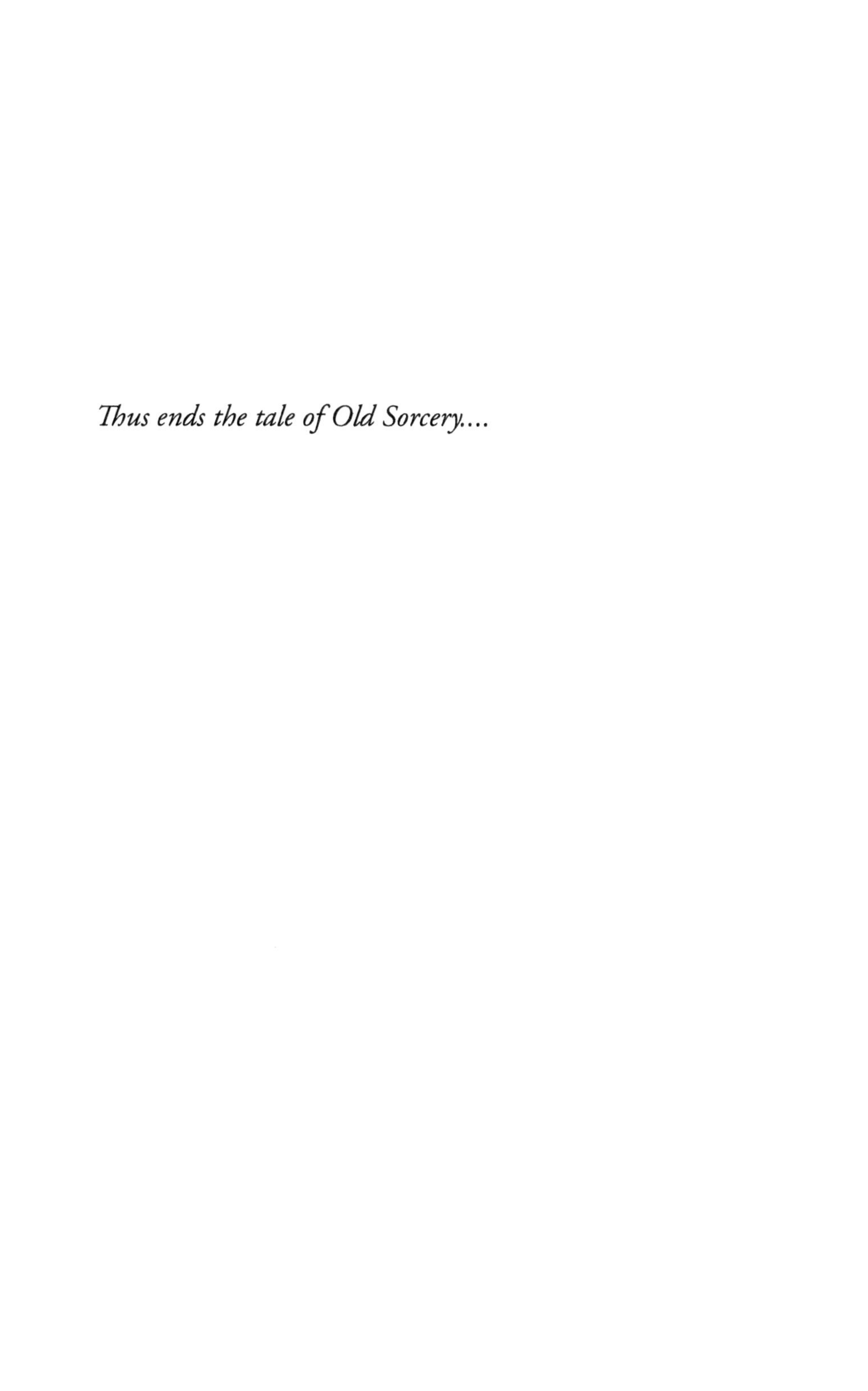

Thus ends the tale of Old Sorcery....

If you enjoyed the book, please support the author by leaving an honest review on Amazon and Goodreads! For more excellent Fantasy written by independent authors, join our mailing list!

www.ingramcontent.com/pod-product-compliance
Lightning Source LLC
LaVergne TN
LVHW010558110826
845149LV00003B/696

* 9 7 8 1 9 7 1 7 0 6 0 1 6 *